As Real As It Gets

As Real As It Gets

Monica McKayhan

sepia

★BET

BOOKS™

BET Publications, LLC

http://www.bet.com

SEPIA BOOKS are published by

BET Publications, LLC
c/o BET BOOKS
One BET Plaza
1900 W Place NE
Washington, DC 20018-1211

All Kensington Titles, Imprints, and Distributed Lines are available at special quantity discounts for bulk purchases for sales promotions, premiums, fund-raising, and educational or institutional use. Special book excerpts or customized printings can also be created to fit specific needs. For details, write or phone the office of the Kensington special sales manager: Kensington Publishing Corp., 850 Third Avenue, New York, NY 10022, attn: Special Sales Department, Phone: 1-800-221-2647.

ISBN 1-58314-605-9

First Printing: January 2005
10 9 8 7 6 5 4 3 2 1

Printed in the United States of America

As Real As It Gets

1

Reece

My sneakers hitting the pavement sounded like music, like drums—tap, tap, tap. A smooth consistent rhythm, and I wanted to dance. My throat was dry and I was panting, almost out of breath, but I pressed on. The last mile and I could still smell the rain from last night. It had rained all night, lightning flashing, thunder roaring as if it were angry. Gram always said that when it rained, somebody somewhere had died and that the rain was washing his or her footsteps away. That's what she said right after Miss Johnson died. Miss Johnson was the first person I ever knew to die, and death is a devastating thing in the life of a twelve-year-old.

I remember the paramedics pulling her out of that old musty house on a stretcher; the bottom of her feet were so filthy. Looked as if she hadn't bathed in days, weeks, or months even. All I could see were her feet, because the rest of her was covered up, but I remember the feet. Remember thinking that they could've had the decency to cover them up. That night, it rained cats and dogs.

The strange thing about it is every person I've ever known to die, died on a rainy day. And I often think about the rain as washing their footsteps away. So to me, rainy days are sad. Rain means death. And death means rain. That's the way I see it. And for that reason, I don't like the rain much. And the thunder and lightning make it worse. Seems like God is scolding us, like he's mad at the world for being so rebellious. The thunder sounds like he's slamming his fist down and saying, "Listen to me, you disobedient people! I wish I'd never created you!" The thunder and lightning remind me of my own life, the part of it that makes me uneasy and fearful. I feel trapped in a lifestyle that affords me very few choices, when I was once so carefree.

"You're slowin' me down." Darren smacked me on my behind so hard it seemed to echo across the city. And I would've smacked him back, but I didn't want to lose my rhythm. Darren, my prince, my armor-bearing knight, my fiancé. His only goal in life right now is to get me to the altar as soon as possible and impregnate me with his babies. A goal that we unfortunately do not share, and one that awakens me in the middle of the night, throat dry, pillow moist from the sweat. Leaves me shaking in my boots! Marriage is a huge step, and one that can't be rushed into. Especially when you're unsure about the person you intend to marry. My head hurt when I thought about it. As long as I wasn't forced to make a decision right away, it didn't exist. So I pressed it to the back of my mind in a file where I deposited all the thoughts I'd deal with later.

Three-quarters of a mile to go, and I was determined to finish my run. My mind drifted as I listened to my feet hitting the pavement. Started thinking about the previous afternoon, in my office, Wanda Manning sitting out there in the reception area. She and the little girl looked like a couple of rag dolls in their second-hand clothing. A black woman and a child with the saddest eyes I'd ever seen. The child was silent. So much so that it rang in my ears. The loudest silence I'd ever heard. Her mother said she hadn't spoken in days, afraid to; wouldn't eat either. Just wanted to be left alone. Wasn't like her, she'd said. She was usually a little chatterbox, but now she wouldn't speak.

Brenda had buzzed me, and I'd asked her to send them in. Wanda plopped down in the chair on the opposite side of my desk and ran the whole story down to me; told me what the little girl had said. That he had messed with her.

"What do you mean he messed with her?" I had to ask, just to be clear about what we were really talking about here.

"He been touchin' her private parts when I go to work at night."

"Your boyfriend, right?" I didn't want to be mistaken.

"Ex-boyfriend," she said, ashamed to admit that she'd once cared for this pervert.

"So what you're saying is your boyfriend . . . excuse me, ex-boyfriend, molested your little girl?"

"The bastard!" she said. "Wanted to kill him with my bare hands."

"Has she seen a doctor?"

"Took her down to the county health department. Doctor even said she been tampered with. Wrote it up in his report too."

"That's good. At least we have record of it. What about a police report?"

"Well that's how this whole thang got started. When I talked to the police they accused me of . . . what is it?" She thought for a moment. "Failure to protect. Said I was just as guilty. The prosecutin' attorney down there tryin' to get that judge to take my baby away from me, can you believe it? Said they investigatin' me."

"Has the perpetrator been arrested?"

"The what?"

"Your boyfriend."

"Ex-boyfriend," she corrected me. "Got out on bail. His family got a little money, and he was out the next day. Ain't that a trip?"

I leaned forward in my leather chair to jot down a few notes. "What's the child's name?"

"Jill," Wanda said.

"Hello, Jill." I smiled at the little girl, her ponytails flying in opposite directions atop her head.

"Say somethin' to the woman, child," her mother said.

Jill just stared at me with those sad eyes.

"She won't talk. Can't get her to say a word. Won't eat," she explained. "That's how I knew somethin' was wrong."

"When did all this take place? When he molested her, I mean."

"Been messin' with her for months. I confronted him."

"What did he say?"

"Denied it. Said she was lying."

"Jill told you he did this?"

"Yes, ma'am," she said. "Lady, do you thank you can help us? The therapist who been tryin' to talk to Jill gave me your card. Said if anybody could help it would be you." She pulled a beat-up business card out of her old leather purse. Handed it to me. I took it, looked at it. It was my card, all right. Gave it back to her.

"I'll see what I can do. Do some checking to see what I can find out."

"Thank you." She smiled.

"If I decide to take the case, are you aware of my retainer?"

"Your what?"

"My fee."

"She didn't tell me anything like that. And I know legal help ain't free, ma'am. But I'm willin' to pay; it'll just take me a little time. I work odd jobs. Don't have nothin' steady yet. But what little I get, I can give you a little at a time."

"There is free legal help, ma'am. Ever heard of Legal Aid?"

"Therapist said you was the best. Don't wanna take my chances anywhere else."

I thought about it for a moment. Knew she was desperate.

"Tell you what. If it's something I can do, I will. If it turns out that you need an attorney, I'll take the case pro bono."

"Pro what?"

"Let's just say, I'll take the case and we'll work something out later."

"God bless you," she said, standing up and reaching out to shake my hand. Her fingernails desperately needed a manicure.

"Leave your name and address with the receptionist."

"We live in a shelter for women and children downtown." She grabbed the little girl's hand and headed toward the door. "You can reach us there."

According to Wanda, they had been living with the boyfriend in a one-bedroom apartment, and when she accused him of molesting her little girl, he threw them both out on the street.

Less than half a mile left. Two miles each morning is what we did, and three miles on Saturday.

"You can give up at any time, sweetheart."

"Never. Lenox Mall and back. That's what we agreed to, right?"

"That's what we agreed to, Counselor."

I hated when he called me that. *Counselor.* He said it with such contempt in his heart. Although he'd tried to convince me that it was an affectionate nickname, I knew the underlying meaning was resentment for my success as an attorney. As if being a woman and being an attorney could never be synonymous. He resented my working altogether; thought a woman's place was in the home, giving birth to a dozen little nappy-headed children, cooking, cleaning, and still finding time to look pretty for a husband when he came home from his nine to five. Men, on the other hand, were the breadwinners, the champions, the heroes.

Darren was sort of stiff in his approach toward life. In a picture full of color, he'd see only the black outlines and the white paper on which the picture was drawn. He often missed the hues that gave a picture life. It was either one way or the other, no in-between. No room for indifference. And he didn't know me at all; not really. He knew I was attractive, intelligent, and successful and that any man would be proud to have me. But he didn't know who I was on the inside, what made me tick, where my strengths lied. And he never took the time to find out.

"I'll meet you at Starbucks. I'll be working on my second Frappuccino by the time you get there." He laughed as he ran ahead of me, his sweats soaked in back.

"You just order me a vanilla latte, and keep it warm."

He threw his hand in the air and continued to run. I watched him from behind, his dark six-foot-two frame bouncing as he kept a consistent pace. His Chicago Bulls cap turned backward on his bald head, his Morehouse T-shirt soaked from his sweat. He was a beautiful man, with a body to die for. Successful dentist. Educated. No vices; he didn't smoke, gamble, or get high. He had a drink socially every now and then.

My husband-to-be. A package every woman in Atlanta wished she could unwrap. Some even tried occasionally, and in my heart I believed that a few were even successful. I had caught Darren in a few compromising situations with women he claimed were only friends. And for the sake of my relationship, I bought it and moved on. Reminded myself of how irresistible he was, and that it wasn't his fault that others wanted him. Because in the end, he was mine. My prize. And I was proud, happy. Wasn't I? Why shouldn't I be, with a man like Darren in my life?

I ran past the Marta station, past the mall, and then crossed Peachtree at the light, until I reached Starbucks, about ten minutes behind Darren. Stood outside for a moment. Leaned over to catch my breath. Then went inside.

"What took you so long?" His long legs were stretched out, his back against the wall as he sat at our favorite table in the corner. When he smiled, his chocolate dimples were deep.

I sat down across from him, removed my sweatshirt down to my leotard top. Loosened my braids, then pulled them back into a ponytail again; tied them with a rubber band. My sweats were cold and wet against my legs. Darren had ordered my latte and a bran muffin.

"Why you so slow today?"

"Didn't feel much like running this morning." My latte warmed my insides as I took a sip. "Got a lot on my mind."

"Like?"

"My case."

"The sexual abuse case?" He asked as if it were ridiculous for me to waste time thinking about it.

"Yep," I said.

"Sweetheart, you can't take on these people's problems. You have to remember, you're just the attorney. Not the savior of the world."

Darren stuffed the remainder of his bran muffin into his mouth. He had a point. "You get too personal with your clients."

"I don't."

"You know you do. It's almost like you're some social worker or something." He laughed, "The homeless guy who was beaten by the police. You took his case pro bono. Reece, you tried to take on the entire Atlanta PD. Then you took the guy into your home to give him a meal."

"Reuben?" I smiled, remembering my friend who was now holding down a job at McDonald's in the West End. "He had no place else to go."

"You treat these people like they're your personal friends."

"Reuben *is* my friend. And thanks to him, you now get free fries at McDonald's."

"Oh, you got jokes?" He said. "What about the woman whose husband was abusing her, and you hid her in your office for two days until they finally arrested him."

"She tried to get a restraining order against him, but we both know what a joke that was. What was she supposed to do? Sit there and wait for the brother to show up?"

"Reece, that was dangerous, and you know it. He could've killed her, then you. You worry me sometimes." He started on

7

his second Frappuccino, took his cap off, and rubbed his bald head. "Now this case. What, are you gonna move the little girl and her mother in with you?"

"They *are* homeless," I said and smiled. "I'm just kidding. I do care, though."

"I know you care. But why can't you just do your job, make your money, and go home? I know you're passionate about your work, babe."

"Is that a bad thing?"

"If it starts to wear you down, it can be. You're a runner, yet you could barely finish your stretch this morning."

"It's not wearing me down. I'm just thinking about how I'm gonna handle the case, that's all."

"I'm sure you'll come up with something brilliant, Counselor."

"What's that supposed to mean?"

"What? That you'll come up with something brilliant?"

"No. 'Counselor.' It's just the way you say it." We always argued about my career.

He struggled with the thought of his woman bringing home her own bacon and not having to rely on him. He'd always taken care of the women in his life, and although he claimed that he admired my independence, deep down inside he resented the day I passed the bar exam. Secretly wished I'd failed, so that I could become his next work of art. He had rescued his last girlfriend, Trisha, from the projects and moved her into a nice little apartment in the suburbs. And once she became too independent and started talking about going back to school, he got rid of her, moved on to his next challenge—me.

He mistakenly thought I was in need of rescue. I was a student at John Marshall Law School at the time and holding down a job at IHOP when he walked into my life. Yes, making manager was one of my short-term goals, because Lord knows I needed the money, but for some reason he thought it was my pie in the sky, my end of the road, my destiny. It was later that he realized that the reason I kept turning down his offers for dinner and a movie was because I was in law school, which was kicking my butt, and that left me very little time for leisure activities.

He became intimidated, mostly because I had my own agenda, and although the pay at IHOP wasn't the greatest, I made it work for me until I graduated. I figured that once he got used to the idea of having a successful woman, he'd change, would support me—but here we were six years later and the idea that I'm capable of making my own decisions still causes him to sweat. I was a challenge for him. I didn't need him, and he knew it. So he stuck around, trying to change me every chance he got. Any idea I came up with that wasn't his, he shot it down. Made me feel downright stupid for aspiring to become a partner at my law firm. Outsiders gave me more support.

I'd have moved on long ago, but first of all, Mama loves him. Already calls him her son-in-law, thinks he'll make her some beautiful grandbabies. And secondly, on a brisk Atlanta night, it's nice to have someone to cuddle with in front of a roaring fire. And thirdly, he's familiar, been around for a while.

"How did I say it?"

"Just forget it, Darren," I said. "Don't you care about your patients?"

"Absolutely. But when I leave my dental office, I leave the work behind. No appointments after six."

"Well, I can't do that. An attorney's job never ends."

"Reece, *your* job never ends. Has nothing to do with the profession. I know plenty of attorneys who actually work a nine to five and actually live pretty happy lives after five." He was getting irritated. And when he became irritated he'd either shut down completely or change the subject. This time he opted for the latter. "Let's talk about something else."

"Like what?"

"Like our wedding date. And why you keep pushing it back."

I was silent. Sipped my latte.

"What are you afraid of?"

"Nothing."

"Then let's set a date."

"Right now?"

"Right now. June twenty-eighth. It's a Saturday. I tentatively reserved the church. Spoke with Reverend Peterson. It's good for him." He often took it upon himself to make decisions for me. I don't know if it was the decisions that he made for me that ticked me off more, or the fact that he didn't bother to discuss them with me first.

"I can't agree to a date without checking my schedule first."

He finished his second Frappuccino. Stood. "Going to the restroom. I'll be right back."

I watched him disappear around the corner. Knew he was mad. The wedding date was a never-ending argument and had gone on far too long. I knew it. He was ready. I wasn't. I needed more time to sort things out in my life. Needed to sell my condo for one. Hadn't even put it on the market yet. Didn't really want to move into Darren's four-bedroom abode in Stone Mountain. I was perfectly happy in my two bedroom with a view of the downtown skyline. I loved the Buckhead area, not to mention my office was downtown, a twenty-minute drive in rush hour from where I lived. Fifteen, if I timed it right.

Darren wanted children. I didn't. Not right now. I was handling two of the largest cases of my career. Winning either one of them would put me directly in line for partner. Making partner at Williams and Schmidt's wouldn't allow much time for a child. Children were Darren's tactic for stagnating my growth. A means for keeping me at home and stripping me of my independence. Losing my independence is what I feared the most. Not to mention, I would barely have time for a husband. Things were fine just the way they were. He knew our schedules were hectic. That's why we only spent time together on the weekends. Plenty for me. Not enough for him.

"You ready?"

"Yep."

We jogged up Peachtree, past Pharr Road toward my condo.

Traffic in Buckhead was congested as people went about doing whatever their Saturday morning thing was. We stopped in the middle of the block, my fingers intertwined with Darren's as we jaywalked across Peachtree, stepping over a puddle that remained from the previous night's rain. We jogged past the storefront businesses, through my picturesque neighborhood of mini-mansions, with their colorful brick fronts and circular drives, just minutes from the governor's mansion. We headed toward my mahogany-colored brick building with a security gate. I punched in my four-digit code, Darren behind me running in place as the huge wrought-iron gate began to open. Still pouting, arms folded. To ask what was wrong would be to open up a whole new can of worms, so I kept my mouth shut. Jogged in silence to the lobby of my building, the only sounds were the ones from our sneakers hitting the pavement. Once inside, we caught the elevator up eighteen flights, to my place with polished hardwoods, charming vintage furniture, and the scent of juniper that greeted you at the front door.

"I'm hitting the shower. Make yourself at home," I said, kicking my sneakers off and throwing him the remote to the television.

"Think I'll head home," he said, kissing my cheek. "Call you later."

"I thought we were getting some Chinese and a couple of movies from Blockbuster."

"Rain check?"

"You mad?"

"Just wanna be alone."

"Okay, baby," I said, heading to the bathroom. "Call me later, then."

There was that pouting again, like a three-year-old who hadn't gotten his way. Of all Darren's little quirks, I think the pouting was the most annoying.

I jumped in the shower, watched the water stream down my mocha-colored breasts like a waterfall. I heard the phone ring but ignored it. Wasn't about to leap out of the shower, butt-naked, only to find that Darren had gotten as far as I-85, then decided he wanted to take me up on that shrimp lo mein with the veggie egg rolls, a couple of fortune cookies, and a bottle of Beringer's to wash it all down. Probably had even swung by Blockbuster to rent the movie I'd wanted to see.

I stood there, eyes shut, water soft against my skin. I got lost in the rhythm of the water bouncing from my body and twirling down the drain at my feet. I drifted away in thought until my toes began to wrinkle. Finally came to and jumped out of the shower, the mirror steamed from the heat. Just as I grabbed a towel and wrapped it around me, the phone rang again, stopped me dead in my tracks. I tiptoed into the bedroom, leaped across the bed, and grabbed it.

"Hello."

"Didn't you hear the phone a minute ago?"

"I was in the shower."

"I'm at Blockbuster. What you wanna see?" I could hear the smile in his voice.

"Thought you were going home."

"Changed my mind."

I laughed inside. Knew him like the back of my hand.

"Changing Lanes."

"What?"

"The movie I wanted to see. *Changing Lanes.*"

"Okay."

"And bring me some egg drop soup."

By the time I'd pulled on a pair of sweats and my Ralph Lauren T-shirt, Darren was walking through the door, the aroma of shrimp lo mein suddenly filling my home, a bottle of Beringer's in one of his hands, a couple of DVDs and Chinese food in the other.

"Here, grab the wine," he said, and I caught the bottle just before it fell to the floor. Took it to the kitchen and grabbed a couple of wineglasses from the shelf.

Steered clear of conversation, waited for him to start one. And once I felt his body against mine from behind as I reached for a couple of plates from the shelf, I knew he was in a better mood. He tightened his strong arms around my waist and nibbled on my ear. His breath was warm against my earlobe, his hands like ice from the cold draft that had followed him inside. I turned to meet his lips with mine, only out of habit.

"I'm gonna hit the shower," he whispered, "and when I come back, I got something for you."

His seductive smile told me what that something was, but I wasn't feeling it. There was a time when making up was the best part of fighting, but eventually I became immune to the temporary fix that sex provided. I realized that once the act was over, the problems remained. The little nagging arguments, the silence, the pouting, and the unanswered questions were all still there, even after I'd screamed and hollered and had found that top of the mountain called ecstasy. And I'd still have to contend with my feelings of irritation after it was all over, still feeling empty inside, longing for something more.

"I'll start the movie," I said, maneuvering my body from his embrace. "Which one you want to see first?"

"No matter." He smiled again. "Won't be watching much anyway."

We kissed once again, and then he disappeared into the bathroom.

I started the DVD, the surround sound filling the room just as he liked it. I piled my plate with shrimp lo mein and egg rolls. Crossed my legs underneath my bottom and ate like there was no tomorrow. Running always stirred my appetite.

2

Maxie

Had just dropped off an article to the senior editor at *Atlanta Style* magazine, a publication that I wrote for occasionally. Had met my deadline well ahead of time. In addition to being a published columnist, and writing editorials and articles for several magazines and newspapers, I freelanced commercially and had a corporate client list that included some of the largest companies in Atlanta. Had been offered several opportunities to work as a staff writer, with a nice salary and a plush office to match, but I preferred working at home. Wasn't much into having a nine to five. Had seen too many people living in corporate captivity, and I wasn't down with that. Besides, I made a pretty good living just doing my own thing.

After standing on the platform at the Marta station for a few minutes, feeling that cold draft up my backside, I finally jumped on the train. It was Saturday afternoon in Atlanta, and it wasn't quite as crowded on the train as, say, a Monday during rush hour, but there was always somebody on there asking for money or acting a fool, no matter what day of the week it was.

"Excuse me, my Nubian sister, can you spare some change so a brother can get somethin' to eat?"

"What?" I took my headphone off my ear so I could hear what he was saying.

"I *said,* can you spare some change for somethin' to eat?" He repeated it, eyes bloodshot.

I stuck my hand down into the pocket of my jeans. I never kept money in my purse, always on my person. Pulled out a dollar.

"Yeah. Here you go." I put my headphone back on and continued to bounce to my India Arie CD. He was saying something else, so I took my headphone off once more.

"A dollar?" He looked at the bill as if I had insulted him. Looked at me. "Don't you have any more than this?"

"What? Brother, you the one beggin'. That's all I got."

"What am I supposed to buy with a dollar?"

Was I supposed to dignify that with an answer? I just looked at him, and then looked around at the other passengers. Their faces blank and unconcerned. A black woman with a Kroger bag full of groceries looked at me and shook her head, then put her head down in fear that he might turn to her next.

"A homeless brother on the street don't have a chance. Black people just like crabs in a bucket. Always tryin' to keep each other down." He started preaching to the rest of the congregation on the train. They were looking at him as if he'd lost his mind.

He reeked of alcohol. The cheap kind. Knew he was looking for a drink before I gave him the money. If I hadn't been on the train, I would've offered to take him to the nearest burger joint and bought him something to eat. That would've really pissed him off, because what he was really looking for was a cheap bottle of liquor to sip on until morning.

"I bet if I go over to Buckhead, I would get paid. The white folks over there give up the money. But you? Look at you. You sit there with your golden locks like you from the motherland or something. But you just a fake sister with your high yellow skin. Think you better than the rest of us, don't you? I bet you never had a hard day in your life."

He didn't know jack about my life and couldn't have been more wrong. All my life I'd had it hard. In and out of foster homes since I was twelve. Never forgave my mother for killing herself. What a selfish person she was. Still remember it like it was yesterday.

Mama's eyes were wide open, looked just like she was staring at the brown water stains on the ceiling. Her long, coal black hair hanging over the side of the tub, bath water red from the blood of her wounded wrists. Her mouth was open, as if she'd tried to ask for forgiveness from her Maker. But it was too late, because her body was cold now. Cold and rubberlike. Just like Aunt Dorothy's had been when she died, lying in the casket at her wake. I'd touched her, just to see if she was really dead. She'd felt cold and rubberlike, just like Mama looked right then. I didn't know for sure what Mama's body felt like, because I just stood in the doorway of that bathroom, tears burning the side of my face, paralyzed. My books were on the floor with my heart; they both had dropped the minute I saw her. Couldn't scream, too much shock. Then the pain set in, and that's why the tears were falling. I knew I should've done something, just didn't know what. So I just stood there, staring at my dead mama. Marvin Gaye's "What's Goin' On" spinning on the record player in our living room. I knew all the words and quietly sang them in my head as I stood there.

"Mama! Look at the picture I drew for you." Button came running in behind me, holding up a picture of something colored in red, yellow, and green Crayolas. She stopped in her tracks at the sight of Mama. "What's wrong with her?"

"Is she dead, Maxie?" That was Alex. I don't remember when she'd come into the bathroom.

"No, she's not dead." Button ran over and shook Mama.

"She is dead! Maxie, why are you just standing there? Do' something! We gotta do something!" Alex became hysterical.

"Mommy, please wake up. It's me. Button." Button was holding up the picture she'd drawn at school. "Look what I drew for you. Mommy, please wake up." She was crying and shaking Mama.

Mama's body lied motionless in that bloody water.

"I'm calling Uncle Walter!" Alex ran out of the bathroom, and I could hear her patent leathers tap-tapping across the linoleum floor and into the living room.

"She's not dead! She's just sleeping." Button was shaking Mama so hard. "Mommy, please wake up!"

I heard Alex dialing that rotary phone in the living room, screaming into Uncle Walter's ear. He must've told her to hang up and call 911, because I heard her dialing again, then screaming to someone that our mother was dead, and giving them our address.

That forty-five started over again. Five times I listened to that song, quietly singing the words in my head, before the sirens drowned the tune.

I was busy taking in Mama's features, her caramel-colored skin and high cheekbones, round lips, long, coal black hair. She was so pretty. Why would anybody so pretty want to die? I wanted to ask her. She had it all, a nice figure, a voice like that of Billie Holiday or Martha Reeves, and every man in South Georgia falling over his feet just for a moment of her time. She was smart, pretty. I wanted to remember her face, wanted to burn a picture of it in my memory. So I stared.

It was Uncle Walter's deep voice that snapped me out of my trance.

"Maxie. Pull yourself together."

For the first time, I focused on someone else's face, other than Mama's. I watched him stare at his sister for a few moments, tears filling his eyes but not falling. He looked a lot like Mama, same caramel-colored skin, mustache, tall and slender, handsome, and always dressed to kill. I often wondered how he could afford to dress so nice, when he barely held down a job for more than a few weeks at a time. Mama was always on his case about not being able to keep a job. And he was always on hers about bringing strange men into our home, around us. Mama would always pull me aside later and explain to me how those strange men were often our meal ticket.

"Uncle Walter?" He was holding Button in his arms; her face was buried in his chest. I was finally able to speak.

"Are you all right, sugar?" He pulled me close, his cologne filling the room.

"She's really dead, huh?" I asked him.

"Come on in here, sugar, and have a seat. Get out of these people's way."

Paramedics rushed into our small bathroom like a herd of cattle.

I sat on that brown-and-yellow plaid couch in our living room next to Alex. I held her hand and tried to be the big sister I'd failed to be earlier. I pushed her bangs from her face and wiped the tears from her eyes. And we sat there together, our ashy legs dangling from that plaid couch, our bobby socks pushed down to our ankles, crying and holding hands, for what seemed like eternity.

"Oh, now you just gon' ignore me?" The beggar on the train was really starting to get on my nerves.

The woman with the groceries looked up at me again, her eyes anticipating my response.

No one else seemed to be concerned, had their own issues, and continued to either read their newspapers or glance out the window.

I snapped.

"Brother, you don't know me . . . don't know jack about who I am . . . how dare you fix your drunken mouth to disrespect me like that . . . take a look at yourself. If you leave the bottle alone and go get yourself a job, then we wouldn't be having this conversation, now would we?" Before I knew it, I was in his face.

His response was silence. Looked at me as if I'd lost *my* mind.

When the train came to a complete stop, I glared at him with the most intimidating look I could give and simply said, "You have a nice day."

He continued to ramble on about something, and I was relieved when I finally got off at the East Point station.

I jogged up the hill, past the old homes with their chipping paint and porches that needed the wooden boards replaced. The senior citizens who lived in my neighborhood were on fixed incomes and couldn't afford the upkeep on their deteriorating properties. And there was only so much assistance they could get. These were people who'd paid taxes and dropped money into their social security funds during their working years, but now that they could no longer work, Uncle Sam's pockets had become a little too light.

I knew them all. Had interviewed them for an article that I wrote for the *Atlanta Journal Constitution* a couple of years back; a piece where I'd made a plea to our local politicians and leaders to take a closer look at the senior citizens in our communities. They were being neglected and nobody seemed to care. The article drew the attention of some local politicians, and all of a sudden there was a little pocket change to go around. Miss Holiday in the green house on the corner—only you couldn't tell that it was green because it was in desperate need of a paint job—received some money to have her house painted. Mr. Roby in the middle of the block got that new roof. And Mr. and Mrs. Cambridge who lived in the white house next to the vacant lot got new windows; the kind that tilt in for easy cleaning.

They loved me, mostly because I was the only visitor that some of them had. And if today had been a beautiful summer day, they'd have been sitting on their porches, waving and yelling hello to me or inviting me over for conversation and an ice-cold glass of Kool-Aid. But since it was cold outside, and I wasn't in the mood for stopping, I passed on by and headed toward my building.

19

Checked my mail and went up the three flights of stairs to my apartment.

"Hey, Greg." He was replacing a lightbulb in the hallway.

"What's up, Maxie? I fixed your bathroom sink this morning. The water pressure should be okay now." Greg was our building super, not to mention one of my closest friends. "Let me know if you have any more problems."

Something was always wrong in our building. It had to have been built in the late 1800s or something, with its Victorian-style balconies, hardwood floors, and ancient plumbing. Once, we had to evacuate the building because the sewage was backing up into our basement each time a toilet was flushed. All this took place while our deadbeat landlord was vacationing in Florida. He put us all up in a Holiday Inn in midtown until the problem was repaired. But it was only as a result of threats by the health department to put him out of business that the problem was taken care of. If it weren't for Greg, nothing around here would get fixed half the time. He did repairs in exchange for his rent. Knew all the tenants personally, and made sure the kids in the building stayed out of trouble. Ran errands for the elderly ladies.

You could usually find him shooting hoops with the teenage boys from our complex or teaching the younger kids how to play twenty-one in the stairwell. Occasionally he'd have all the kids in the neighborhood outside picking up trash, or they'd be teaching him the latest dances. Everybody knew Greg.

"What you drinking over there?" I asked him. He lived in the apartment across the hall from me.

"I think I got a bottle of Hennessy tucked away somewhere. Let me go find out." He smiled, his gold tooth sparkling like sunshine. "Why? You want to get whipped in some dominoes again?"

"What you mean whipped?" I laughed. "You know I put it on you the other day. Took all your money."

"Whatever. I'll bring the Hennessy. You just pull out the dominoes and get ready for your beat down, girl. Ain't no mercy this time."

"Put your money where your mouth is," I said, and shut my door.

My apartment. A small two bedroom with mustard-colored carpet in the living room and bedroom, faded linoleum in the kitchen and bathroom. My walls were a dull off-white, but I brightened them with my art; my *Jazz Spirit* print on one wall—a man blowing on his horn, his woman beside him, the bluest sky in the background. And on the other wall hung a couple of my *Buffalo Soldiers* prints. Got a great deal on them at the Sweet Auburn Festival last year. In front of my picture window in the living room sat a very tasteful black leather sofa and loveseat to match. When I entertained company, they raved about my African art. I'd spent many a Saturday at some of the finest art galleries and antique shops in Atlanta, seeking pieces that would make my collection complete.

Most often, that's where you'd find me—art galleries, antique shops, cultural festivals, museums, or events like the Black Expo or For Sisters Only. In the summertime you might catch me at Piedmont Park checking out the local jazz talent, or at Chastain Park on a blanket, sucking on crab legs and being wooed by Luther, Will Downing, or whomever decided to breeze through the city for a live concert. Or you might find me licking my fingers at a barbeque joint on Auburn Avenue, grubbing at a soul food spot in the West End, or at Gladys Knight's and Ron Winan's Chicken and Waffles on Peachtree. I frequented the poetry readings downtown and participated in the different reggae events held to raise money for AIDS awareness, child abuse prevention, and other benefits held for meaningful causes. Sometimes I would simply sit on a park bench in Centennial Park and watch the children run through the musical waterfalls.

I lit some sandalwood incense and a few candles, put on a Coltrane CD, and pulled the dominoes out. Threw some leftover ribs in the microwave. Put on a pair of sweats and my

Malcolm X T-shirt. It was on. I was the queen of dominoes and Greg knew it, he just didn't want to admit it. I would have to show him up again, challenge his manhood. Send him across the hall later on, defeated.

In my dining room, we slammed bones on the table and talked junk. We sipped on glasses half filled with Hennessy and Coke.

"Fifteen, Maxie," Greg boasted, as he made his first play and scored. "Write it down, girl. Write it down."

I jotted his points down on the page where I kept score.

"I got it," I said, and then silently made the next play.

"East Point's finest had to escort Mr. Hardy from two-twenty-two off the premises this morning." Greg began to tell me about all the drama I'd missed in our building in just the few hours I was gone. Our building was usually pretty quiet, but every now and then somebody had to show their behinds.

"Beatin' his wife again?"

"To a pulp." He shook his head. "Paramedics took her away."

"She gon' live?"

"Far as I know," he said.

"I don't know why she puts up with him." It was me who slammed a domino this time and quickly wrote my points down.

"Mr. Williams in one-thirty-eight wandered off again. Had to look for him myself."

I laughed at the thought of the elderly man wandering around East Point a few weeks back and ending up at Hooters, where his wife and two police officers found him greasing down on some hot wings and being a little too friendly with the waitresses.

"Where was he this time?" I had to laugh.

"Had walked over to Kroger's to get groceries but didn't bother to tell his wife," he said, and slammed another domino on the table, smiling at the fact that he'd scored again.

"Sounds like you had an exciting day, my brother."

"Other than that, it was pretty quiet around here." He smiled. "You gon' eat that rib?"

"Help yourself. Wouldn't want to send you home hungry *and* defeated." We both laughed. "Dag, I missed all the fun."

"Did you hear that our landlord is thinking of selling this old place to a developer? There's a new development company in the area, buying up properties, trying to get the homeowners around here to sell too; you know, the elderly folks who been in their places for years. Planning on building a commercial plaza."

"They can't do that." I was annoyed, and Greg knew that if he shared that piece of information with me at the right time, he'd distract me from my game.

"It's already in the works. I even heard that a few of them have already signed their properties away."

"Are you serious?"

"As a heart attack." He stirred the ice around in his drink with his finger. Took a sip. "Offered them a few thousand dollars and got them thinking they can take the money and go put it down on a property somewhere else."

"Why would they go put money down on a new property, when they own their properties free and clear?"

"Got me."

"That's jacked up. Something's got to be done!"

"What?" he asked, sucking the barbeque sauce off of the bone until it was dry. His skin dark and shiny. His hair in an old-school afro that looked as if he still combed it to the front, his jeans a little too snug for a man, and his beard needing to be trimmed. Greg was an older guy; wasn't the most fashionable or the most fine brother, but he was what you called "good people." And I liked him.

"I don't know yet, but something." He had me off my game for a moment, but I focused again and began to put that whipping on him like I'd promised.

He grabbed a paper towel and wiped barbeque sauce from his mouth.

3

Charlotte

"When you see the master bedroom, you'll fall in love with this place. I guarantee it."

"I'm already in love." He smiled a seductive smile.

I knew his taste. Knew everything about him, down to how much he was worth, how much he tipped at restaurants, what his favorite color was. Studied my clients, researched, so I knew exactly what they wanted in a home. Then I closed the deal with a happy client passing my name along to his or her wealthy friends. My career was booming. Salary already well into the six figures.

"Charlotte, how is it you know me so well?" I never knew which way Patrick went. He always traveled in circles with men; saw him at Centennial Park once, at one of the summer concerts, nestled in a compromising embrace with another very attractive white male. Yet he was always flirting with me.

"I've done my homework, sweetheart," I boasted.

"You certainly have. I'll take it," he said, after looking around at the master bedroom and taking in its breathtaking beauty. The view alone was enough to put on a postcard and mail it to your relatives.

"I knew you would," I said, and shook his hand. "I'll send the contract over to your office by messenger this afternoon. Don't delay in signing it, sweetheart."

"Why don't you join me for lunch, Charlotte?"

"Wish I could, honey. But I'm meeting another client in thirty minutes."

"You said that last time," he said with a sly grin. "What are you afraid of?"

The way he said that was way too feminine for my taste. But for an older white gentleman, I had to admit, he was handsome. Tall, medium build, graying sideburns. Always looked and smelled nice, and was worth a lot of money. CEO of one of the largest investment firms in the country. I'd sold him his vacation home in Rio.

I'd never dated a white man before. Never even had an interest in one. As a matter of fact, I couldn't remember the last time I dated anyone since William. Not enough time. Too busy building my career. My goal this year was to earn a million, and I was close to it. I could see it, smell it, and even taste it. My name was on the tongues of all the wealthy homebuyers in Atlanta. I didn't just sell real estate, I lived it, breathed it. It was my life.

"Rain check?" I asked, offering him my best comforting smile.

"Rain check," he said. "Great doing business with you, Charlotte."

"You too."

"See you soon?"

"Okay, honey." I pushed him out the door. "Call if you need me."

When he left, I did a Toyota jump in the living room. Knew I was too big to be jumping my behind in the air. Had gained too much weight. The extra twenty or so pounds came after my break up with William. He had been recently divorced when we started dating, but then in midstream, decided he wanted to go back to his wife. Said he couldn't handle the alimony and child support he was paying her, and it was cheaper to just go home. And besides that, he wanted to be able to see his son every day. Tired of living without him. The Negro just woke up one morning and realized this. I was lying in his arms, and he just dropped it on me like a ton of bricks.

"Charlotte, this is not about us. This is about my son," he'd said. "I really love you, but I love him too."

"You just realized this today, right?" I'd asked.

"Been thinking about it for a while. Just took me some time to piece it all together. I'm driving down to New Orleans in the morning to pick her up."

"Her?"

"My wife. Tonya," he'd said in a matter-of-fact sort of way. "Bringin' her back to Georgia to live."

"With you? At your place?"

"For now," he'd said. "But my little man is getting big and we'll need a bigger place soon. Probably be in the market for a house. I was hoping you could show us something, you being in the business and all."

"I think you should leave," I'd said. "I need to be alone."

"That probably wasn't a good thing to say, huh?" he'd said, pulling his pants on. "I'm sorry, honey. I didn't mean for this to hurt you."

"Can I have my key please?" I held my hand out, fighting the tears that were burning my eyes.

He stood. Turned to look into my eyes as if he'd suddenly had a change of heart. That all he'd just said was just a bunch of nonsense, and he'd come to his senses. Or maybe it was a practical joke. He was good at playing those. "You think we could still see each other?"

He was serious.

"Get out."

"Is that a no?"

"Give me my key and get out of my house."

He got dressed. Threw the key on the dresser and walked toward the door.

"I'll call you tomorrow," he'd said, searching my face for a response. "Give you some time to think about it."

The vase I threw just missed his head as he ducked and darted out the door.

I was depressed for weeks. Some women shop when they're depressed. I eat. I began eating everything in sight. Went from a size seven to a size twelve in three months. But I was working on it. Took an aerobics class at Curves twice a week and walked through my subdivision every night.

After my Toyota jump, I pulled my cell phone out to call my girls. Needed to share my excitement with someone.

"Reece. It's Charlotte, what you doin'?"

"Watchin' a movie."

"With Darren?"

"Alone. He's asleep. What's up?"

"I just closed one of the biggest deals of my career. Can you get away to celebrate for a minute?"

"Where?"

"Meet you at Justin's in thirty minutes."

"I think I can get away for a minute. I'll see you there."

I knew Reece and Darren were attached at the hip most weekends until he got mad at her and went pouting back to his oversized home in Stone Mountain, but I knew I could count on her to be there for me. Knew she would want to share in my excitement as if it were her own.

I hung up and dialed Maxie's phone number.

"Maxie, it's Charlotte. What you doin'?"

"Whipping Greg in some dominoes. Why, what's up?"

"I just sold a three-million-dollar home to one of my wealthiest clients. Reece is meeting me at Justin's in thirty minutes. Can you come?"

"I'll see what I can do. It might take me longer on the train, though."

"Maxie, for God's sake, buy a car! It's not like you're broke."

"I don't want a car. I'm not contributing to the already esca-
lating pollution in Atlanta. Not to mention, I'm not down with
the traffic and the idiots that travel these roads every day."

"I'll swing by and pick you up."

"No, thank you. I'll ride Marta." She roared with laughter,
as if she'd just heard a joke.

"Have you been drinking, girl?"

"Why? Are you my mother now?"

"Quite the contrary," I said. She was so pitiful. "And what's
up with you and Greg? Why is he always hangin' out over
there? Are y'all dating or something?"

"Am I all up in your business like that?" she said. "Oops, I
forgot. You don't have any."

"Whatever, Maxie. Are you coming or not?"

She said, "I'll see you in thirty. Better yet, make it forty-five."

"Bye."

She had already hung up.

Don't know why I even bothered. She was bound to get
under my skin before the day was over.

When I pulled into Justin's parking lot, Reece's silver Range
Rover was already there, and she was at the bar sipping on a
zinfandel and talking to the bartender. She raised her glass to
me when she saw me walk in.

"Hey, girl," she said, and we hugged. "What's up?"

"I closed the deal, and the ink is still wet on the contract. A
three-million-dollar contract!" We both screamed and hugged
again. People in the place were staring at us like we were crazy.

"Who would spend that kind of money on real estate?"
Reece asked.

"Those who have it," I said. "You're starting to sound like
Maxie. Her trifling behind won't even invest in an automo-
bile."

"That's just Maxie." She laughed. "What you drinking?"

"A ginger ale," I told the bartender, who was waiting to take
my drink order. "I'm meeting a client later."

The hostess seated us at a table across the room.

"Is Maxie coming?"

"Yeah. Sometime tomorrow, whenever the Marta gets her here."

"Cut her some slack. Maxie's had a hard life, you know."

"We've all had a hard life. But you don't see me running around on Marta all the time. There comes a time when you move up from the poverty level and do things different. Buy a car and get a decent apartment," I said. "It ain't like she's broke. She makes a nice salary. She's a journalist for crying out loud. Some of my wealthiest clients are journalists."

"I don't think it has anything to do with money. Maxie is just Maxie. She wants people to accept her for who she is. Not what she has."

"Whatever," I said. "What's up with you and Darren? When y'all gon' set a date?"

"Not the wedding date issue again."

"Reece, what are you waiting on? Do you want to marry the man or not?"

"I don't know."

"You don't know?" I couldn't believe my ears. "Reece, are you serious?"

"I'm not ready."

"Does he know how you feel?"

She shook her head.

"You can't keep stringin' the man along. You have to be honest with him. If not with him, with yourself."

"There she is," Reece said, cutting me off. "Over here, Maxie."

"I'm not finished with you," I said.

Maxie walked in, her golden locks needing to be redone, as usual. She was wearing jeans, a Nike sweatshirt, and sneakers. Always wearing jeans and sneakers. Never took the time to make herself look nice. Never an occasion for that.

"Dag, I said Justin's."

"I'm here, ain't I?" Maxie asked. "This *is* Justin's, right?"

29

"It ain't a jeans and sneakers kind of place, Maxie."

"Sorry, Charlotte. Didn't realize there was a dress code. Last time I checked, there wasn't," she said.

"Not like you would care if there was."

"I can just go back home, you know. I was in the middle of something anyway."

"That's cool," I said.

"No. Maxie, have a seat." Reece was always playing referee. "Charlotte, chill out!"

"Reece. I don't belong here." She ran her fingers through her locks. She was actually a very pretty girl, and the world could probably see it if she took the time to fix herself up. She was about five foot three; a perfect size seven. I would trade my size twelve for hers any day. Light brown eyes; perfect honey-colored skin; not so much as a blackhead or pimple on her face. I often wondered what she used to keep her skin so beautiful. And her smile lit up a room. People were drawn to her, even me. Though I couldn't figure out why. Especially since we always fought. Six years I've known her, and we've fought for at least five and a half.

"Of course you belong here," Reece said. "What you drinking, Maxie?"

"Water with lemon." The waitress took her drink order and disappeared.

"Charlotte got a three-million-dollar contract on a house today," Reece said. "We proud of you, girl."

We gave each other a high five.

"Got something I wanna talk to y'all about," I said. "I'm working on a real estate deal in the Bahamas. Need to fly over for a week. Maybe two. I'm leaving next week," I said, and took a drink of my ginger ale. "Why don't y'all come with me? We can make it a vacation. The three of us."

"Can't," Reece said. "We go to trial in a few weeks. And I really need to focus on this one. Otherwise, you know I would, girl."

"I can't go either," Maxie said.

"Why not?" I asked.

"I don't want to." She rolled her eyes and stuck out her tongue.

"Figures." I grinned sarcastically at Maxie. "Marta doesn't go there."

"Girls. Girls," Reece said laughing.

"You don't know what you're missing. I'm staying at a mansion overlooking the beach."

"For real? Whose mansion?" Reece asked.

"Got a wealthy client over there. Remember my friend Ramsey? I sold him a piece of real estate about a year ago. He'll be in London for the next few months but is giving me free access to his home while I'm there closing some deals."

"Girl, you are ballin' out of control. A mansion?" Reece asked.

"Come on, Reece. You know you need to get away. You can prepare for your case while you're there. I know they have a law library somewhere. Lock yourself away in one of the offices in that big mansion. Or sit by the pool and work. Or lie on the beach, whatever, just say you'll go. It's not like you can concentrate here anyway." I was trying desperately to convince my friend to step outside of her box. "Besides, it'll give you some time to think about what's going on with Darren."

"What's going on with Darren?" Maxie jumped in.

"Nothing," Reece said, rolling her eyes at me.

"She still scared to set a date." I answered the question for her.

"Girl, what's up? Why are you stringin' that man along?" Maxie asked the same question.

"Same thing I asked," I chuckled. "I know a lot of women who would love to get a piece of that chocolate thunder."

"Um hmm. He is fine," Maxie agreed.

"Let me think about your proposal, Charlotte," Reece finally said.

"What about you, Maxie? You know you need a vacation. Some new dreads too. And maybe some new clothes, but a vacation would do you some good. Come on and go."

"I'll have to check my schedule and get back to you."

"Do that," I said. "Let me know something soon. I'm leaving on Thursday, and I need to know in advance so I can book the airline tickets."

I stood and placed a ten dollar bill on the table. "Well, it's been real, ladies. But I have to run. I'm meeting a client."

"I'll call you after church tomorrow." That was Reece.

"Yeah, I'll call you tomorrow too," Maxie said.

I already knew they were going. Called my travel agent on my way to Decatur to meet my client. Booked the tickets.

4

Reece

When I got home, Darren was gone, and the red light on my answering machine was flashing out of control. I checked my messages. There was only one.

"Reece, it's your mother. Will I see you at church in the morning? You missed last Sunday, and I don't want this to become a habit. Reverend Peterson wants to know when you and Darren will be coming in for marriage counseling. You know that's so important, sweetheart. A marriage without counseling is doomed for failure. And when on earth are you two going to set a date? And where are you at this hour? Give me a call when you get in."

I opted not to call back, at least not right away. Mama had a bad habit of trying to run my life. It was as if I'd reached adulthood so quickly that someone forgot to notify her.

I grabbed some yogurt from the fridge and stepped out onto the balcony. The moonlight was beautiful. It was a chilly March night, and I leaned over my balcony to look at the stars. Never noticed how beautiful they were before. Thought about Charlotte's offer; the Bahamas. I could use a vacation. Couldn't remember the last time I'd had one. Could spend time working without interruptions. Not to mention, I needed some time to think about my situation with Darren. I'd been trying for weeks to tell him I just wasn't ready to get married. But at the same time, I was scared of losing him. He was definitely a great catch. Everything a woman wanted in a man. Couldn't figure out what was wrong with me. I loved Darren. Whatever that meant. Everybody had a different way of defining love. If it meant that I genuinely cared about his well-being, wanted him to succeed, cared about his hopes and dreams, then I guess I loved him. But then, I cared about the homeless man who slept on the pavement below my office window. Would take him in if I thought it was safe. There was nothing any different with Darren. It was the same kind of love, I thought. And that's what confused me. If you were in love with someone, weren't you supposed to feel a tingle in the pit of your stomach? Aren't you supposed to be blinded by uncontrollable feelings that cause you to do stupid stuff? I hadn't experienced any of that with Darren. He was a logical choice. Made sense in my life. Fit into the scheme of things. Besides, Mama was crazy about him. Wanted me to settle down and give her some grandchildren, especially since there wasn't much hope of my younger sister Sheila giving her any.

Sheila was happily single and let you know it every time the conversation of marriage and babies came up. She'd shown up at Mama's with three different guys within the past three months and none of them were marriage or fathering material. First there was Dexter who rode a motorcycle, wore earrings in both ears, tattoos covered his sleeveless arms, and he'd spent the evening bragging about doing time for armed robbery. He actually tried to fire up a joint in my mother's house, and then apologized for not stepping outside on the porch instead. Bobby was the short Keith Sweat look-a-like who claimed he was awaiting a record deal with Columbia Records. Swore he had passed his demo along to someone who worked there and they couldn't stop talking about it. He was just waiting for the contract to come through. Then there was Larry. Larry seemed normal at first, even after I got past the silver caps on his teeth. He was a Morris Brown graduate who was working on his masters. But when he kept telling me how he could hook my braids up and kept calling me girlfriend, I knew something wasn't quite right about that brother.

"I think he swings both ways," Sheila whispered when we were alone in the kitchen.

"You think?" I asked, already coming to that conclusion an hour before.

"Yeah. His roommate is gay, and that's all he talks about. Gary this and Gary that," she said. "I think his roommate is more than just a roommate, if you know what I mean."

"You're not serious about this man, are you?" I'd asked her.

"Nah," she said, "just looking for casual sex."

"Sheila. Are you serious? Please tell me you haven't slept with him."

"Thinking about it."

"Well think again," I warned her. "Ever heard of HIV?"

"He's been tested," she said in a matter-of-fact tone. "Got his results back last week."

"Did you see them?"

"He told me, and I believe him."

"No matter," I said. "If he swings both ways, he's more susceptible to the disease than a straight guy. And just because he tested negative doesn't mean the disease won't show up later. Takes years sometimes."

"I don't know if he swings both ways, Reece. I just suspect it."

"Well, whatever the case, be careful. Casual sex is nothing to play around with. Use protection, girl."

I couldn't sleep that night for worrying about my sister. I was relieved to find out she never slept with Larry and that he and Gary ended up moving to Miami together.

I grabbed the cordless off the base. Speed dialed Darren's number. No answer. Which was strange because he said he'd be at home all evening, and I'd already tried his cellular twice. If it were two or three years earlier, I might have driven to Stone Mountain just to pay him a surprise visit. But my days of checking up on my man were long over, especially since the last time I decided to drop in at his place, I'd received my own surprise. And although I swore it was forgotten, I thought of it often, and it only added to my reluctance to marry. It had rained most of the day, and I'd driven the two hours to Augusta to interview a witness for a case that was going to trial. Once I'd finished up and grabbed a bite to eat, I hopped on I-20 and headed west toward home. It was late, sometime after midnight, and my good sense warned that I should get a room for the night and make the drive the next morning; but I ignored my good sense. Once inside the Atlanta area, right outside of Stone Mountain, I began to doze at the wheel and thought it would be a good idea to stop at Darren's and crash. I had clothes there and could easily get dressed for the office the next morning at his place. I listened to the Quiet Storm on V-103, Luther getting me in a mood that made me anxious to get to my man. As I maneuvered my Range Rover into his driveway, I sat there for a moment, shut my eyes and took in the words of the sweet love song. I realized that I didn't have the garage door opener he'd given me, so I decided to use my key instead. I hit the alarm on my truck and walked across the lawn to the front door. Turned the key and tiptoed in, careful not to make too much noise. Knew Darren had an early morning and didn't want to wake him. Took my shoes off at the door and headed toward the kitchen to grab a light snack before surprising my prince by snuggling into bed beside him.

"Hi, Reece." The voice was so soft and timid, I barely heard it. My heart began to pound rapidly. She startled me.

"Hi," I said, not recognizing the beautiful stranger who was standing in my man's kitchen wearing my bathrobe. "Who are you?"

"I'm Cathy," she said, smiling as if it were perfectly natural for her to be standing there. Extended her hand to me. I looked at it, then at her face.

"And what are you doing here?" I asked, trying to remain calm while I collected the facts.

"I'm a friend of Darren's."

"Yes, but what are you doing here?"

"Visiting. We're old friends. Go way back." She smiled. "Darren didn't tell you I was coming? He can be so forgetful sometimes."

"Where's Darren?"

"In the bedroom. We were watching a DVD and I needed a snack," she said cheerfully.

"Watching a DVD, huh?" I said, remembering that the only DVD player in the house was in Darren's bedroom.

"I'm just gonna go get Darren."

"Don't you move!" I screamed, and dropped my briefcase, my purse, and commenced to take my earrings off. I had visions of my skinny fingers tightly wrapped around her neck, squeezing the life from her. Thought of pinning her to Darren's double door refrigerator until she began to grasp for breath.

I hadn't fought since grade school but knew that it was my duty to beat this woman's behind and show her that she was intruding in my life. However, my good sense kicked in and told me it wasn't worth it. This time I listened. I picked up my belongings from the floor and left without another word; I ran past Darren who was coming to see what the commotion was, wearing silk pajama pants and no shirt.

"Reece!" He ran outside trying to stop me from leaving. But I kept moving, fighting back the tears. "What's going on?"

"You tell me, Darren."

"It's not what you think."

"Then what is it?" I waited for an answer.

"Reece, she's just an old family friend. Her mother knows my mother."

"Have a nice life, Darren," I said, and ran to my truck.

"Reece, let's talk about this."

I jumped in my vehicle and burned rubber through his quiet upscale neighborhood, leaving Darren standing in the center of his yard, yelling my name. Dogs began barking, lights from curious neighbors suddenly blinked on, shining through closed blinds.

I ignored his calls for a month, and even ignored the dozens of roses that had been delivered to my office each day, and the cards that cluttered my mailbox. I finally allowed him the opportunity to explain that Cathy was an old friend of the family, who was in town for the night and needed a place to stay.

"She couldn't find a Holiday Inn anywhere?"

"Reece, there were plenty of hotels in the area, but my mother asked me if she could stay with me. I'm the only person she knows in Atlanta. She wanted us to catch up on old times."

"And you didn't see fit to tell me she was coming?"

"It was last minute."

"She said you knew," I said.

"I didn't know," he pleaded. "I swear I didn't know she was coming until the day of."

"She was wearing my bathrobe, and you were wearing . . . almost nothing."

"I didn't think you'd mind if she borrowed your robe. And the reason I was dressed that way, was because I heard loud voices coming from my kitchen. I ran down to see what was going on."

He had an answer for everything. And the truth was, I hadn't seen anything more than a woman in his kitchen. Cathy had even called my office twice to apologize for startling me, and swore that she and Darren were just old friends. I never believed any of it. Too many questions left unanswered, but I let it go. And although I eventually forgave him, the thought of it never left my mind.

I put the phone on its base so it could charge. Took a shower and put on my plaid flannel pajamas. Caught a *Sanford and*

Son rerun on TV Land. It was hilarious. It was the episode where Fred and Julio, the Puerto Rican neighbor, were arguing over where their property line was. Fred hired a surveyor to come out and measure the property line, so that he could force Julio to remove his junk from what he thought was his side of the property line. But as it turned out, Julio's property line stretched clear to Fred's front door. So his plan backfired. Fred was a trip, always giving that Puerto Rican a hard time. If it wasn't Julio, it was Aunt Esther. I'd seen just about every episode, but each time I watched, I'd laugh uncontrollably until tears filled my eyes.

After the credits went up, I hit the power button on the television, said my prayers, and shut off the lamp. I stared at my ceiling fan in the dark for a moment. Darren had installed it last summer. Said I needed it to conserve energy. Said my electric bill would be lighter if I used the fan instead of the air conditioner. He was right. I'd seen a tremendous difference when I got my next bill. He was Mr. Fix-It man. Spent so many hours at Home Depot, I was sure he'd bought stock in the place. If he could fix my bathroom showerhead or replace my garbage disposal, why couldn't he repair my heart? Why couldn't he make me love him the way he loved me?

I closed my eyes, but it took hours to fall asleep.

My alarm hadn't gone off, and when I glanced at the red numbers on my digital clock, I knew I would be running late. Mama would be fussing and giving me a lecture about being on time to the Lord's house. I could see her now, checking her watch and calling my cell phone every five minutes.

"You can be on time for work, why can't you be on time for the Lord?" she'd ask. And I'd just stand there looking sheepish because I really didn't have an answer.

I stood in the shower, eyes closed, mentally picking out my gray-and-white pinstriped suit. Thanked God that I'd caught it on sale at Rich's a few days before, because everything besides my jeans and sweats was still at the dry cleaners waiting to be picked up. I did something quick with my braids, got dressed, grabbed a bagel, and dashed out the door.

Mama was wearing her blue hat. I could see it a mile away when I drove up. Had on a navy blue suit to match. She was outside running her mouth with Sister Phillips. I was blasting a Mary Mary CD but turned it down as I maneuvered into a tight spot in the church parking lot. Parked next to Deacon Jones; his old Chevy had been driven since he bought it new in the sixties. Had it for as long as I could remember, and it was in tip-top shape, the prettiest blue I'd ever seen. Some youngster would love to own it, soup it up and claim he'd done something by throwing some expensive wheels on it and throwing in a sound system that he'd pump so loud you could barely hear yourself think. I was willing to bet Deacon Jones hadn't put more than twenty thousand miles on it, driving it back and forth to church on Sunday morning. He ran around to the passenger's side of the car, opened the door for Sister Jones. She stepped out as if she were stepping onto the red carpet at the Emmys, clean in her Sunday suit, hat to match. They were the epitome of marriage. I watched them stroll into the church like royalty, her arm in his. I smiled.

"Now that's what love is, Reece," I told myself. "Deacon and Sister Jones."

The way they looked at each other, you could tell they were in love.

I climbed out of my Range Rover, careful not to run my pantyhose, and grabbed my Bible off the leather passenger seat.

"I thought you'd never get here," Mama started fussing right away. "Don't you come to Sunday school anymore?"

"Hello, Mama." I kissed her cheek. "Hi, Sister Phillips."

"Hello, Reece. Nice to see you, honey."

"Where's your sister? Have you talked to her?" Mama asked. "I have all these different numbers for her—pager, cell phone. I don't know which is which."

"She'll be here, Ma. Let's go in and find a seat before it gets crowded," I said. "You worry too much."

"Reverend Peterson wants to talk to you after church."

"Okay, Ma."

We found a seat about three rows from the front. They were already into the praise and worship part of the service, so I joined in. Lifted my hands and gave God praise for all that he'd done for me. I was truly blessed and let him know it every chance I got. After the visitors were greeted with a warm welcome, we took our seats.

"It's offering time!" Minister Davis shouted, and the congregation started cheering. We were cheerful givers at the Christian Center.

As I sat down and filled out my tithes and offering envelope, Sheila slid in beside me.

"Hey," she whispered.

"Hey."

"Mama been looking for me?"

"About to send out the dogs."

We both snickered and Mama cut her eyes our way. When the offering plate came around, I put my envelope in. Sheila threw in a dollar and stuffed a piece of gum into her mouth. The choir rendered a selection and got us all worked up. People were dancing and shouting in the aisles. One of the ministers took off running at full speed, down the center aisle, clear to the back of the church and back up into the pulpit. A woman with a hat on bigger than Mama's started shouting.

"Hallelujah! Hallelujah!"

Sister Smith was jumping up and down so hard, I thought for sure she'd fall through the floor and into the church basement. Mama just waved her hand, tears streaming down her face. She was conservative when it came to the Holy Ghost. I couldn't wait to see it hit her hard; she'd fall out in the floor, or take off running through the church. That would be a sight, my Mama lying out in the spirit. I would need my camcorder for that one.

Just before the choir's selection was over, Darren squeezed in between Mama and me. Kissed Mama on the cheek, then me.

"Sorry I'm late," he whispered.

"You missed the offering."

"Did I miss Sister Smith's Holy Ghost break dance?"

"Shhhh." That was Mama.

"At this time, I would like to present our pastor. Reverend Peterson. Let's receive him with a warm Amen," Minister Davis said. He shook the pastor's hand, and then sat down.

"Amen." The congregation said it in unison.

"Good morning, saints." Reverend Peterson wore a gray suit, with a colorful pink-and-gray tie. His hair perfectly lined, and mustache trimmed. He was a handsome man, brown skinned, tall, single. All the older women in the church mourned the day of Sister Peterson's death, but rejoiced at the fact that the good reverend was now a bachelor. They fought for the front row seats, and nearly knocked each other over after church just to shake his hand or invite him over for a nice hearty Sunday dinner.

"Good morning, Reverend!" the congregation shouted.

"God is good!" he said.

"All the time!" the congregation responded.

"Let us bow our heads for a word of prayer," Reverend Peterson started. "Father God, we thank you for this new day. A new opportunity to worship you and give reverence to your name. Father God, we ask that you bless the Word and open up our hearts to receive it. These and all other blessings we ask in your Son, Jesus' name. Amen."

"Amen," the congregation said.

"How many of y'all came armed and dangerous with the Word?" We all waved our Bibles in the air. "Let us open up our Word to Proverbs twenty, verse twenty-two."

Pages were rattling as we searched for the scripture. Sheila forgot her Bible, so I shared mine with her.

"It reads, 'He who finds a wife, finds a good thing. And obtains favor from the Lord.' "

The women on the front row shouted "ooohs" and "ahhhs" and "Amens," as if he were addressing them personally.

Mama leaned over and peered at me.

"What?" I mouthed to her.

Darren gave me a smile with those dimples.

Reverend Peterson went on to talk about holy matrimony and the things that each partner in a marriage are expected to do. He talked about how family comes first, then careers. I couldn't tell if this was a Sunday morning service or premarital counseling. I wondered if God were trying to tell me something or if Mama had pulled Reverend Peterson aside before the service and whispered in his ear. I threw my finger in the air, a sign that I needed to be excused, and tip-toed to the restroom.

I leaned over the face bowl and freshened my lipstick. Straightened my pantyhose, then took a seat on the sofa. Needed to get myself together before going back into the sanctuary. I found a piece of chocolate in my purse and popped it into my mouth, sat there for a long while and enjoyed the peace. A couple of sisters came in, handled their business, and went back to the sanctuary. I sat there a little while longer but knew Mama would come looking for me if I were gone too long, so I made my way back. When I opened the doors, the service was over and the congregation had been dismissed. Sheila had already taken off. She never stuck around for the socializing that went on after church. I found Mama, Darren, and Reverend Peterson at the front of the church huddled in what seemed like a secret conversation. I approached with caution.

"I've invited the Reverend over for dinner." Mama smiled at me and commenced to straightening my collar. "You and Darren are coming, aren't you?"

"Of course we are, Mother Jameson," Darren answered for me.

"That's good, good." Reverend Peterson was grinning like a proud father. "Look forward to speaking with you both over dinner."

"And we look forward to hearing what you have to say." Darren shook the Reverend's hand.

"You all right, honey?" Mama asked.

"I'm fine, Ma," I said. "I'll meet you at the house."

"You have your key, don't you?" she asked. I nodded a yes. "Go on in and check on the collards. Make sure they're tender. Okay, honey?"

"Yes, Ma."

"And if you don't mind, could you make a pan of corn-bread?"

"Consider it done, Ma," I said.

Darren walked me to my car, he couldn't open the door fast enough before I was inside, with the key in the ignition, my foot on the brake, and the gear in drive.

"You all right, Reece? You look a little flushed." He moved a stray braid from my face and kissed my cheek.

"I just needed some fresh air. I'll see you at Mama's, okay?"

"All right," he said. "Drive safe."

As soon as he stepped away, I drove out of the parking lot and took off down 75, blasting my Mary Mary CD.

At Mama's, the Reverend blessed the food. Mama commenced to passing dishes of fried chicken, greens, macaroni and cheese, and cornbread around the table. And we all placed healthy portions of it on our plates.

"When y'all planning on coming in for counseling?" The Reverend started up the conversation that I'd dreaded all the way home.

"I told Reece that we need to schedule a time as soon as possible," Darren said. "What's good for you, Reece?"

"I . . . uh . . ."

"I'll be at the church all day Wednesday. Got another couple comin' in that afternoon. Tryin' to save their marriage, you know. It's always good to get counseling when your marriage is in trouble, but ain't nothing like marriage counseling before-hand, though. That way you don't fall short once you get in it." He stuffed a piece of cornbread into his mouth.

"Wednesday's good for me, Reece. What about you?" Darren asked.

"I'll have to check and see. What . . . what time are you thinking of?"

"Oh, say, five o'clock or so." Reverend Peterson could put some food away and was working on his second helping of greens. "I ought to be finished with my other couple by then."

"I'll let you know by Monday, you know, if I can make it at that time or not."

"That'll be just fine," he said. "And have y'all decided on a date yet?"

"June twenty-eighth is good for me. What about you, Reece?" There was that date issue again, lingering in the air, awaiting my submission to it.

"Uh, sure." I gave in, and immediately wished I could take it back. "June twenty-eighth is okay with me, I guess."

There. It was out there. A date had been set.

"That's good. I had already penciled you in. Don't have any other engagements. The church is available all day too. And you shouldn't have any problems getting Sister Green to play the organ for you, if that's what you choose."

"I'll give her a call tomorrow," Darren volunteered.

Darren had barely touched his plate; he was so busy planning my life for me that his food was getting cold in the process. Mama kept smiling and bouncing her head back and forth between all of us as we talked. She hadn't bothered to add her two cents as I'd expected.

"The two of you make such a fine couple." Reverend Peterson smiled. "Don't you think so, Sister Pearl?"

"Yes, yes," Mama said.

"Fine couple," Reverend Peterson said again.

"Reece, you all right honey? You don't look like you feeling good at all."

"I'm fine, Mama." I put my fork down. "Excuse me, please. I need to go to the restroom."

45

I locked the door behind me; sat on the toilet with the lid down. Thought I would pass out in there, the air was so thick. I pulled my cell phone out of my purse. Dialed Charlotte. It rang twice before her voice mail picked up. I knew she was still at her AME church in College Park. They usually went until three o'clock, sometimes longer if it was communion Sunday.

"Charlotte. It's me, Reece. Book my ticket, girl."

5

Maxie

I grabbed a glass of milk and warmed it before going to bed. Pulled out my notepad and jotted down a few things I needed to remember. I was doing some research to try and find my sisters. All I had was the name of a lady I thought had adopted them some years back, and the woman at social services couldn't seem to place the file. Had been looking for them for at least six years. Kept running into dead ends. I wondered if they were even in the country. Nobody seemed to know anything. I'd cried myself to sleep so many nights. And tonight was no different.

It was late, so I turned off the television. Listened to a little Miles Davis. Couldn't sleep, though, for the bright streetlight that was blaring through my window. Even after I shut the blinds, it still seemed to creep in. The streetlight reminded me of that night; the night that changed my life.

Uncle Walter's one-bedroom apartment was the closest thing we had to home. The three of us cuddled together in his king-sized bed, and he usually took the couch in his living room.

I never slept much after Mama's funeral. Couldn't. Most nights I would stay awake, staring at the streetlight outside

Uncle Walter's bedroom window. Some nights I was entertained by the arguments of Miss Bessie and Mr. Paul who lived below. They'd get drunk, cuss and throw things at each other at least twice a week.

"Maxie, you still up?" All I could see were the whites of Alex's eyes looking at me.

"Yeah, I'm up."

"What you thinkin' about?"

"Just wonderin' what could've been so bad that Mama wanted to leave us. Were we really that bad?" I sat up and leaned against the headboard.

"I think it was because I kept getting in trouble for talking in Miss Johnson's class. Maybe if Mama didn't have to go down to that school so often, she'd still be here."

"Maybe it was because it was so hard for her to feed us and stuff. Maybe she was tired of sleeping with those men just to provide for us."

"Or maybe she just had some things going on in her life that didn't have a thing to do with you!" Uncle Walter startled us as he came into the room and turned on the light. "What are you girls doing up at this hour anyhow?"

"Can't sleep."

"What happened with your mama didn't have a thing to do with y'all, you hear me?" Uncle Walter had a serious look on his face. "Sometimes grown folks just get to a point in life where they feel like they can't move forward. Life just gets too hard for 'em and they take the easy way out."

"But what about us?" Button was missing her two front teeth. She'd lost them the day she turned six. She sat up in bed, and I'd wondered how much of the situation she truly understood.

"Your mama loved you. Every one of you. Don't you ever forget that." Button crawled up into his lap. "You hear me?"

"Yes, sir." We said it almost in unison.

"Now, Uncle need to make a run somewhere. I don't wanna leave y'all here by yourselves, so put some shoes on."

"Where we going?"

48

He started cheesing, and his gold tooth twinkled like a star in the night. "I got a horse that's about to make me a whole lot of money."

"I like horses." Button clapped her hands.

"We goin' to the track?" I asked. I knew Uncle Walter spent a lot of time at the horse races. He was always losing money there. Mama had helped him pay off some of his debts, and he'd promised to pay her back as soon as his horse came in the next time around.

"Yes, sugar. My girl Buttercup is definitely comin' in tonight." He stuck his hands in his pockets and jingled his change around. Then he took some Visine out and put two drops in each of his eyes. "Now get some shoes on; we goin' for a ride."

We did as Uncle Walter told us, the three of us piling into the backseat of his brown El Dorado. He had two big fuzzy dice hanging from his rearview mirror, and his eight-track was playing some tune by Curtis Mayfield. I recognized his voice because Mama had some of his music. I even knew some of the words, especially the part where he talked about being somebody's pusher man.

"Uncle Walter, what's a pusher man?" Alex was always the curious one.

He looked at her and roared with laughter.

"Somebody you don't need to know nothin' about." He took the eight-track out and put another one in.

"I know what it is." Since I'd turned twelve, I thought I knew just about everything there was to know. "It's a drug dealer."

"You mean like Mr. Sam who used to bring them pills to Mama?" Alex was always running off at the mouth too.

"What pills?" Uncle Walter looked right at me, as if I'd been the one who'd intentionally kept this information from him.

"Just some pills to help her nerves." I repeated what Mama had told me when I asked her about it.

"Did Mr. Sam come around a lot?" he asked.

"About two or three times a week." I wanted to put my hand over Alex's mouth. "He always told Mama he wasn't coming back until she paid him for the other stuff. He spent the night sometimes too."

"Shut your mouth," I told Alex. I didn't want anyone knowing about Mama, not even Uncle Walter. Wanted to protect her. She'd told me things in confidence, and I swore I'd never share them with anyone.

Uncle Walter peered at me through the rearview mirror. It was a look that told me he knew what I was thinking.

"You really are growin' up, Maxie. I'm real proud of how you take care of your sisters and all. I used to take care of my sister that way. It was hard, too, 'cause she was just so hard-headed. Your mama was somethin' else." He chuckled a little. "It ain't easy being the oldest, is it?"

I shook my head.

The siren and those blue lights startled me.

Uncle Walter became panicky as he pulled the El Dorado over. It was dark on that dirt road, but the lights from the police car brightened it up.

"Were you speeding, Uncle Walter?" Alex asked.

"Just a little," he said.

"Then he'll just give you a speeding ticket and send you on your way," I tried to assure him. "Right?"

"Well, it's not that simple, sugar." He looked really scared and I couldn't figure out why. "You girls just sit back and be quiet, okay?"

We did just that.

The officer shined his flashlight right in Uncle Walter's face, then in each one of our faces.

"You got a driver's license, boy?" A toothpick hung from that white officer's lips.

"Yes, sir." Uncle Walter pulled his wallet out of his back pocket and handed the officer his driver's license.

"I'll be right back." He went back to his car for what seemed like an eternity.

There were more sirens, blue lights, and two more police

cars surrounded the El Dorado before long. The officer showed back up at the driver's window.

"You wanna step out of the car, boy?"

Uncle Walter cooperated. The minute he stepped out, the officer told him to place his hands on top of the car, frisked him, and then handcuffed him.

"We have a warrant for your arrest." The other two were holding guns in our uncle's face. "Is there someone we can call for those children?"

"What are you arresting me for?"

"Is there someone we can call for the children?" the officer repeated, ignoring my uncle's question. My eyes begged for an answer as well.

Uncle Walter looked at each one of us; maybe he was hoping we knew someone. But the truth was, our Mama was dead and he was all we had.

"No one," he said, dropping his head. "What's gonna happen to my girls?"

"They'll be just fine," the officer snapped. "You have a right to remain silent. Anything you say can and will be held against you in the court of law."

"Where are we going?" I wanted to know. Alex and Button were crying hysterically. I was fighting back the tears. I had to stay strong for them.

"You have a right to an attorney. Boy, you got a lawyer or someone you wanna call?"

"No," Uncle Walter said to the officer. "Where are you taking them?"

"Social services. Probably be placed in foster care until their mother or another relative can come and pick them up."

"Girls, I'll pick you up first thing in the morning. I promise."

"I don't think you'll be picking anyone up in the morning." The officer grinned and flipped that toothpick around in his mouth.

"Their mother is dead," Uncle Walter pleaded. "I'm all they have."

"Oh yeah? Well, they'll be all right."

I was in tears by then.

"Uncle Walter?" I looked into his eyes for an answer.

"Be a big girl, Maxie. And take good care of your sisters for me."

"When are you coming to get us?" Alex's nose was snotty.

"As soon as I can, sugar. I promise." He didn't sound convincing at all.

We were on our knees in the backseat, looking out the back window as the officer pushed Uncle Walter's head down into the backseat of his patrol car.

Another officer opened the back door of the El Dorado.

"Let's go, girls." His shirt barely covered his stomach as he escorted us into his car.

"I want my mommy," Button whined, and put her finger in her mouth.

"Your mommy? Where's your mommy?" He asked as if he didn't already know.

"She's dead," I explained to him, and grabbed Button's hand. I held on to it the whole way.

When I woke up, the digital red numbers on the alarm clock were flashing three o'clock, Miles Davis was still playing, and the glass of milk was still on the nightstand untouched, cold now. I booted my laptop and starting working on my editorial piece that I was writing for the newspaper; a piece that would warn its elderly readers of a greedy new developer in the land and hopefully protect them from being stripped of their investments. Some of them just didn't know any better, and I felt it was my duty to get the word out. After a few pecks on the keys, my mind began to drift. I found myself thinking too much, hoping, and longing for my sisters. Could actually see their faces. Had a picture in my mind of what they would look like all grown up.

All the tension was keeping me awake most nights. Knew I needed a vacation and planned on calling Charlotte the first chance I got.

6

Charlotte

"Why can't she be on time?" I paced the floor. "If they start boarding, I'm leaving her behind right here at Hartsfield Jackson Airport. She can walk to Nassau for all I care! I told her our flight leaves at five."

"Charlotte, she'll be here. Just relax." Reece was calmly typing away on her laptop, and I was pacing the floor waiting for Maxie to show up. I checked my watch again. It was four thirty. Checked it again at four thirty-eight.

"We will now begin preboarding for American Airlines flight nineteen thirty-three to Nassau, Bahamas. If you're traveling with small children or if you need special assistance, you may begin boarding now," the woman announced over the intercom.

A couple with three small children rushed over to the gate, followed by an elderly woman with a cane. My eyes searched Hartsfield Jackson for Maxie. Reece continued to type on her laptop; in-between answering calls on her cellular phone, her eyes searched the airport too. Once preboarding was complete, the tall slender redhead in the American Airlines uniform came back over the intercom.

"At this time, we will begin our general boarding. Please

have your proper identification ready and your boarding passes available. We will begin our boarding with rows fifteen and higher. If you're seated in rows fifteen and higher, please come forward at this time."

Reece finally looked up from her laptop, then looked at her watch, then looked at me. I had already left three messages on Maxie's home phone and one on her cellular. I started looking around the airport again, pulled the itinerary out of my purse, read it, wondering if I'd given her the right flight times.

"Looking for me?" Maxie startled me.

When I turned to look at her, she took my breath away. She looked amazing, actually wearing something that enhanced her appearance. She had on a black pinstriped suit with wide-legged pants and a lime green silk blouse underneath. Her golden locks were redone, and she was wearing a sexy brown-colored lipstick and even eyeliner.

"Where have you been? I told you the flight leaves at five!"

"Maxie, you look amazing!" Reece had packed up her laptop, and threw her laptop bag across her shoulder.

"Yeah, yeah. You do look good," I said, "but you're late!"

"I'm here now, Charlotte," she said, "and the plane's still here, so what's the big deal?"

"What's up with the new duds?" Reece asked.

"The big deal is we have been here for over an hour waiting on you," I said.

"Charlotte, let it go," Maxie said.

"No. I won't let it go. You are so irresponsible sometimes. Having us all worried about you."

"Where did you get the suit?" Reece was totally ignoring the matter at hand. Maxie was late.

"I went shopping. What's the big deal?" she said. "Let's go. We have a plane to catch."

"Oh, now she's rushing us." I picked up my carry-on and headed toward the ramp.

* * *

I rested my head against the leather seat in first class. Began to think about the hectic morning I'd had. Remembered zipping through traffic on 285 headed east before it had come to a complete standstill. Knew I had an appointment in Dunwoody and should've left long before I did, but forgot to set the alarm clock. My pager going off was my only salvation. I signaled to get over into the fast lane, attempting to pass up gramps, who was moving along at a snail's pace. The minute I swung into the passing lane, Suzy Homemaker with her three kids in the back of a Volvo rammed me from behind.

"No, she did not hit my Lexus!" I screamed and pulled over. She pulled over behind me, got out and started apologizing.

"I'm so sorry, ma'am," she'd said.

I assessed the damage to my vehicle and looked at her. The damage was minor, just a few scratches of paint, but enough to make a report and to get her insurance information. She continued to apologize and explained that she had been tending to a choking child in the backseat and had turned her head for just a minute. A minute was all it took to put a few red paint scratches on my white Lexus.

"I've already called the police," she said. "They should be here any minute."

Well wasn't she efficient? I didn't have the strength to tell her what I really thought of her negligence.

A minute turned into thirty minutes before the officer arrived. By the time he took a report and I merged back onto 285, I was already fifteen minutes late for my appointment. I called my client and explained the situation. Unfortunately, he was on a strenuous time frame and couldn't wait. So we rescheduled, and I headed to my OB-GYN's office for my ten o'clock appointment instead. Fortunately, a nine thirty had canceled, and I was able to squeeze into that time slot.

Gwen hadn't looked happy when she walked in with my chart.

"Good morning, Charlotte." She was a small woman, from Kenya, and wore a short fro perfectly trimmed, which was perfect for her face. I loved her African accent. "I'm glad you could come this morning. I have the results from your mammogram here."

"Good. What's up, Gwen?"

She shut the door.

"We have a problem."

Gwen Hayes had been my gynecologist for the past six years, and I loved her because she always took time with her patients to explain things and to make sure they understood everything about their health. Always answered questions, straightforward, honest. Knew her profession well.

"As you remember, during your clinical breast exam, we found an unusual lump. Which is why I ordered a mammogram. Because there's a lump present, further tests are needed to find out if it's benign or malignant."

"Gwen, what are you saying? Are you telling me I have breast cancer?"

"No. I'm saying that further tests are needed, Charlotte." She was always so calm. "I can't make a complete diagnosis at this point."

"Okay, when?"

"I'm going to refer you to a surgeon who will perform a biopsy as soon as possible. Here's his name and number." She handed me a card. "His office is less than a mile from here. He has more experience with breast diseases and breast biopsies than me. He will be able to determine which exam is best for you. I would like for you to go over to his office right now, if you can. My nurse has already set up a tentative appointment for you."

Tears were beginning to fill my eyes. Gwen grabbed my hand.

"The biopsy will give us more information, Charlotte. Let's not worry until then. Okay?"

"Okay," I said, attempting to get myself together. "When will I know the results?"

"Couple of days."

"I'm leaving town this evening."

"I'll call you myself. As soon as I get them. Leave me a number where I can reach you."

"What if it's cancer?"

"Then we'll know how to proceed from there," she said in her Kenyan accent. "Relax, sweetheart. Let's take this one step at a time. Okay?"

I nodded my head in agreement.

When we began landing, I looked over at my girls. I hadn't shared my medical findings with them. Didn't want them to worry. Reece was busy, still punching the keys on her laptop, engaged so deeply in whatever it was she was working on, she only looked up occasionally. Maxie was reclined in the aisle seat next to me, light sounds of snoring escaping from her open mouth the entire flight. I nudged her with my elbow.

"Maxie, stop snoring," I whispered.

Her head shot straight up and she looked around, trying desperately to remember where she was. Checked her mouth for drool.

"You were snoring the whole way. Couldn't hear myself think," I said to her. "Didn't you sleep last night?"

"Of course I slept last night," she said, and placed her seat in the upright position. "Where are we?"

"We're about to land."

I looked over at Reece who was putting her laptop away. "Are you planning to work the entire trip?" I whispered to her.

"Just tying up some loose ends, that's all," Reece said.

"You're gonna have some fun, right?"

"Of course," she said, and locked her tray in position.

I stuffed a piece of Doublemint into my mouth, leaned my head against the back of the seat, and prepared for landing.

57

7

Reece

Nassau was a beautiful seventy-six degrees. A picture book, fairy tale sort of place, with its pastel-colored buildings and the scent of the ocean floating through the air. It screamed of romance, culture, and history. I could even visualize the candy-striped lighthouses that stood firm in the middle of the ocean. The ones that caused so much grief some years ago to those who had made a lucrative living by salvaging from the unfortunate ships that ended their sailing days on the shoals of the white beaches.

I observed the islanders at the airport with their dialect and idioms that reminded me a little of the South Carolina Gullah people. Only their dialect was the melodic English you heard only in the islands of the Bahamas, spoken with such precision and clarity, but you almost had to ask them to repeat it, if you weren't familiar.

I took off my jean jacket and tied it around my waist. Charlotte hailed us a cab at the airport, her Louis Vuitton luggage stacked at the curb: two large suitcases, a carry-on bag, and a make-up case. It was a wonder she made it through customs with more than one suitcase.

"Dag, how long you planning to stay?" I asked, pulling my one suitcase on wheels behind me and throwing the strap of my carry-on onto my shoulder.

"A week, maybe two," she said. "I actually packed very light."

"Yeah, right. Light, Charlotte?" That was Maxie.

"I can't help it if you chose to pack your clothes in a backpack," Charlotte said.

Maxie had one carry-on gym bag and a backpack.

"Got everything I need," she said. "Ain't trying to impress nobody."

"That's dreadfully apparent." Charlotte rolled her eyes. "I'm not trying to impress anyone either!"

"Oh really? Two oversized Louis Vuitton suitcases, Charlotte?" Maxie snapped back.

"Everything I brought is necessary," she said. "You should take notes. I can only imagine what you have all crumpled up in that duffel bag of yours."

"Everything I need."

"Can we get something to eat? I'm starved." I interrupted their bickering. "Let's get something authentic, like some conch fritters or some pigeon peas and rice."

"That sounds good to me," Maxie said. "Nothing like the native eats of the island."

My mouth watered for the taste of fresh seafood. The infamous pigeon peas and rice or whatever the fresh catch of the day was, accompanied by a plate of hot grits. Or my all-time favorite conch fritters with a bowl of conch chowder on the side; so spicy it would cause my eyes to water.

"I don't eat that." Charlotte turned her nose up. "I just want a salad, with a light ranch dressing on the side."

The dark gentleman with a graying beard loaded our bags into the trunk of his car. Driving his taxi along the left side of the street, we ended up on Delancy at the Buena Vista, one of the finest restaurants in Nassau. A pink-and-white historical mansion that was built in the early 1700s. I would've been fine at a small neighborhood joint where I could roll up my sleeves and get busy, but Charlotte's taste for their Bahamian lobster bisque prevailed. We weren't even dressed for the occasion. The Buena Vista wasn't a jeans sort of place, and the stares we received only solidified that fact.

After dinner we made our way over to Cable Beach, an area just west of Nassau, to the beautiful beachfront estate that would be our home for the next week or so. It was breathtaking, palm trees all around it, manicured lawn, and both indoor and outdoor pools. The mansion was situated on a huge golf course. Charlotte found the key, and when we entered, my mouth fell to the floor. I could see my reflection in the marble floor in the foyer, and the winding staircase was more than my heart could take. The three of us were shocked into silence, hesitant to speak for fear that we might wake up and find we were dreaming.

"Wow." Maxie broke the silence, but that was all she could muster up.

"Ramsey is living quite large," Charlotte said. "Well girls, don't just stand there. Let's take a look around."

We ventured upstairs first. Peeked into each bedroom. Eleven of them altogether. We counted.

"Who on earth needs eleven bedrooms?" I gasped for breath.

"Wait a minute. Nine bathrooms?" Maxie said after we had counted them too.

"That's what I'm sayin', " I agreed with Maxie, and took a peek into the study, which was furnished in beautiful cherry wood. "Nice office."

"Keep moving, Reece," Charlotte said, pushing me along to the stairwell. "No more working today. I say we put on our bathing suits and go for a dip in that pool."

"Sounds good to me." That was Maxie. "As a matter of fact, I'm taking the room on the end overlooking the pool."

"I'll take the one with the view of the rose garden," Charlotte said.

"Not sure which one I want. So many to choose from." I was still in awe of the place.

"Oh, girl. Just pick a room. There's like a hundred to choose from," Charlotte said.

"For real." That was Maxie.

I finally decided on the one adjacent to the study. It was decorated with Victorian-style furniture. Reminded me of *Gone with the Wind,* or the quaint little bed and breakfast Darren and I frequented in the French Quarter in New Orleans.

My cell phone buzzed and I knew who it was before I even looked at the number on the screen. I silenced it and made a mental note to call Darren back later.

I chose my white bikini for the pool and jumped in for a swim. Maxie jumped in after me, and Charlotte sat on the side with her feet dipped in the water. She was a million miles away in thought. I could tell by the distant look on her face that something was on her mind. Something serious.

"Hey, Pookie," I said teasingly to Charlotte. She hated when I called her that.

"That name is so ghetto, Reece. Please don't call me that," she said. "What is a pookie, anyway?"

Maxie and I fell out laughing. I only called Charlotte that to annoy her or to get her attention. Sometimes I called her that in public places just to embarrass her in front of some of the bourgeois people she hung out with.

She was unusually quiet, and I knew something was wrong.

"What's on your mind?"

"Nothing."

"Come on, girl. We been friends for ten years. I know when something's up."

"Nothing's up. I'm just taking in the view."

"Liar." I splashed water on her, and she tried to duck, but it got her right in the face. I knew her better than she was giving me credit for, and it pissed me off. "Tell me or I'm pulling you in."

"Don't."

"Tell me, then."

"Nothing to tell."

"Let's pull her in, Maxie."

Maxie grabbed one leg and I grabbed the other.

"Don't!" she screamed. "I just got my hair done!"

Too late. She was in. Her hairdo that was once a short and sassy cut tapered all nice in the back, was now a flat mess on her head. Maxie and I laughed until our stomachs hurt.

"You heifers are in trouble!" she gasped. Her dark chocolate skin changed tones. "I'm too old for this crap!"

"Have a little fun, Charlotte," Maxie said. "Life is too short not to."

"Yeah, life *is* short, ain't it?" Charlotte screamed. "Grow up, Reece."

She got out, grabbed her towel, and dried off.

"You ain't mad are you?" I teased. "We were just having some fun, Charlotte."

"Reece, you're doing my hair later."

She ran into the mansion, the towel tied around her waist. Maxie and I couldn't help but laugh as she tripped over a lawn chair, stumbled, then stomped on inside.

Maxie and I stayed in the pool until our toes began to wrinkle. Later, we went inside where I found my home in Ramsey's study. It was the most interesting place in the entire house. All sorts of books were on the shelf, James Baldwin's *If Beale Street Could Talk,* Maya Angelou's *I Know Why the Caged Bird Sings,* several Harlem Renaissance personalities such as Langston Hughes, Marcus Garvey, DuBois. The music collection boasted of artists like Duke Ellington and Louis Armstrong.

"Hey Charlotte, is Ramsey black or white?" I yelled it down the hall and almost heard an echo.

"White, why?" she yelled back.

"Because he has all these books and music by black people."

"What kind of music?" Maxie asked, coming into the study where I was and checking out the collection.

"Here's Miles Davis." I knew he was on her list of favorites.

"Get out of here. Miles Davis?" She took the CD. "This dude has great taste in music."

"Put it in," I told her.

She went over and studied Ramsey's expensive stereo for a moment, popped the CD in, and we looked at each other and smiled at the beautiful sound of it. We sat in the middle of the floor in our bikinis; with towels wrapped around us, we looked through the books and found several autographed copies. Made ourselves right at home.

"My mama used to play this song all the time." Maxie closed her eyes, and I could tell that she was far away. "Reminds me of when I was little. My sisters and me would sit up half the night listening to Mama and her friends Reba and Maydella from down the street, playing cards and telling lies until the crack of dawn. Drinking and cussing." She smiled. "They used to wear those records out. Marvin Gaye and Curtis Mayfield. Sometimes a little Miles Davis. She thought we were sleep."

"How's your research coming?" She had drifted away, but I brought her back to the present time.

"Empty. Social services can't seem to find any record of who adopted my sisters. The records were purged and no one can seem to find them. All I remember is we stayed with a woman. Her first name was Sarah. A black woman. Never knew her last name. We just called her Miss Sarah. She adopted my sisters. Didn't want me," she said, and I saw a sort of sadness in her eyes that I hadn't seen before. "Said I was too old. I was almost a teenager and she thought I might be trouble. I was sent away."

"Sent away where?"

"To another foster home. Wasn't there two months before my foster father raped me. After that, I was removed from that home and sent to another one." Her eyes were closed as Miles serenaded us. "This time I was beaten. By Miss Fisher, my foster mother. She would hit me with a broomstick across my back if I looked at her wrong. Or if I mouthed off to her, which I often did. I would mumble things under my breath, because I hated her so much. I was very rebellious and had a lot of anger. She said I was too old for anybody to adopt me, so she was all I had. Said I should be grateful somebody wanted to put up with me at all. The abuse continued at every home I ended up in. If it wasn't physical, it was sexual abuse. For years I thought it was normal to be abused by adults. Because it happened so often."

"That's awful, Maxie. I didn't know."

"When I turned sixteen, I ran away from my fifth home. Got myself a job."

"Whatever happened to the uncle you told me about? He never tried to find you?"

"Haven't seen Uncle Walter since that night he was arrested. He promised to come back. But he never did."

"What about Miss Sarah's house? Do you remember where it was?"

"I was twelve, Reece. Don't remember much at all. Just that it was in South Georgia somewhere. Don't even remember the name of the street. Wasn't there long before I was shipped away to another home."

"There's got to be some record somewhere."

"I've been down this road so many times. Telling myself there's got to be some answers somewhere. And I keep coming up empty."

"What about school, Maxie? Did you go to school from Miss Sarah's house?"

"It was the summertime."

"What about the social worker who took you there?"

"Hispanic lady. Miss Hernandez. They never heard of her at social services."

"They never heard of her? Surely if she was employed by them, her signature is on some paperwork somewhere."

"I'm telling you, Reece. They said they never heard of her. It's like pulling teeth to get answers from them."

"Let me make some phone calls. I have a private detective friend who can find out just about anything about anybody."

"Who you looking for?" Charlotte came into the study, a towel wrapped around her freshly shampooed hair. Caught the tail end of our conversation.

"Talking about looking for Maxie's sisters."

"Again?" Charlotte rolled her eyes.

"Yes, again," Maxie said.

"Why do you have to be so insensitive, Charlotte?" I asked her.

"I'm not. It's just that she's been tormenting herself with this issue for as long as I've known her. It's time to move on. Find a man, settle down. Have some babies."

"Like you, Charlotte? Where are your husband and babies?" There was hurt in Maxie's tone.

"All I'm saying is you should get on with your life, that's all."

"I can't move on until I get some closure."

"Closure, Maxie?" Charlotte asked. "What's it gonna take to put closure to a situation that's not even open?"

"Charlotte, shut up!" I wanted to stop her before she hurt Maxie any more than she already had.

"No, Reece. She needs to hear this," Charlotte insisted. "Maxie's thirty-four years old. How long has she been waiting for Uncle Walter's return? Six years I've known her. And six years she's been waiting. He ain't comin' back, Maxie. And your sisters? Surely they know they have an older sister out there somewhere. Why haven't they tried finding you? After all this time, why aren't they out pounding the pavement looking for you? You know why, Maxie? Because they've moved on with their lives."

"Charlotte!" I couldn't believe her.

"No, let her finish, Reece. Maybe she's right. I've asked myself the same questions. Why haven't they tried to find me? I've spent my whole life worrying about them. Who ever took the

65

time to worry about me? I was the big sister. Always had to be the strong one. Who was supposed to take care of me?"

"I'm telling you, Maxie. Life is too short," Charlotte continued. "You should be enjoying yourself instead of tormenting yourself over your past."

I looked into Charlotte's eyes and saw something I'd never seen before. Compassion.

"Look at me. I'm forty years old. Can't keep a man to save my soul. No children to pass anything along to. Nothing in my life means anything to me, except my career and the two of you. My mother, with her Alzheimer's, doesn't even know who I am half the time. Pretty pitiful, huh?"

Maxie and I looked at Charlotte, searched her face for where all this was coming from.

"You're not pitiful, Charlotte," I said.

"Oh yeah? Then why don't I have anything to show for my life?"

"You do, Charlotte. Look at the career you've built for yourself," Maxie said.

"Who cares about a career when I might have breast cancer?" She just blurted it out. Then sat on the floor with us, her back against the wall. She said it so quickly, I thought I'd heard her wrong.

"What?"

"Dr. Hayes found a lump that she thinks might be early signs of cancer. I had a biopsy done this morning."

"Oh, Charlotte, I didn't know." I reached over to hug her.

"Me either," Maxie said, and we gave her a group hug.

"Don't be getting all mushy and stuff. That's why I didn't want to tell y'all. I'll be fine."

"Of course you will," I tried to reassure her.

"When will you know the results of the biopsy?" Maxie asked.

"Couple of days."

"Why didn't you tell us sooner?"

"Because y'all worry too much." She pulled herself up from the floor. "Reece, you need to come on and do my hair."

"Okay, but you have to promise you'll keep us in the loop. We wanna know what the results of that biopsy are. We wanna know everything that goes on from here on out. You understand?" I sounded like my mother.

"I'll keep you in the loop if you promise not to make a big deal out of everything."

"Okay, Pookie." I tried to cheer her up.

"And stop calling me that!" she said and stormed out of the room.

8

Maxie

I bought some Cuban cigars at the straw market. At least a half dozen, and the brother who sold them to me assured me they were really from Cuba. Charlotte had a straw bag full of jewelry and clothes that she had bought. And Reece was trying on some shades.

"What about these, Maxie?"

"Too big on your face," I said as I tried on the ugliest straw hat I'd ever seen in my life. It had huge red and green flowers made of straw all over it.

"These?" Reece asked, trying on a smaller pair of black shades.

"Those look good on you, girl."

"I'll take these," Reece told the young Bahamian woman, who was sitting in a chair fanning from the heat.

"Very nice choice," the woman said, and took Reece's money. "What about the earrings, my lady?"

"Yeah, I'll take them too," she said. "And give me the necklace too."

"And I'll take this hat," I told the woman after she made change for Reece.

"What you gon' do with that hat, Maxie?"

"Piss Charlotte off with it," I laughed. "Wear it at the most inopportune time. Maybe if she takes us to one of her stupid parties for the rich and famous, I'll throw it on my head."

"You wouldn't," Reece said.

"I would," I said. "You know me. I would."

We both laughed.

"Did I hear my name?" Charlotte said, walking up.

"Nope. You hearing things," I told her.

"Can we get something to eat?" she asked. "I'm hungry."

"Yeah, but not at one of your bourgeois restaurants again," I said. "Let's go to the hood and get some real down-home cooking this time."

"I'm down with that," Reece agreed, and her cell phone buzzed again. It had been ringing off the hook since we got to Nassau and she kept silencing it. I noticed, but I didn't ask any questions. Wasn't my business.

"The brother who sold me the cigars told me about a place. He said to take the ferry over to Paradise Island."

Reece was wearing her cheap shades, a pair of white Capri pants, and a blue blouse that tied at the waist. Charlotte wore a multicolored sundress that hugged her full-figured body. And I wore my jean shorts with the T-shirt I'd brought back from the Million Woman March back in ninety-seven. We looked like tourists with our bags of loot from the straw market, especially with Reece snapping pictures of every pastel-colored building we passed along the way with her disposable camera. With palm trees swaying in the wind, the Bahamas were a picture of beauty. But what I found more beautiful than the scenery, were the people. Just being themselves, speaking in their lingo that belonged to only them, and accentuating the pride of their culture. They seemed to be happy people, though most all poor, tourism being their main source of income. That's why they peddled their handmade items on the street. For most it was the difference between making ends meet or not. They lived in small houses, often one-room abodes, with several family members sharing the small space.

I gave change to the gentleman with the thick white beard, plucking on his banjo for the people passing by on the street, and singing a song that sounded so familiar that before long I was singing along.

We found fried fish, macaroni and cheese, fresh conch salad, and pigeon peas and rice for lunch. Charlotte was even sucking on the bones of her short ribs and tried some conch fritters and actually liked them. There was a Caribbean rake and scrape band playing their traditional goombay and calypso music at the little restaurant we'd stumbled upon along the street, with their saws and goombay drums. Reece wasn't shy about shaking her booty with a very handsome man who was teaching her a dance he called the Bahamian Quadrille.

"She is so fast," Charlotte said, waving her fork in the air. "Look at her."

I looked at Reece and smiled. She was having a good time.

The place was packed with mostly natives. I got the feeling it was the best-kept secret on the island, and tourists didn't frequent there. Dull hardwood floors, the walls were covered with pictures of famous Caribbean artists and grease stains, and the smell of enticing spices floated through the air. The tables were old wooden pieces covered in red-and-white-checkered cloths. The chairs were rickety, which was fine, because few people were sitting down anyway. Most were dancing, or just standing with hands raised, and hips swaying to the music.

Charlotte was finishing every bit of her pigeon peas and rice. "I have to admit, this is good, Maxie."

"I know," I told her. "You should really broaden your horizons a little more, Charlotte. I think you'll find that life is a little more interesting than you think."

"I'll keep that in mind." Her smile told me she was happy at that moment. I couldn't remember ever seeing true happiness on Charlotte's face before. She was always so shallow and pretended to have fun with people I don't even think she liked. Attending fancy dinners and eating at places simply because they got rave reviews in the newspapers. A shame she really never let her hair down and hung out with some people who were full of culture.

"Would you like to dance?" The gentleman with the ragged beard was holding his hand out to Charlotte. And I'm sure she had immediately assessed his appearance from head to toe and decided he wasn't worthy of her time.

"No, thank you."

"Go on, Charlotte. Dance with the man," I told her.

"I don't know how to do that . . . uh . . . dance they're doing."

"You just move your body, girl," I said, running my fingers through my locks. "Do you think Reece knows what she's doing? Look at her out there."

Charlotte and I both had to laugh at the sight of Reece.

"I'll show you." He pulled her onto the dance floor even though she resisted. She started moving to the music and kept up with the rhythm until the same man came back for me. He danced with both of us. Showing us the Quadrille and another dance called the Heel and Toe, which were both very similar to African-style dances.

We danced for what seemed like hours, Charlotte and I sharing a man, whose name we never knew. We were too busy having the time of our lives.

When we were too tired to dance to another beat, Reece's new friend, Kevin, took us on a tour of the island. We visited the huge Atlantis Hotel and Resort, checking out the enormous glass-paneled aquarium with its kaleidoscope of sea life—sea horses, stingrays, and swarms of goldfish and silverfish. We strolled through the breathtaking hotel lobby. There was a band in the lobby playing old Luther tunes, and we stopped and listened for a while. Kevin and Reece slow danced.

"I'm tired," I hinted. "Can we go home now?"

"I second that," Charlotte said.

Reece was having a hard time prying herself from Kevin's embrace, but Charlotte's and my raised eyebrows convinced her that we needed to call it a night.

We took in some scenery as Kevin drove us back to the mansion.

"That was so much fun!" Charlotte kicked her sandals off at the door of the mansion. "Tomorrow, we check out the beach."

"Um, I might have a lunch date tomorrow." That was Reece.

"Excuse me," I said.

"With Kevin. Um, he asked me what I was doing tomorrow. At the time, I didn't have any plans."

"I guess you just forgot you're engaged, huh?" Charlotte asked.

"He knows that. And so do I. It's just lunch, Charlotte."

"I ain't mad at you, Reece," I told her. "The brother was fine."

"It's really not what you think. We just had a good time, good conversation, and I want to see him again. That's it. No strings."

"Have you even talked to Darren since you been here?" Charlotte was our mother hen.

"This morning," she said. "Are we going for a swim or what?"

"I'll meet y'all at the pool," I said, quickly taking a sniff of my armpits. "I'm feelin' a little funky after all that movement. Think I'll hit the shower first."

I bounced up the steps of the mahogany staircase and felt just like Cinderella. That is, until I decided to slide back down the railing. Whatever cool points I'd gained with Charlotte, I lost within those few moments, as she gave me a look of displeasure. I laughed anyway. The day had been a good day.

9

Reece

I checked my cell phone for missed calls. Checked for messages. Cell phones were tricky; sometimes you heard them ring, sometimes not. Sometimes you had messages even when you hadn't heard it ring. Neither scenario was the case this morning. It simply had not rung, and the only messages I had were the ones that Darren had left the night before, wondering why I hadn't returned his calls, and that annoyed me. One message was from Wanda, who had been arrested but was out on bail. I'd decided to take on the case as her defense attorney after the boyfriend had made claims that Wanda knew about the molestation that had gone on with her child. Claimed that she'd known for months, and if he was going down, he was taking her with him. Wanda called him a liar, and a few other choice words, and denied his claims. The investigators had reason to believe that she'd been negligent, and that prompted the arrest. The prosecution had plans of sending them both to the penitentiary. My job was to get her off with a small charge of failing to protect; one that would carry maybe a few months probation or community service. I would plea bargain with the prosecuting attorney and had already set up a lunch meeting to discuss

Wanda's options. She was guilty of leaving her child with a pervert, and though that was bad enough, I wasn't totally convinced that Wanda was guilty of any more than that. I felt sorry for her; wanted to help her get on her feet. If only I could get that child to talk. Would've made my job so much easier. But the prosecuting attorney owed me a favor, so I worked with what I had.

I wished like crazy the phone would ring, and, like they say, a watched phone never rings.

I was anxiously awaiting Kevin's call. Longing to hear his voice again, kept trying to remember what it sounded like. Tried to picture his face in my mind all night. Just met the man, but had all these thoughts and desires. I knew he was a churchgoer but couldn't remember if he'd said he would call before church or afterward. He was also a runner like me. Said he got up at seven to run and was usually home by eight. Went to church by nine on Sunday. It was eight thirty. Thought he might call before service. But maybe not.

I jumped in the shower, and when I stepped out, caught the smell of sausage cooking. Took me back to Philadelphia; Gram's house on Sunday morning, fresh smell of sausage and hotcakes cooking. Gospel music would be playing. She would have on her slip, running through the house trying to get dressed for church. Sheila and I would get on her last nerve, but she had the patience of Job she said. And she did. Helping us with our tights and fastening our patent leather shoes around our ankles. Of all her grandchildren, I was her favorite. I knew it, and the rest of them did too. She was my favorite too. Nobody like Gram; she was the one and only. That's why I took it so hard when she was gone. A rainy day in June had washed her footsteps away. Couldn't quite get it together after that. She was my rock, and without her my life began to crumble. Right in the middle of law school and I lost focus. Luckily, Darren came along at the right time to help me piece it all back together. I owed him for that, and he reminded me of that debt often.

When my cell phone rang, I checked the number. Darren. I answered.

"Hey."

"Hey, yourself. Why haven't I heard from you? I was worried."

"Sorry," I said. "It's been hectic."

"You could've let me know that you made it, Reece. That was just downright thoughtless."

"You're right. I'm sorry. Won't happen again."

He was mad.

"So, you havin' a good time?" He tried to change the tone of his voice.

"Yes. This is just what I needed. I'm glad Charlotte talked me into it."

"You miss me?"

"Of course," I lied.

"Yeah, I miss you too," he said. "I'm hanging out with Nate and some of the other guys later on tonight. Going to the game."

"That's cool. Who's playing?"

"The Hawks and the Bulls."

"Have fun, baby."

"Yeah, you do the same. I just wanted to hear your voice," he said. "I'll call you tomorrow."

He was gone.

A hefty plate of sausage, pancakes, and scrambled eggs met me at the kitchen door.

"Your breakfast is getting cold, chile." A round black woman with a Bahamian accent was handing me a plate of food. Maxie and Charlotte were already at the table, putting food away as if they hadn't eaten in days.

"Reece, this is Miss Pauline." Charlotte introduced us, waving her fork in-between bites. Barely looking up from her plate. Thought she was on a diet. "She's Ramsey's housekeeper and cook."

"Raised his children myself, ya know. With my own hands." She held her heavy, dark hands in the air for us to see. "Chip and Doug. They're away in college in the states now. Chip at Harvard. Doug at NYU. I love those boys."

"Glad to meet you, Pauline. I'm Reece," I said. "I usually just have a muffin or some fruit for breakfast. Have to watch these hips, you know. Sorry you went to all this trouble."

"No trouble at all. A muffin or fruit? Ha! That's why you don't have no meat on ya bones, chile." She started laughing. "Sit down and eat the meal I prepared for you."

I was taught to respect my elders and did what she said.

"Ramsey told me you were coming and said to take good care of you girls." She finished washing the dishes that were stacked in the sink. "Sorry I wasn't here yesterday to greet you with a hot supper. I play poker on Friday nights."

"That's okay," Charlotte said. "You don't have to go out of your way for us."

"I want to," she said. She dried her hands with a dishtowel, and then leaving the kitchen said, "I'll make sure your beds are turned down now and that you have fresh linen. Enjoy your day, babies."

She was gone in a flash.

"She's sweet," I said.

"She nearly gave me heart failure this morning. I stepped out of the shower and poof, there she was, pulling sheets and pillow slips off my bed!" Maxie said. "I didn't know who she was."

"She sure knows her way around a kitchen," I said.

"Wonder how long she's been cooking and cleaning for Ramsey," Charlotte said, getting up to refresh her plate. "Don't she know that we've progressed as a people?"

"For real," Maxie said.

"Breakfast is good," I said, throwing scrambled eggs down my throat.

"There went my diet," Charlotte said. "And I haven't exercised since I been here. I know I've gained ten pounds."

"You're on vacation. Who cares if you gain a few pounds?" Maxie drank down a glass of milk.

My cell phone startled me. I checked the number and excused myself from the table. Went out into the sunroom.

"Hello."

"Reece?"

"Yes. This is Reece."

"It's Kevin. Good morning, sunshine." I loved the sound of my new nickname.

"Good morning to you."

"I'm running late for church but wanted to give you a call to let you know I was thinking of you."

"Glad you did."

"Will I see you this afternoon?"

"I hope so."

"Where would you like to go?"

"You choose," I said.

"Let's go to the beach, okay? I'll cook for you."

"You cook?"

"I dabble a little." His Bahamian accent sent chills down my spine. "Pick you up at two?"

"I'll be ready."

"Bye now."

He was gone.

He looked even more handsome than the day before, in his white linen shorts. They fit his behind so nicely and his olive-colored silk shirt was unbuttoned just enough to reveal a few chest hairs. He wore brown sandals that revealed his toes. Hated to see a man with ugly toes, but his were nice, dark brown to match his face. I could tell he took care of his feet, and wondered how often he received a pedicure.

We drove down Bay Street in his old Mercedes, stopping at a fish market that resembled the farmers' market in Forest Park, Georgia. This place sold fresh seafood and reeked of fish. Kevin bought whiting, jumbo shrimp, whole crabs, and fresh oysters.

"You like oysters?" he asked.

"Only the smoked ones in the can."

"In the can?" He frowned. "I'm talking about fresh raw oysters on the half shell."

"Never tried them."

"I'm going to show you how to eat them," he said, and paid the woman with a Bahamian bill. "Let's go." He grabbed my hand.

When we got to the beach, he spread a blanket out on the sand. Fired up the grill and seasoned the food. He cracked open a few oysters and arranged them on a plate. Began to slow cook the food, and in the meantime poured two glasses of wine. Handed me one, then sat on the blanket next to me. Placed the oysters in front of me. Took a small bowl and a few sauces.

"This is how you eat oysters," he began to explain. "You take some hollandaise sauce, a little cocktail sauce, and a dab of Tabasco." He mixed it all up in the bowl. "Then you take a fork, pull the oyster out of its shell, dip it in the sauce."

He popped the raw oyster into his mouth. Pulled another one out of its shell, dipped it into the sauce, placed it up to my lips, and I took it, tasted it, tossed the slimy little creature around in my mouth.

"Not bad." I tried to be calm as my mouth was on fire from the Tabasco. Took a long swallow from my wineglass, tears forming in my eyes. I could feel the tears as the wine went straight to my head.

"It's an acquired taste," he chuckled. "Want another?"

You would think I'd say no, but nodded a yes. He placed another one in my mouth. Fire again, but the more I ate, the more I wanted.

I sat quietly, watching him finish the other two.

"What are you thinking?" He smelled so good, and I tried to figure out what brand of cologne he was wearing.

"Thinking that I'm having a very nice time."

"That's good," he said. "You're very beautiful, you know?

I smiled, my cheeks turning red from blushing so hard.

"What do you do for a living?"

"I'm an attorney." I took a sip of my wine.

"An attorney? Wow. I would have never guessed," he said. "Are you good at it?"

"I think so," I said boastfully. "What do you do?"

"I'm an attorney as well. Studied in England."

"Get out of here!"

"Handle mostly corporate law. Wills and things of that nature," he said. "But in my heart I'm an artist."

"An artist, huh? What type of artist?"

"I'll show you. Wait right here." He went to his car and came back with a sketching pad and pencils. Sat back down on the blanket and began sketching. When he turned it around to show me, it was the exact replica of the ocean and the sky above. In the center of the page was a picture of me, a glass of wine in my hand. His eye was keen, his hand precise, because he captured me with such exactness.

"It's beautiful," I said.

"You're beautiful, Reece." It threw me off guard when his lips touched mine. And I felt that feeling in the pit of my stomach. That feeling that I'd heard so much about, but had never experienced. "What's your last name?"

"Jameson."

"Reece Jameson. Attorney Jameson. That has a nice ring." He said it and smiled. "I'd better get my food before it burns. See what you do to me? Get me all off course."

He hurried to the grill, flipped the fish with tongs, his eyes affixed to mine. His glance moved from my eyes, swept over my body, taking in the curve of my breasts, the muscles in my legs, settled on my lips, and then finally back to my eyes.

"Going for a swim," I said. Needed to cool off. Slipped my

khaki shorts off down to my one piece. Jumped in the ocean and swam out about twenty feet. Came up for air. Looked back at Kevin, watching him flip seafood on the grill. His eyes met mine and I trembled. Dated Darren for years and never once trembled when he looked at me.

After the food was done, and he had lifted each piece from the grill, he removed his linen shorts and shirt, until he was wearing only black trunks. The curve of his muscular arms and legs left me in awe. He jumped in the water and swam toward me, grabbed me from behind, his arms strong and heavy around my waist. He kissed my cheek. It was then that I recognized the cologne he was wearing. Polo.

"Dinner's ready," he whispered sensually in my ear.

"You came all the way out here to tell me that?" I teased.

"Yes." His hot breath in my earlobe was more than I could stand. "Are you hungry?"

"Yes." The way I said it was not how I meant to, at least not how I wanted him to hear it. I was feeling him, but it was way too early for him to know how much.

With one swift move, I was facing him, his fingers stroking my spine, his tongue probing the depths of my mouth. And I lost track of where I was. I'd never wanted anyone more. But my good sense told me to back up. Moving too fast. Desire was all over his face like a hungry animal, but he remained a gentleman.

"I'm sorry," he apologized after I backed away.

"Don't be," I said. "I'm not. I am so attracted to you."

"The feeling is mutual." His goatee was trimmed so nicely.

"But I don't want to move too fast."

"I completely understand," he said. "Your fiancé, right?"

"Partly," I said. "And partly my own good sense."

"Does he know that you don't love him?"

"What?" Where had that come from?

"Never mind," he said. "Let's go eat. Our food is getting cold. Last one's a rotten egg."

We would definitely revisit that comment.

He jogged toward the grill. I followed, pulling up the rear. Guess I was the rotten egg.

He fixed our plates, and we sat on the blanket eating grilled fish, shrimp, crabs, and fresh conch salad, sipping wine and enjoying each other's company. After I was full, I stretched my body out across the blanket, my eyes toward the sky.

"What are you thinking?" Kevin stretched out on the blanket beside me.

"That I could stay right here forever." I listened to the sound of the waves from the ocean bouncing back and forth upon the shore. It was a calming sound, created a peace that I hadn't felt in so long.

"Do you mean here as in this beach, here as in the Bahamas, or here as in this place of tranquility?"

"Here as in this place of tranquility."

"Then stay here forever." He smiled and I noticed how beautiful his teeth were. Perfect and white.

"As nice as forever may sound, it's not realistic," I said. "As soon as I get back to Atlanta, it's back to life as I know it."

"I still say stay here forever. Why can't your life as you know it be peaceful and tranquil just like this?"

"Because it's too complicated. It's not like this."

"Then make it so, Reece. You're too young and beautiful to have a complicated life. Life is a gift."

"Yeah. That's what they tell me."

"What's making your life so complicated?"

"Just is, that's all." Wasn't ready to share my confusion about Darren.

"Wish I could show you something different." His eyes met mine and we held the stare for the longest time.

His lips brushed against mine. He moved a braid from my face and I touched his strong chest. His mouth began to engulf mine, and I got lost. Closed my eyes and got lost. That tingle in the pit of my stomach told me that this was exactly where I should be, but I wasn't totally convinced yet. Seemed more like a fantasy to me, and I was way too practical to fall for some fantasy. But it felt good for the moment, and I didn't resist. I just allowed this beautiful creature, a stranger no less, to gently caress my breasts with his fingertips. To take all my power away, to make me weak.

The clouds began to grow dark, but I was too busy falling in love to notice.

"Looks like rain," he said, drawing my attention to the sky. "I'd better get you home."

"Probably a good idea." I cleared my throat, but didn't move.

He lowered his head, and I closed my eyes as his tongue probed the inside of my mouth once more. He then stood and pulled me up from the blanket.

"Let's go, sunshine."

We loaded the car with leftover food, the blanket, and other items we'd brought to the beach. He opened my door; I hopped in and snapped my seatbelt on. As we drove down Bay Street, I leaned my head back, kicked off my sandals, and closed my eyes for a moment. I felt like the sunshine, even on a cloudy day.

10

Charlotte

Monday.

I had missed Gwen's call, but she left a message.

"Charlotte, it's Gwen. I have the results of your biopsy. I need for you to call me as soon as possible. Thanks."

I dialed the doctor's office and my hands were trembling. Mostly from fear. Some from anticipation.

"This is Charlotte Daniels. I need to speak with Doctor Hayes, please," I said. Reece and Maxie were hanging on my every word.

"She's expecting your call, Miss Daniels. One moment, please." The nurse who answered had put me on hold; jazz from Atlanta's 107.5 was playing as I waited to hear Gwen's voice.

"This is Dr. Hayes."

"Gwen, it's Charlotte. I got your message."

"Ah, yes, Charlotte. I need to see you in my office the moment you return."

"You have my results?"

"Yes."

"Well?"

"I'd rather not discuss this with you over the phone, honey. I really need to see you."

"Gwen. You've known me for a long time. Please just give it to me straight."

"Charlotte, this is extremely unorthodox. Not something I would like to discuss with a patient over the phone."

"Please, Gwen. Yes, I'm a patient, but I'm also a friend," I pleaded. "Tell me."

"You're putting me in an awful position," she said as she relented. "The lump we found is malignant. You do have breast cancer. Not only that, the cancer has spread a little farther than we had anticipated. I need you to come into the office right away when you return. We need to sit down and discuss some options."

I was silent. Closed my eyes. Shock rushed through my body like a bolt of lightning. Reece and Maxie tried to read my face. I had replayed this day in my mind over a million times. Had prepared myself for the worst, I thought. But never had I expected the worst. Guess I'd just hoped, prayed, trusted that God would work things out. He always had in my life. Had always taken care of Charlotte, even when she was careless, heartless, and so many other things. But today I'd been abandoned, forgotten, unworthy of another rescue. He was fed up with me, and I knew it. I felt the emptiness.

"Charlotte. Are you there?" Gwen asked.

"I'm here."

"When will you be back in town?"

"Sometime next week." I managed to get it out. There was a lump in my throat, preventing me from speaking clearly.

"I need you to come in to the office as soon as you get back to Atlanta. Okay?"

"Okay."

I dropped the phone, lost control of my legs.

"Charlotte, what did she say?" My girls helped me up and over to the sofa.

I started crying uncontrollably. Reece cried too.

"What did she say?" she asked in-between tears.

"The biopsy results...I...the cancer spread." I stared at the Thomas Kincaid on the wall in Ramsey's den.

"Sweetie, I'm so sorry." Reece hugged me so tight, and I was glad because I needed to feel her strength in the absence of mine. Maxie wanted to say something, but didn't know what. She just hugged me too. The three of us just sat there in silence for the longest time, rocking, hugging, tears streaming down our faces.

Spent the entire afternoon and most of the night in that spot in the den. Sat there on the leather sofa mostly in silence. At one point, Reece started praying, and I was glad because I didn't have the strength to. Felt betrayed by God. The God I served each Sunday morning at my small AME church; I didn't know him anymore. Where was he when I needed him most? I didn't understand why, out of all the women in the world, I was being singled out. Reece tried to explain it, but I was only confused more.

"Sometimes it's just not about you, Charlotte."

"Well if it's not about me, Reece, who in the world is it about?" I cried out for an answer. "I'm the one who it's happening to."

"Sometimes God allows you to endure certain things, so that you can touch someone else's life."

"So you're saying this is about someone else?"

"Could be."

"Reece, that doesn't make any sense. If this is about someone else, then why is it that I'm the one enduring the pain?"

"You have to be strong, Charlotte. That's all I'm saying."

"Strong for whom? Someone else?"

"Strong for you. It's not the end of the world. I've seen many women fight this disease and win," she said. "You have to hold on to your faith. God has not abandoned you."

"You sure about that?" My eyes met hers, searching for an honest answer. "Feels like he has."

"He hasn't."

It was three o'clock in the morning before long, and the bags under her eyes were from the same deprivation of sleep that mine were from. She and Maxie had been up with me most of the night. Crying, praying, talking, debating.

"I'm turning in." Maxie stood and headed toward the door.

"Me too," Reece said. "You should try and get some sleep too, girl."

"What if we all just sleep here in the den?" I said it quickly. Wanted them to stay. Realized I was too afraid to be alone. "Like a slumber party."

"I guess that would be cool," Maxie said. "I just need to get some sleep. I don't care where it is."

"Let's go grab some pillows and stuff," Reece told Maxie.

We spread comforters and pillows out on the floor. Wasn't long before Maxie was snoring, mouth wide open. I kept thinking of things to debate with Reece about, just so she'd stay awake. She fell asleep in midsentence while trying to get a point across. I watched them both sleep. Thanked God for them. Finally dozed off myself around five. At six, I was awakened by the rattling of pots and pans coming from the kitchen. Realized it was Pauline.

"I'm sorry, honey. Didn't mean to wake you." She was startled when I walked into the kitchen.

"You didn't. I was up."

"At this hour?"

"Couldn't sleep."

"Man trouble?"

"No ma'am. Nothing like that." I poured a glass of orange juice and sat at the kitchen table. Watched her cook. "Other troubles."

"Like what?"

"Found out I have breast cancer."

"Yeah?" She seemed unalarmed by my news. Way too calm. Hadn't she heard what I said? "They going to remove your breast?"

"Don't know yet," I said. "Need to see my doctor when I get home."

"Which one is it?"

"Which one?"

"Which breast? Right or left?"

"Right." I cupped my breast with my hand to show her which one.

"Mine was the left," she said. "You see this?"

She unbuttoned her housedress, stuck her hand against her bra. "It's just padding, you see. Had my breast removed five years ago. Spread clear down to my lymph nodes. But no more. No more cancer. No more chemo. I was completely healed."

"How?"

"Faith." She said it with so much confidence. Straightened her clothes.

"For real?"

"For real," she said. "Got faith, don't you, baby?"

"Yes. I think I do."

"If you got faith, then you needn't stay up all night worrying. Worrying about something you can't change."

"I know." I really did know all of this, but it just made more sense when she said it. I knew God. Had known him all my life. Rarely missed a Sunday at church, spent many a night on my knees.

"When you pray, chile, you got to leave it there. Can't keep taking it back." She washed her hands and kneaded some dough to make homemade biscuits. "Now go get yourself some sleep. Need all the strength you can get. Got a long road ahead of you, ya know."

She reminded me of Mama. So much like her. That is until the Alzheimer's set in. Now I wasn't so sure who my mother was. One minute we'd be discussing real issues, about real people. The next minute she'd start talking about something off the wall, and asking me who I was. When she started wandering off in the middle of the night, I knew I had to place her in a home.

"Yes, ma'am." I got up, placed the glass in the sink, and headed back toward the den.

"Hey," Pauline called out to me, "I know one thing for sure. With God, a few good friends, and a little faith, anything is possible."

"Thank you, Miss Pauline." I went over and hugged her.

"You're welcome, baby."

I slept most of the day. In the afternoon, I got up, showered. Felt revived. Refreshed. Renewed. I met my clients at the breathtaking estate that they'd admired and wanted to buy. They loved it and immediately signed the contract, and sealed the deal with a firm handshake. The business part of my trip was a breeze, and afterward I went for a walk on the beach. Sun beaming down on my face, I rolled up my pant legs, walked through the water. Wanted to swim, but didn't want my clothes to get wet. Instead I strolled across the water's surface, sand in-between my toes, lifted my eyes toward heaven.

"I do have faith, Lord. I do."

Reece's words rang in my ears. "It's not about you, Charlotte."

Then who is it about, I wondered. I watched the water brush across my toes, and listened to the chirp of the seagulls as they played in the sand. I needed some answers.

I pulled my cell phone out and called Mama. Needed to hear her voice. Although she probably wouldn't know who I was, there was something about talking to your mama when you were facing life-altering situations that makes you feel better inside.

"Mama?"

"Hi, baby," she said, and I was relieved that she recognized my voice. "How you doing?"

"I'm fine, Mama. What about you?"

"Fine, except these nurses won't leave me alone. Always in here makin' a fuss about somethin'. I can't even go to the toilet in peace." She paused for a moment, and I could hear her roommate, Miss Hattie, mumbling about something in the background. "This arthritis gettin' the best of me too. Hurt real bad this time of year, you know, when it's cold outside. Can barely pick things up anymore. But I'm feeling okay outside of that."

"That's good, Mama."

"Doctor took me off of them water pills too. I'm so glad. Had me peein' all the time. Morning, noon, and all through the night, I was peein'."

"Mama, I'm coming to see you in a couple of weeks. I'm on vacation in the Bahamas right now, but I promise I'll get over there to see you as soon as I get back."

"Your father's been asking about you. You need to call and talk to him sometime." I knew I was losing her when she began talking about Daddy as if he were still alive.

"Mama, Daddy passed away already," I reminded her.

"What's this nonsense you talkin', child? Your Daddy was just here yesterday." She was becoming annoyed, and I just decided to play along.

"Okay, Mama. You're right. I'll call Daddy as soon as I get a chance."

After Daddy was gone, I'd moved Mama out of her two-story, three-bedroom house that she'd shared with Daddy for many years and into my place. It soon became too much for me to care for her and to keep up the maintenance on the house. I finally convinced her to sell it, and she'd reluctantly agreed. It sold in less than two weeks.

It was a breeze at first, actually very nice having her at my place. The company was good for both of us. But once her health began to fail, her care was more than I could handle. I hired a nurse to come by each day while I worked. Mama had gotten so she would wander off and the nurse would call me, in a frenzy, and I'd rush home to find that she'd been found. Twice in one week I'd met the fire chief at my house, because Mama had attempted to cook and had forgotten to check on the pot. She'd nearly burned the house down. She was beginning to forget things on a regular basis. At first they were just subtle things, like where she'd left her eyeglasses or what day it was.

Then she began forgetting where she was, and who she was. And worse: who I was. She often accused me of stealing her money, or trying to convince me that someone was after her, watching, lurking in the house. She heard noises, and swore that Daddy had visited her room every night. I knew then that something had to be done. I found a place that could take care of her and that had experience in dealing with people with Alzheimer's.

"Mama, I have to go now," I told her. "I'll see you soon, okay?"

"Okay, baby."

She was gone, but just hearing her voice made me feel a little bit better inside.

11

Maxie

I sat in a lawn chair next to the pool, watched palm trees blowing in the wind, sun beaming down on my forehead. It had stormed in Nassau last night, and the aftersmell of the rain still tickled my nose. When the phone rang, I picked it up on the first ring. Reece had contacted her detective friend and asked him to help me out in locating my sisters. He'd finally turned up with something.

"Did some checking," he began. "Found an Alexandria Hunter. Used to be Alexandria Parker. But her adopted family changed her name to Jones. Hunter is her married name now. Married to Nicolas Hunter. Lives in Los Angeles, California. Beverly Hills to be exact. Went to UCLA. . . ."

He ran down her entire M.O. Couldn't believe my ears. Wanted to talk to her at that moment. Wanted to see the face of the woman he was talking about, just to make sure. I would know her if I saw her.

"Get a pen. Write down her phone number and address."

I grabbed a pen from my purse and found a pad. Wrote down every number, every word. Read it back twice to make sure I had it.

"What about Button? I mean, Beatrice Parker?"

"Nothing yet," he said. "I'll keep checking, though. Let you know what turns up."

"Thank you so much." What he gave me was enough to get started. Much more than I had. "You don't know what this means to me."

"Glad I could help," he said. "And tell Reece to call a brother sometime. Other than when she needs something."

"I will."

I hung up, but held the receiver to my chest. Devastated and delighted, all at the same time. Reece's detective friend had found my sister. The one I'd been searching for most of my life. So much anxiety. My hands were numb. A million thoughts rushing through my head. Wanted to be in LA. Needed the fastest way there. I couldn't wait. Afraid I might lose her again. Wondered what she looked like all grown up.

Began dialing her number, but hung up before anyone could answer.

I didn't want to do this over the phone. Wanted to see her with my own eyes. Called Delta, booked a flight.

I found Reece and Charlotte in the den and couldn't wait to share my news.

"Maybe you should call her first, Maxie. Just to make sure."

"Reece is right," Charlotte said. "You can't just hop a flight to LA. What if she's out of town or something?"

"Too afraid to call. Dialed the number five times already. Hung up each time. I don't even know what to say."

"You just tell her who you are," Reece said. "Want me to call for you?"

"Nope. I can handle it."

"God forbid she doesn't want to see you or something," Charlotte said.

"Charlotte!" Reece snapped.

"I'm just playing devil's advocate."

"Why wouldn't she want to see me, Charlotte?"

"I'm not saying that's the case. I'm just saying call first."

"She's right," Reece said. And I knew they were right.

"Okay, I'll call first."

"Want me to go to LA with you?" she asked.

"Got to do this on my own," I told her. "You understand?" She did.

"What time's your flight?"

"Tomorrow morning at eight. Staying at the Airport Hilton."

"Write it all down for me before you leave. Your flight numbers and your hotel information."

"I will," I told her. "Now can I have a little privacy? I'm about to call."

"Fine," Reece said. "I got to get showered anyway."

"Another date with Kevin, huh?" That was mother hen, Charlotte.

"As a matter of fact, he's teaching me how to play golf this afternoon," she said. "Not really a date. Just a round of golf."

"Talked to Darren lately?" I had to ask because she was behaving as if he were nonexistent.

"Yesterday." She bounced out of the room, swiftly avoiding the next round of questions she knew would follow. "Holler at y'all later."

Charlotte hit the power button on the remote, putting an end to the antics of the *Jerry Springer* show, where trailer park trash were distastefully displaying their body parts, and some fat woman was cussing her man out. Couldn't understand why people watched that show, wasting valuable time they could spend educating themselves. The only thing I've ever learned from *Jerry Springer* is that the world is way more screwed up than I could've ever imagined.

"Hey, Maxie. I'm sorry about the other day. What I said about you looking for your sisters and all. It was thoughtless and insensitive."

"It's cool, Charlotte."

"I'm glad something turned up. I hope it all works out for you."

"Thanks." It was all I could say as I awaited the second part of the sentence, the smart remark, the "but" that would follow with a slap in the face. But she was sincere and showed it with a hug.

When she left the room, I dialed the number and held my breath. Third ring. Fourth. A male voice greeted me on the other end.

"Hello." He sounded out of breath, like he'd run to the phone.

"Hello. May I speak with Alexandria, please?"

"Hold on a minute." He set the phone down and I could hear him shouting her name. "Alex! Pick up the phone! It's for you."

The sound of children in the background, laughing, playing. Something falling.

"Stop running, I said. And take that ball outside. You know better than to play in this house," the male voice addressed the children. "Alex!"

Someone picked up the receiver. The male voice again.

"I'm sorry. She can't come to the phone right now. Is there a message?"

"Um." I wasn't prepared to leave a message. "Could you ask her to call Maxie Parker, please?"

"Maxie?"

"Yes." Had he known? He said my name as if he'd heard it before.

"Spell that for me, please."

"M-A-X-I-E," I said, and gave him my cell phone number. "Have her call me at seven, seven, zero. . . ."

He was writing it all down. She would call when she saw my name on the paper. Would recognize it immediately and know it was me. I knew it was her; her husband, her children, her family. My sister, Alex. I knew it in my heart.

12

Reece

Gentle hands. Smooth touch. Ninth hole.

Right shoulder lower than left. Head behind the ball. Ball opposite left heel. I had it memorized but pretended not to remember. Wanted him to stand behind me and show me again. Wanted to feel him close.

"You need the nine iron for this shot, Reece," he said, breathing into my ear. "Narrow your stance. Keep your weight forward. Swing back with your arms and shoulders."

"Like this?" I swung at the ball. Missed.

"Try again."

I did. Missed again.

"Like this." He took the club, swung, and the ball went flying through the air like a missile. Kevin wore black slacks, a red golf shirt, a white glove on his left hand, and a Nike cap that fit snugly on his head. Lips pursed. Serious eyes. He was good. Golf was definitely his game.

I was glad to see the eighteenth hole. It was over, and now I could exhale. Golf was a breeze. Keeping my hands to myself was the real challenge.

* * *

I kicked my sandals off as he drove me to his place. A beach-front condo on Cable Beach. Decorated richly in burnt oranges and hunter greens. Felt warm and inviting; his place. Definitely had a masculine flavor. Exuded character.

"Get you something to drink?"

"What you got?"

"Tea, water, grapefruit juice," he said. "Might even have some Kool-Aid."

"I'll take the Kool-Aid." Plopped down on his sofa; my toes caressed his plush beige carpet.

He put on some nice Caribbean sounds.

"You were good out there on the course," he said, handing me a refreshing glass of cherry Kool-Aid, a slice of lemon swimming around in it. "Next time I'll teach you how to play cricket."

"Cricket?"

"An outdoor game, sort of like baseball. It's fun."

"I'm leaving on Saturday."

"So soon?"

"Got work," I explained.

He sat next to me on the sofa, placed my bare foot in his hands and began to massage it.

"Can I ask you something?"

"Anything."

"Do you enjoy living your life as a lie?"

"What?"

"Let me see. How can I word this?" He contemplated, chose his words carefully. His thumb began to slowly caress the heel of my foot, then the grooves in between my toes. Drove me crazy. "Can I just be frank?"

"Please do."

"Reece, you don't enjoy practicing law. Your true love is helping people. You're a nurturer, a caregiver. Why then, do you continue to practice law? Knowing your heart's not there?"

"I love the law."

"Taking cases pro bono tells me you're not in it for the money. What is it that you really want?"

"What do you mean?"

"Tell me what your dreams are. Your passion," he said. "What is it that would make your life worthwhile, fulfilled?"

No one had ever probed my heart and mind this way. I had dreams but dismissed them as just that, dreams. Needed a nine to five to pay the bills. No time for what's in your heart. Darren taught me that. The fact that I was his fiancé was enough to know that you don't follow your heart. You do what makes sense and hope that your heart follows.

"I like helping people."

"Okay."

"I volunteered for several years at a shelter in downtown Atlanta. The problem is, homelessness is not concentrated in just one area. For instance, in one of the counties in the metro area, they have only one shelter throughout the whole county. It's overpopulated, can't serve everybody."

"Go on."

"There has to be a way of targeting that group of people who can't get help. You know, where help's not available. I want to be the one to do that. Run a homeless shelter. One that would also be available for abused women and children. Would have a food kitchen."

"What else?" He was hanging on my every word.

"People need job skills. Would have a professional on staff to teach them how to complete job applications, tell them what to expect at interviews, teach them office etiquette. There would be child care available for working mothers. Parenting skills classes for new mothers."

"You've thought this through," he said. "What are you waiting for? Need some start-up cash?"

"No. Got some money put away."

"Well, what then?"

"I'm an attorney. I have a degree in law, a flourishing career with a successful law firm. Make a nice salary. I'm this close to making partner." I showed him how close with my two fingers. "I wouldn't have time to do both."

"Then quit."

"Quit?" I asked.

"The firm."

"It just wouldn't make sense." Had he read my mind? Had he known how many times I'd actually considered just that?

"Make sense to whom?"

"Me."

"Life doesn't always have to make sense, Reece. You should always follow your heart. You'll only be passionate about what's in your heart." He took my hand and placed it over my chest, his on top. "You might love the law, but it's not where your heart is."

"You think you know me so well?"

"I know enough," he said. "You should seriously give it some thought at least. There are a lot of people out there who need someone just like you. You're limiting yourself. Wouldn't take much to begin. You just need a building. Could get some funding from your government. Lot of grants out there to be had."

"How do you know all of this?"

"I read a lot," he said. "The resources are there. You just have to find them."

I saw my vision coming to fruition through Kevin's eyes.

"Now for the big question," he said.

I closed my eyes. Knew what was coming.

"Tell me about your fiancé. What's his name, Darren?" He knew his name. We had discussed this issue at length.

"What is there to tell?"

"When are you going to tell him the truth?"

"About?"

"About how you feel. You don't love him."

"You're wrong. I do love Darren."

Then why am I here? Wanting nothing more than for this man to take me into his arms and make passionate love to me?

"Do you?"

"Do I what?" My mind had drifted for a moment.

"Love him?"

"Yes."

"Are you in love with him?"

"Whatever the case, I'm going to marry him."

"When?"

"Well, um. June twenty-eighth."

"That's what, three months from now?" His smile was the sunshine. "Can I come to the wedding?"

"Yeah. I don't see why not."

"I'll be there." He laughed. "June twenty-eighth, right?"

"Yes."

"You'll send me an invitation so I won't forget?"

"Yes."

"Then you'll need my address, right?"

"How else will I send you an invitation?" I said it with attitude.

He immediately got up, found a notepad, scribbled something on a piece of paper, folded it, and handed it to me. I snatched it, stuffed it into my purse.

"I really should be going." I slipped my sandals back on, stood, purse in hand.

"Are you mad?"

"No."

"You sure?"

He stood, pressed his body against mine. Took my face into his hands and kissed me.

"Forgive me?"

"Shut up and kiss me again," I said.

We both knew it wasn't Darren I was in love with.

When I returned to the mansion, I sat outside on the patio for the longest time. Couldn't get Kevin's smile out of my head. It was there, day and night. The crickets chirped in a harmonious tune, a warm breeze blew through my braids. I thought of Darren and my calmness was shaken, stirred. I'd betrayed him with my heart. He was at home loving me, and here I was, a million miles away fantasizing about another man.

My cell phone buzzed as I sat there. I answered it before checking the number.

"I've tried reaching you all night. Where were you?"

"I was out for a while."

"Did you have your cell phone with you?"

"Had it turned off."

"Reece, I told you I would call. Why would you turn off your phone?"

"What is this third degree?"

"Just miss you, baby, that's all," Darren said. "When are you coming home?"

"Saturday."

"Pick you up at the airport?"

"Catching a ride with Charlotte." I wanted nothing more than to get off the phone. "But I'll call you when I get in."

"Got a surprise for you."

"What is it?"

"If I told you, it wouldn't be a surprise, now would it?"

"Guess not."

"Well, I won't keep you. Get yourself some sleep. I'll call you in the morning."

I was glad to finally hang up. I pulled the piece of paper out of my purse, the one that Kevin had scribbled his address on. Read it: *I think I'm in love with you, Reece Jameson.*

"Well, I'm not in love with you, Kevin whatever your name is," I whispered.

But the little voice inside my head shouted, "Liar!"

13

Maxie

LAX.

Long flight, but smooth, enjoyable. Especially after the conversation I had with the vanilla brother with shoulder-length dreads, a precisely trimmed goatee, and pearly whites so perfect, I swore he'd worn braces as a child. We talked about the war in Iraq, why children in South Africa are starving, racism, Malcolm X, who would be the first black president, jazz, blues, reggae. Told him about my sisters. He told me he'd recently gained custody of his eight-year-old daughter. Told him I was living in Atlanta. He was on his way home to LA. Before long, we were old friends. I knew him from another life it seemed. He was me. I was him. Conversation flowed like the rhythm of a smooth Marvin Gaye tune.

"Where you stayin'?" We both waited at baggage claim for our luggage to appear on the carousel.

"Airport Hilton."

"You play spades?"

"You know it."

"Want to get whipped?"

"If you think it's possible."

"I do," he said, throwing his garment bag over his shoulder. "I'll call you and we'll set something up."

His smile was the sunshine, the moon, and everything beautiful. He disappeared through the automatic doors and caught a taxi.

I stepped outside, took in the beauty of LA, the majestic, arrogant palm trees that almost gave you the impression that they would wear sunglasses if they could, the ocean air that made you feel free and laid back. I breathed it in and found a secret heaven.

Hailed a taxi at the curb, hopped in the backseat, and told the driver where I was going.

"Hey, partner, I did a MapQuest from the airport to my hotel," I told the foreign taxi driver. "Know exactly how many miles it is. So don't be trying to take me the scenic route. All right?"

"Ma'am?" he said. "I'm sorry, I don't understand."

"Straight to the Airport Hilton."

"Airport Hilton. I know where Airport Hilton is."

"Straight there, dude. No variations."

"Ma'am? I don't understand."

Now he was playing dumb. Bet he would understand if I slighted him a few dollars on his fare. Slipped back in my seat and relaxed. Dialed Reece, and left my flight and hotel information on her voice mail.

I checked into the hotel, got my key, and headed down the corridor to my room. I walked in and immediately assessed the quality of the carpet, the comfort of the bed, and the overall cleanliness of the place. It was cool. I dropped my bag and decided I would shower, change into my boxers and T-shirt, and get some shut-eye. Wouldn't make sense to call Alex until morning. Saturday morning. Even though she hadn't returned my call, I wouldn't give up until I made contact. Had to see her for myself. In person. Face to face. Sister to sister.

* * *

The phone rang first thing. It was the wake-up call I'd requested. I caught the local news just to see what sort of crime they had going on in LA compared with that in the ATL. Folks killing other folks. Same old stuff, just a different venue. I pulled Alex's number out of my purse. Dialed it. Third ring and someone picked up.

"Hello."

"Hello," I said.

"Hel-lo." The voice said it with attitude. "Is anybody there?"

"Alex?"

"Who is this?"

"May I speak with Alex?"

"You're speaking to her. Who is this?"

"This is Maxie."

"Maxie who?"

"Maxie Parker."

"Is this some sort of sick joke?"

"No," I said. "Alex, this is your sister Maxie. Do you remember me at all?"

Bang. She hung up. If she wasn't going to talk to me, I needed an explanation. Like Charlotte said, I needed closure. And I had flown too far and too long to be hung up on. I dialed again. Second ring.

"Hello."

"Alex, please do not hang up that phone again. I've flown a long way to come here. The least you can do is talk to me."

"Who are you?"

"I said my name is Maxie Parker."

"That's not possible!"

"Why is that?"

"Because my sister Maxie Parker is dead."

"Excuse me?"

"She died when we were children. And if you think this is a joke, it's not very funny."

103

"Alex, I assure you. I'm not dead. It's me, Maxie."

"Prove it." Her voice began to tremble. "Tell me something only you or I would know."

"Like what?"

"Anything. If you're Maxie, you'll know what to say."

I sat there for a moment. Thought about it.

"Our birth mother's name was Brenda Parker," I began. Obviously, that wasn't enough. Anybody would know that. "You had this doll, you called her Rebecca. A black ugly thing with nappy hair. Stood about three feet tall. Her eyelids moved up and down. Got her for Christmas when you were five. She was so big and ugly; she scared our little sister to death. She would scream whenever she saw it, that is until she got used to her."

Silence.

"And . . . and you have a scar on your knee, about two inches long. Running through Miss Booker's backyard, you fell on a huge rock, busted your knee wide open, down to the bone. Needed stitches. Mama was drunk that night and said for you to just put some alcohol on it and a Band-Aid, it would be just fine. Said for you to stop crying before she beat your behind. It was Mr. Sam who finally convinced her that you needed to go to the hospital. Remember Mr. Sam?"

"With the jacked-up hair?" she asked softly.

"Yep. It wasn't his hair, though, it was a toupee," I told her.

"It looked like a press and curl or something," she said, and we both laughed.

"When you came home it was after midnight, and we ate macaroni and cheese for dinner. And we had cherry and grape Kool-Aid mixed together. Remember how we used to mix the flavors to see what we could come up with?"

"We called it a Suicide."

"Yep."

"Oh my God," she whispered as she was crying.

"Alex, this is Maxie," I said, tears in my eyes too. "You still got that scar on your knee?"

"Yep."

"I've been looking for you for a long time, my little sister. Six years."

"They told me you were dead. Didn't tell me how or when. Just dead."

"Who told you that?"

"My adopted parents."

"When I called, they couldn't find any records on you and Button. Said the records had been purged. Had to get a private detective to find you," I told her. "Where's Button?"

"She lives in San Diego with her husband."

"Husband, huh?"

"Yeah."

"Kids?" I smiled at the thought of my baby sister being married.

"Nope. They're trying, though."

"I know you got kids," I said. "I heard their little bad butts in the background tearing up furniture when I called the other day."

"Ashley and Nicolas Jr.," she laughed. "When you called the other day, I thought it was somebody playing on the phone. That's why I didn't call back. I'm sorry."

"It's okay."

"Where are you, girl? You want me to come get you?"

"Yeah! About time you asked. I'm staying at the Airport Hilton."

"Let me throw on some clothes, and I'll be there in about an hour."

"Okay."

"We can drive down to San Diego to see Button." I could hear the smile in her voice. "It's really you, huh?"

"It's really me."

"I'll see you in a minute."

I had to pinch myself, just to make sure.

* * *

I changed clothes three times. Waited. Checked my watch. Waited some more. Checked my watch again and it was two o'clock. Five hours since I'd hung up with Alex.

"See you in a minute," she'd said.

Called her house, left two messages. No response.

By five I realized she wasn't coming. The phone startled me. Maybe it was her and something had come up.

"Hello." I picked it up by the second ring.

"You expecting a call?" The voice on the other end, a smooth vanilla milkshake. Rico from the plane.

"I was."

"Disappointed?"

"Not totally," I said, and tried to brighten my tone. "Was waiting for my sister."

"Oh, you finally reached her?" The excitement in his voice was genuine.

"Yeah. She was supposed to pick me up at my hotel five hours ago. She was a no show."

"I'm sorry to hear that," he said. "Guess that means you're free, then, huh?"

"Guess it does."

"Meet you in the lobby?"

"When?"

"Is now too soon?" he said. "I'm downstairs."

A little sunshine after the rain.

14

Reece

It's always such an ordeal traveling through Hartsfield, one of the largest airports in the world. So hectic. Took the escalator up to baggage claim. I stared at the mural on the wall above the escalator, which depicted children of color from every nation of the world. My carry-on thrown over my shoulder felt heavier than before.

Tried twice before I left Nassau to reach Kevin. Left a sweet good-bye message the second time. Thoughts of him filled my head all the way home. In between naps, I pulled the folded-up piece of paper out of my purse, read it. Missed him already. Confused.

"What's up with you, girl?" Charlotte had asked. "You haven't said two words since we took off."

"Just tired."

"Whatever. I know you thinking about that man."

Silence.

"Please tell me you did not fall in love with him, Reece."

"What if I did?"

"You did." She knew me. "And him?"

"What?"

"He in love too?"

"Could be."

"So, what now?"

"Could never work. We live two worlds apart," I said. "I'm not trying to move to Nassau. And I'm sure Atlanta's not an option for him, either. So, we go back to life as we know it."

"Dag, girl. I see so much pain on your face. You were somebody different over there in the Islands, chile." She pretended to have a Bahamian accent. "I didn't even know you. And come to think of it, I don't even think you pulled that laptop out of its bag once."

"Hard to work when you're having so much fun."

"You know what? In all honesty, you looked happier than I've seen you in a long time, girl. Just in those few days."

"Vacations do that for people."

"Kevin must've put it on you." When she laughed this time, people turned to look.

"Shhhh. You're embarrassing me."

"I'm sorry. It's just that you look so pitiful now, girl. Look like somebody died. I wish I could go back and get that man for you." She sipped on her ginger ale. "You tell him good-bye?"

"Couldn't reach him. Left him a message."

"What happens to Darren now?"

"What you mean?"

"Surely you're not still thinking about getting married." She leaned over and lowered her voice. "Did you sleep with Kevin?"

"Of course not," I whispered back. "I ain't no hoochie!"

We both laughed.

"I really don't know what to do. My feelings are all out of whack," I admitted to my girlfriend of ten years.

"You need to tell Darren the truth. That's what you need to do. Be up front. Can't play with people's feelings. He'll go psychotic on your behind."

"What if I end up alone?"

"It's better to be alone than to spend the rest of your life with someone you don't love. Even if you never see Kevin again, Darren deserves the truth. And he deserves to have some-one who loves him." She made sense. "And so do you, Reece."

"You're right."

"I know I'm right." She reclined in her seat.

Silence.

"When are you going to see Dr. Hayes?" I asked her.

"As soon as I drop your butt off in Buckhead."

"Can I come?"

"If you want to."

"You scared?"

"Yeah, I'm scared!" she said. "But I'm positive."

"That's my girl." I grabbed her hand and held it tight. "I'm positive too."

We held hands for the longest time.

I spotted my black suitcase right away and lifted it off the carousel. Waited for Charlotte's bags to turn up.

"Welcome back." I turned to find the most beautiful black man in all of Atlanta. He wore black jeans and a gray Ralph Lauren shirt. His bald head and beautiful dimples were a sight for my tired eyes.

"Darren. What are you doing here?" I asked.

"I have missed you so much." He held me so close and kissed me with intensity. "I couldn't wait for Charlotte to bring you home. Had to pick you up myself."

"Hey, Darren." That was Charlotte.

"What's up, Charlotte. Long time, no see," he said. "Did you take good care of my woman while she was gone? Made sure she had a good time?"

"Oh, she had a good time." Charlotte gave me a little smirk. "Didn't you, Reece?"

I nodded.

"She didn't spend the whole time working, did she?"

"Didn't pull her laptop out once that I remember." She was really laying it on.

"That's good," he said. "Is this your only bag, Reece?"

"Yes," I told him. "It was a nice gesture for you to show up, honey, but Charlotte has a doctor's appointment, and I've made plans to go with her."

"It's okay, Reece. You go on ahead with Darren," Charlotte said. "I'll let you know how things turn out."

"But I really wanted to go with you." I clinched my teeth and made faces at her.

"You really need to go with your man." She gave me a look that said "handle your business."

"You sure?"

"I'm positive, Reece." She pulled her last bag off the carousel. "I'll call you later."

"You call me the minute you get home." I gave in.

"I will."

"I guess I'm ready, then," I told Darren.

"Nice to see you, Charlotte." Darren threw my carry-on over his shoulder.

"You too, Darren," Charlotte said. "It was fun, Reece."

"You call me."

"I will," she said, as she shooed us off.

My body sank into the passenger seat of Darren's convertible Mustang. We flew up the I-75/85 interstate headed north. My body jerked each time he shifted gears, past the WE'RE GLAD GEORGIA'S ON YOUR MIND sign that greeted newcomers to the city, caught a quick glimpse of Turner Field, flew past the Westin standing tall in Atlanta's downtown. Once inside the perimeter, we veered onto I-85 toward Buckhead. I kicked my shoes off.

"I have a surprise for you." Darren smiled.

"You said that on the phone," I said. "You're gonna tell me what it is?"

Darren hit the four-digit code on the security gate, and we drove through as it began to creep open. Darren had been given the four-digit code as well as a key to my place back when we'd decided to get serious. I was also given a key to his house, although I rarely used it. We pulled up in front of my carport.

There was a white minivan parked where my Range Rover was supposed to be.

"Where's my truck?"

"It's at the dealership. I'm test-driving the van. Figured if we're going to be married and start having kids, we're gonna need something a little more practical. While your Range Rover is roomy, the van is more of a family vehicle. Gets better gas mileage. More conservative. Would drop your payment down tremendously. What you think?" He sounded just like one of those fast-talking car dealers who trapped you into purchasing a vehicle you really couldn't afford.

"I think you need to go back to that dealership and get my vehicle!"

I suddenly regretted giving him my extra set of keys.

"Thought you would be happy."

"About a minivan, Darren? I am not a minivan kind of woman. Look at me; do I look like a soccer mom?"

He looked as if he were really contemplating an answer.

"And not only that, what gives you the right to shop for a vehicle for me without my consent or input." I was livid.

"Reece, I didn't buy the van; I'm just test-driving it."

"Good thing. Make it that much easier to take it back," I said. "And as far as the kid thing, I'm not ready for children at this time in my life. There are so many other things that I really would like to do first."

"What's up with the attitude, Reece?"

"What's up with the attitude?" I answered his question with a question. "Darren, do you know who I am?"

"Of course I know who you are."

"I mean, do you really know me?"

"What are you getting at, Reece? Stop with the riddles."

"Darren, you really don't know me at all," I said. "Because if you did, you would've known the van was a bad idea."

"Sorry."

"And you would know that I'm not happy."

"Okay, the van was a bad idea."

"Not just the van, Darren. I'm not happy about a lot of things."

"Like what?"

"My career, for one. Did you know that I really don't enjoy practicing law? That what I really want to do is help people."

"I know you like to help people, Reece."

"I'm seriously considering a career change."

"To what?"

"Thinking about opening a shelter."

"A what?"

"A homeless shelter, Darren."

"Are you crazy, Reece? You would be crazy to give up a lucrative career to go chasing after some pipe dream. The only way you would quit practicing law would be to stay home and raise our children. And that's what you should be focusing on right now anyway!"

"What?" I was getting angry. "What gives you the right—"

"You really need to get a grip on reality."

"Oh, and what you're proposing—my staying at home to raise babies after I've put so much time and effort into building a career—is reality?"

"More so than this shelter nonsense," he said. "Many of my colleagues' wives stay at home, raise the children, homeschool. I've done some asking around. Many of their wives don't even have college degrees that they're attached to. And they are grateful to have husbands who can afford them such a lifestyle. One that would allow them to stay home. There's nothing wrong with that."

"You're right, there is nothing wrong with it if that's what they choose to do. But for me, that's not what I want."

"Reece, what kind of income would a homeless shelter net you anyway?"

"Probably nothing but fulfillment. But it's not about the income, Darren," I said. "I've been putting some money away over the years. Not to mention, Daddy left me a nice little nest egg when he passed away. He invested his money well, and I could live off of that alone."

"Reece, a homeless shelter?" He shook his head. "I'm sorry, but I won't agree to that."

"You won't agree to it?"

"It's not realistic. And I'm sure that after you think about it for a while, you'll get past this crazy idea of yours."

"It's not just an idea, Darren."

"When we get married, this is something we'd have to discuss."

"That's another thing, Darren." I paused. Chose my words. "I like my life, just the way it is. I like Buckhead. I like my little condo, with the view of the Atlanta skyline. I don't want to move to Stone Mountain."

Horror was on his face.

"Surely you don't expect me to move into your little place," he said. "I've got all my weights and stuff, not to mention my workbench and tools. There's no room."

"I don't expect you to move in with me."

"Then what are you saying?"

"Darren, I can't marry you." I slid the stone off my finger. "Not right now."

He wore his heart on his face, wanted to cry, but resisted with everything in him. His manhood was at stake.

I handed him my engagement ring. He didn't reach for it, didn't even look my way, just stared straight ahead. Hurt in his eyes. Anger too. I placed the ring on the dash. Opened my door slowly. Heart racing. Wanted him to say something.

"You've thought about this?" His words were softly spoken, but intense.

"Yes." I said it softly. "For a very long time."

"I hope you know what you're doing."

"I do."

"So this is what you really want?"

"Yes." I didn't hesitate, and it was the first time in a long time I'd been completely honest with myself. I'd been living a lie for so long, I didn't know where to find the truth. "This is what I want for now."

"I'll go get your vehicle back." He got out of the Mustang, got into the van, and drove off. Never said another word.

15

Charlotte

I sat in the waiting room reading a magazine, legs crossed, looked cool on the outside, but my insides were in turmoil. I flipped through the pages of the *Newsweek* with nervous energy, eyes lifting each time the door opened and the nurse called someone back.

"Charlotte Daniels." The nurse finally called me, held the door, her eyes searched the waiting room. I stood, followed her to a cold room in the back and waited for Gwen. The nurse's smile was reassuring, my chart in her hand. Rolled my sleeve up so she could check my blood pressure. Wrote it down. Stuck a thermometer under my tongue and wrote that down too.

"Dr. Hayes will be with you in a moment." She shut the door behind her.

My eyes searched the room. Gauzes and rubber gloves were set in glass canisters on the counter near the sink. A poster on the wall encouraged its readers to maintain a healthy, well-balanced diet. Torn magazines had been flipped through by hundreds of readers while they awaited their destinies.

"Hello, Charlotte." Gwen's fro was always in place. "How was your vacation?"

"I can't complain." I became fidgety and began to pick at my nail that needed to be repaired. I was planning on visiting my usual little Asian spot for a manicure and pedicure the minute I left Gwen's office.

"Well, now," she said, shutting the door, my chart in her hand. "Let's get down to business."

She studied it.

"Your vitals are good."

"You said something about discussing some options, Gwen."

"Let me first say that you're certainly welcome to be re-diagnosed, as well as get a second opinion. In fact, I encourage it."

I nodded.

"There are a wide range of choices for you, and when I introduce you to our treatment team, you will certainly be involved in the decision-making process.

"Will they have to remove my breast?" I wanted to cut to the chase.

"Not necessarily, honey. Treatment has changed over time, and just because you're diagnosed with breast cancer, doesn't mean you have to lose a breast. There are improved ways to treat breast cancer nowadays. Working with our team of medical specialists, you get to play a key role in choosing the treatment that is best for you."

"I get to choose, huh?"

"Absolutely." She smiled. "Now if you're ready, I'd like to introduce you to the oncologist."

"Okay."

She walked toward the door.

"She's going to discuss with you the types of treatments, like surgery, radiation, and things of that sort."

"Hey, Gwen?" I stopped her. "Thanks. This is very scary for me, but you make it seem so, you know, less scary."

"Relax, honey." She rested her hand on mine. "Just know that most women who are treated early for breast cancer go on to live healthy, active lives."

* * *

I spent most of the day talking with doctors about treatments and taking in an abundance of information about my disease. *My disease.* That was a frightening phrase. *Treatment* and *surgery* and *cancer* were becoming words that I was forced to become familiar with as well. Words that described or went hand in hand with *my disease.* It became painfully obvious that I was facing one of the hardest situations of my entire life. Having to make decisions that would affect me physically, emotionally, and mentally. Questions were haunting me. If I had a breast removed, would I be able to have a relationship with a man again? What would he think of a woman with one breast? Would he find me less attractive? Would he care? Would I tell him up front or wait until we were into the relationship? I was trippin'. Who was I kidding? Since William, I couldn't remember when I was last in a relationship and had no intentions of being in one now. So why was I even stressing that issue? Squashed that thought. Still others haunted me. If they removed the cancer cells, was there a chance they would return? Or spread? If I had surgery and followed up with radiation, would I lose my hair and be forced to wear a wig? Or maybe a short fro like Gwen's? Or maybe just go bald like Shaq. Oh my God, I was starting to sound like Maxie. She would just go bald, wouldn't think twice about it. Wouldn't care what people thought, either. I envied Maxie sometimes. Wished I could be so free.

This was all too much, too soon, but I scheduled my surgery before I left, and braced myself for what was ahead. I feared the worst—that once they went in, they'd find that the cancer had spread all over my body. And they'd give me so many months, maybe weeks to live. And I'd be facing my Maker sooner than I thought. I wondered if I would take the news like a woman, or if I'd crumble and fall. Wondered if I'd have a nervous breakdown, or if I'd be relieved. I just didn't know what I'd feel, how I'd react, what I'd do. All I knew was I was afraid. Afraid of knowing, afraid of not knowing, but most of all, afraid of dying.

Once inside my car, I called Reece.

"Charlotte, you're tripping over nothing," she said. "You'll be just fine."

"You promise?"

"I promise," she said with such confidence. "And I'll be right there with you. You won't have to do this alone."

"You can't fix this, Reece," I told her. "It's between me and God now."

"It always has been. You just got to keep the faith."

It was a huge promise she'd made, and although she sounded convincing, I still trembled inside at the thought of it.

"When's your surgery?"

"Week from today. Nine o'clock in the morning."

"Fine. I'm taking the whole day off, just so I can be there with you."

"That's sweet. But I'll be fine if you can't make it."

"I can make it," she said. "Matter of fact, I'll spend the night with you the night before. Drive you over to the hospital myself. How 'bout that?"

"Sounds like a plan."

I was thankful for Reece. She was my family, my sister. And I needed her more than ever now. And just as always, she was there.

16

Maxie

Rolling through the hood.

Just to check things out. Wanted to see what my people were up to on a beautiful California day. I went to a couple of museums in the Miracle Mile district. Afterward caught some lunch at Reign, Keyshawn Johnson's place in Beverly Hills. Rico was able to get us reservations at the famous restaurant with a renaissance Etta James, Billie Holiday sort of flavor. White architecture with chrome trim and hardwood floors adorned the place. Southern cuisine with an upscale twist. Reminded me of a place Charlotte would frequent. The food was good, but I would have been happy with a greasy burger joint in South Central myself.

"How about the beach?" Rico asked after lunch, wheeling his Ford Explorer through traffic on Wilshire, then onto La Cienega. "There's a beach in Orange County, but I really think you would enjoy Venice Beach more."

"Why is that?"

"A lot more culture," he said. "You'll see what I mean."

We jumped onto Rosa Parks Freeway for a hot minute and then onto the 405. Caught some smooth jazz on the Wave 94.7.

I'd decided to give the jeans and T-shirt a rest and actually looked good in my cinnamon-colored capri pants with matching halter top, sandals with my toes out, my golden locks still freshly done. My girls would be so proud. We strolled the boardwalk on Venice Beach, taking in the shops, watching the folks on Rollerblades, bounced to the rhythms from the drum circles, and was entertained by the dancers and artists. So much culture, I closed my eyes for a minute and took it all in.

"What you thinking about?"

"Just taking in the beauty," I said. "Why are the people here always in a hurry? Never taking the time to enjoy life. Always got a *thing* to get to."

"That's just LA," he said. "Some people do have a *thing* to get to. Others just pretend they do. It's crazy."

I laughed. "So what's your thing?"

"Just a regular guy, Maxie. Got a real nine to five. Trying to take care of my daughter and make ends meet." His smile was the moonlight. "What about you?"

"My life is pretty uncomplicated. I'm a journalist. Live in East Point, Georgia, in an apartment where the plumbing is terrible and the landlord is a fat white dude who don't care two cents about his tenants. Tenants who, by the way, are making him rich."

"Why don't you move?"

"It's important for me to maintain contact with the real world."

"I like you, Maxie."

"Why, because I'm uncomplicated and most of the women you meet are high maintenance?"

"No." He grabbed my hand and threw me way off course. "Because I think you have a great deal of character, and I really would like to get to know you better."

"Yeah?"

"Yeah. And I think you're very beautiful too."

"You're making me blush." I smiled. "Please stop before I blow a gasket or something."

"You should blush more. It looks good on you."

"Why you flirtin'?"

"Can't help myself," he said. "Let me ask you something. What would make your life complete?"

"Let me see, what would make my life complete?" I looked to the sky as if the answer were there. "My sisters. I've been searching for them for a long time. Finding them, I guess, would make my life complete. Think that being with them would make me whole or something. Everybody has family they can call their own. I never have. I bet you go to your mama's on Thanksgiving and pig out, huh?"

"You know it. Every year she has a big spread. Turkey, ham, cornbread dressing, collard greens. The works."

"Your whole family there?"

"A house full. And, you talking about some fun? Play a little spades. Eat until we don't have room for anything else."

"See, I don't have that. Miss Jones down the hall from me usually sets me a plate aside. And I might catch a matinee at the movies with my buddy Greg. That's if he doesn't go home to Chicago to be with his family. One year, my girls Charlotte and Reece and me attempted to cook our own Thanksgiving dinner. Now keep in mind that none of us can cook, but we sure tried. Turkey half done, cornbread dressing overcooked. We ended up ordering a couple of pizzas and finishing off a bottle of wine. But we had fun, though," I said. "Charlotte and Reece pretty much have become my family. We've been through a lot together. They been like sisters to me."

"See, there you have it. Family is not necessarily people who are blood related to you." Rico wore khaki shorts with a cleaner's crease in them and a black tank top, advertising the fact that he'd spent some time at the gym. "Sounds to me like you've already found your sisters."

A concept I'd never considered.

"I never really thought of it that way," I said, taking my sandals off to feel the sand between my toes.

"Well, you should," he said, grabbing my hand again. This

time his fingers intertwined with mine. "Where you wanna go now?"

"Home," I said, referring to my hotel. "I need to get some rest. Think I'll rent a car and drive down to San Diego tomorrow morning. Need to track down my other sister."

"I can drive you down there if you want me to. It's not that far, about two hours," he said. "That is, if you don't mind my daughter Brianna tagging along."

"I don't mind. You sure you want to drive down there?"

"Be my pleasure."

We headed back to my hotel in Inglewood. He walked me to my door and planted a kiss on my cheek.

"I'll see you in the morning," he said.

"Good night." I watched him walk toward the elevators and disappear.

I checked my phone for a blinking red light. There was one message from Reece, checking to see if I'd made it safely and how things were going. One from Charlotte telling me about her visit to the doctor. And one from Button, my baby sister. She said that Alex had called and told her I was here. She wanted to see me. Gave me directions to her place. No messages from Alex, no apologies, no promises to make things right. I didn't understand but was too tired to lose sleep over it. Hearing from Button was enough. I replayed the message again, just to hear her voice. Grabbed the notepad from my nightstand and jotted down the directions. I smiled with anticipation, changed into my workout clothes, and bounced to the hotel fitness center for a round on the weights before turning in.

This had definitely been a good day.

17

Maxie

First thing Sunday morning we hopped onto the Santa Ana Freeway heading south.

Rico's daughter Brianna was way too grown for her own good. And I kept trying to remember if I was that sassy at eight.

"Daddy, can you please take the child lock off my window? I really need some air," she said.

"Bri, if you're hot, take your jacket off."

"I thought we were going to church with Grandmommy today." She unsnapped her seatbelt and took her jacket off.

"Well, we had other plans instead. Grandmommy will understand." Rico was good at this father thing. "Now sit back and be quiet for a while."

"For how long?"

"Until we get to where we're going."

"Which is where? I forgot."

"Bri, let's play the quiet game for a while. You be quiet for at least ten minutes, and I'll give you dollar."

"Daddy, you know I can't buy anything in LA with a dollar."

"She has a point," I interjected, and we both laughed.

She was cute. Not quite the vanilla that Rico was, but more a chocolate brown with two long ponytails on each side of her head and two big front teeth.

We finally pulled into a residential neighborhood in College Grove. Palm trees standing tall and alert. Found the address we were looking for. It was a gray stucco house; a Nelly CD pumped up so loud you could hear it from the street. Cars parked in the driveway and lined all the way down the block. I checked my handwritten directions to make sure I had the right address. It was the right house.

Rico parallel parked his Ford into a tight spot between a black Maxima with dark tinted windows and a green lowrider Chevy that had been fixed up with expensive wheels and black tint on the windows.

I walked toward the door and could smell marijuana coming from the house through the screen door. Loud masculine conversations and laughter filled the room. I walked up onto the porch, Rico and Brianna stood on the sidewalk. I was met at the door by a dark brother with braids and pants hanging off of his behind, revealing his red-and-black checkered boxers.

"Hi. I'm looking for Button," I said.

"She around back," he said, pointing us in the direction of the backyard. "Y'all can go around the side of the house."

We hesitantly followed the brick sidewalk on the side of the house to the back, the smell of smoked barbeque floating in the air. I opened the gate. People were everywhere, some were eating, others dancing. Others just stood around engaged in conversations with each other. A tall brother with a doo rag on his head and a bottle of Miller beer in his hand looked our way.

"How y'all doing?" He raised his Miller to us, and then headed our way.

Rico nodded that we were all right.

"I'm looking for Button," I said, attempting to be heard over the music.

"Aw, man. You must be Maxie!" He smiled and was actually quite handsome. Stepped back to get a good look at me as if we were old friends. "She told me all about you. Said you were coming."

"Is she here?"

"She went down the street to do this girl's braids," he said. "She'll be back soon. She been gone a long time already."

"Okay, we'll come back then, when she's here."

"Please don't leave," he pleaded. "Have some grub. We got ribs, chicken, potato salad. Can I get y'all a brew?"

"No, thank you," I said.

"I'm cool," Rico said.

"She's been waiting for you to get here," he said. "She would be heartbroken if she missed you. I'll call her."

He pulled a cell phone out of his pocket and dialed a few numbers, mumbled a few words to someone on the other end.

"She's en route. She said for y'all to have a seat, fix yourselves a plate, and get your groove on. Whatever, just make yourselves at home." He disappeared into the house.

Rico and I found a couple of seats on the back patio. No one seemed to notice we were there, all wrapped up in their personal conversations and food. We watched people dancing like they were at the club. One girl was shaking her booty so hard, I was sure it would fall off her body. A brother next to the grill was flipping some ribs with tongs. Four brothers stood in a circle, each had a beer in hand, and were laughing and talking about whatever men discuss when they're together. A picnic table was set up next to us; two brothers and two girls were playing a game of spades.

"What y'all bid?" the dark sister with too much lipstick asked the other team.

"Give us six," the brother with the perfectly trimmed Afro responded.

"Six? That's all?" Lipstick asked.

"That's it." Afro's sexy partner answered with attitude, as her breasts spilled over onto the table. "Give us six like he said."

Lipstick wrote it down on a notepad. "We'll take six too, then."

We watched them play. Afro and Breasts had underbid their hands, and Rico told them so.

"Man, you had at least six books by yourself. Y'all underbid," he said, and I wanted to shut him up. We didn't know any of these people from Adam, and they didn't look very friendly. I waited for Afro's response as he handed Rico the meanest look I'd ever seen. I felt helpless. Knew I didn't have my .38 with me, as I'd been forced to leave it at home due to tightened security at the airport.

"Well, you think you can do better?" Afro asked.

"I know I can."

"Y'all wanna play?" Lipstick asked, smiling seductively at Rico.

"No, we don't really have time," I said.

"What, y'all scared?" That was Afro, standing now.

"You wanna show them what we got?" Rico looked at me. We'd never played together before, so I didn't know what he had. I knew I could whip the best of them under the table myself, and I only assumed that he could do the same. I gave in.

"You can be my partner." Lipstick smiled at Rico again, and I'd had about enough of her. Rico must've anticipated that I was about to set her straight, because he stepped in.

"That's all right. I brought my partner with me," he said, grabbing a hold of my hand, and her smile dropped as she cut her eyes my way.

When the losers got up, we took their places at the table. Bid our hands like pros and commenced to whipping Lipstick and her partner. Brianna had found a group of little girls her age and went to play baby dolls.

"I got four, Maxie," Rico said after observing his hand.

"Then we'll take eight," I told Lipstick, and she wrote it down, rolling her eyes.

We beat them at every hand from the minute we'd sat down.

Someone from behind covered my eyes, and I almost jumped up ready to fight.

"Guess who?" The voice I remembered from my voice mail. I turned around.

"Button?"

"That's me."

She wore a pair of bell-bottom jeans and a cropped top with spaghetti straps, revealing her pierced belly button. She looked a lot like Mama, caramel skin, long coal black hair that hung on her shoulders. Perfect shape.

"Give me a hug, girl." We embraced for the longest time.

"I see you made yourself at home," she said. The brother with the doo rag who'd greeted us when we got there was standing next to her. "Did Earl offer you something to eat?"

"Yes. He was the perfect host," I told her.

"He's my husband," she said, smiling at him as if they were falling in love for the first time. "Earl, meet my sister, Maxie."

"Already did," he said, shaking my hand anyway.

"Glad to meet you, Earl."

"This is my friend, Rico."

They each shook Rico's hand.

"Let's go somewhere so we can talk," she said.

"Y'all done playing?" Lipstick asked, disappointed to see Rico go.

"We'll be back for another round," I promised.

"Brianna!" Rico called her and she looked disappointed to have to leave her newfound girlfriends.

"Daddy, I'm not ready to leave yet." She came bouncing over to where we were.

"Let her play if she wants to," Button said. "Niecy can keep an eye on the girls."

Niecy was a heavy girl, the stitching on her stretch pants was screaming for mercy on her behind. But she seemed safe.

"She'll be fine," Niecy said. "Let her stay and play with Shamika and Nay Nay."

127

"Please, Daddy," Brianna pleaded.

"All right, go ahead," Rico said, "but you'd better behave."

Earl pulled Rico over to the garage to show him the sixty-seven Chevy he was fixing up. I followed Button inside to the kitchen. Took a seat at the table.

"You look different than I expected," she said, staring at me.

"What did you expect?"

"I don't know," she said. "Do I look like what you expected?"

"You look like Mama."

"Yeah?" she asked. "I have a picture of her."

She looked around in her purse, grabbed her wallet, and pulled a black-and-white photo out. I got chills looking at Mama in the photo. The only photo I have is the one burned in my memory.

"Where did you get this?"

"I've had it since I was little. Used to sleep with it under my pillow. Even after Alex and I were adopted, I would hide it and look at it every now and then. Didn't want to forget what she looked like."

We just smiled and looked at each other for a few seconds.

"What's Alex's story?" I began. "She called me yesterday and promised to pick me up at my hotel. Never showed up."

"That doesn't surprise me." She got up and poured herself a glass of orange juice. "Want something to drink?"

"No. I'm fine."

"I don't know why she didn't show up. But I'm guessing that it was because of Nick."

"Nick?"

"Her husband." She placed a large pill on the tip of her tongue and washed it down with the juice. "He's very controlling. She can't leave the house without his knowing her every move. And if he knew she was coming to see you, he might have protested."

"Why?"

"Old wounds, girl. He's a politician. Running for some office," she said. "Can't risk his wife running into her long lost sister, from a past life filled with orphanages and foster homes. Would only complicate things for his campaign."

"I didn't come here to complicate her life. Just wanted to see her."

"I'm sure she knows that. But she's not at a place in her life where she can welcome you."

"I don't understand."

"She goes to all these fancy fundraising events, hanging out with her bourgeois socialite friends, living in the upscale part of town. Your being here really puts a twist on things," she said. "You have to understand what sort of life we had growing up, Maxie. The kind of person Alex is."

"Tell me about it."

"From the beginning?"

"From the beginning."

"Let me see," she said. "I was six. Alex was ten. Sarah and William Weaver adopted us. The only parents I ever really knew. They were good parents, gave us a great life. We lived in the largest house on the block in Georgia, in an all-white neighborhood. Dad was an engineer. The first black man at his firm. We had a pool in our backyard, had a beach home in Hilton Head that we visited every summer. Went to a private school. We lived a life that other black children only dreamed about."

"How did y'all end up in California?"

"Dad's job transferred him out here. Mom didn't work. Stayed at home to raise us. When she wasn't home with us, she spent time with her bridge clubs and socialite friends, throwing and attending big parties. I hated California at first. All my friends were in Georgia and I hated having to leave them behind. I was about fourteen then, and going through puberty. I became rebellious, started hanging out with the wrong crowd. Smoking weed, drinking, and having unprotected sex. Luckily I didn't get pregnant."

"Or worse," I said.

"Freaked my parents out! They didn't know what to do with me. Dad was worried that I was headed down a road of destruction. Mom was worried about what her bourgeois friends would think or say. I was more of an embarrassment to her. We weren't allowed to tell people we were adopted."

"What about Alex? What was she like as a teenager?"

"She was a nerd." She chuckled a little. "Always into the books. Played by the rules. Made our parents proud. She always warned me that if I didn't behave and get myself together, they would send us away, and we'd be out there with no one to care for us . . . like you were. I didn't care. Wanted to do my own thing regardless."

She sat quietly for a moment, finished her juice.

"Alex ended up going to UCLA. Graduated at the top of her class. Went to graduate school, too, but is doing absolutely nothing with her degree. Married Nicolas right after college and got pregnant right away. Became a stay-home mom, started homeschooling her kids. Travels in social circles with the wives of some of the biggest moneymakers in LA. Spends all her time at museums and raising money for Nick's campaign. It's all about Nick, you know."

"I'm starting to get the picture," I told her.

"She's so unhappy."

"Why?"

"I don't know. She's always been that way. Always had a chip on her shoulder."

"What about you, Button? Did you go to college?"

"Did a semester at UCLA before realizing that college was not for me. That's where I met my boo, Earl." She smiled when she said his name. "He's from San Diego, and I moved down here with him. Went to cosmetology school, got my license. Got my own shop now. I'll have to hook your locks up before you leave, girl."

"I'll take you up on it," I said, running my fingers through them. "You and Alex close?"

"As close as any two sisters can be. But we're two totally different people."

"You sound a lot like me, little sister," I said.

"Tell me about you, Maxie," she said. "What's your story?"

"I remember when you and Alex were adopted. Remember Miss Sarah. Didn't know her last name until now. I was twelve. They didn't want me because they said I was too old to be adopted. Spent most of my life in foster care. Finally got a job when I was sixteen and ran away. Quit school, but went back later and got my GED. My girlfriend, Reece, showed me how to apply for some grants and scholarships, and I put myself through college and grad school. Now I'm a journalist. Worked for a couple of large magazines and newspapers. But I freelance most of the time. Prefer to do my own thing."

"That's cool," she said. "Can I come see you in Atlanta?"

"Of course you can. Whenever you want to."

"I will." She smiled, placing her hand over her stomach. "But it'll have to be after the baby is born. I'm seven weeks pregnant."

"Get out of here!"

"It's true," she said. "You're the first to know, except Earl. I haven't told my parents or Alex yet."

"I feel privileged."

"Hey, Maxie." That was Rico, sticking his head in the door. "Can you come out here and dance with me? Let's show these youngsters what old school is all about."

"I'll be out there in a minute," I laughed.

"That your man?" Button asked after Rico was gone.

"Just somebody I met on the plane ride here." I couldn't help blushing.

"For real?" she said. "He's cute. And y'all look good together."

"He's cool. But I'm not really looking for a man in my life right now," I said. "It could never work anyway. He lives in LA I live in Atlanta. Worlds apart."

"Never know," she said. "Sometimes life surprises you."

"You're right about that."

"I really want to get to know you, Maxie." Button stood. "I really don't remember much about my childhood, but I remember you. I've always known I had a big sister out there somewhere. I often wished you were a part of our lives. And you seem like somebody I could really hang out with. Talk to."

"I want to get to know you too." I hugged my little sister. "Let's just take it one step at a time, though, okay?"

"Okay," she said.

This was our moment in history, and I didn't want it to end.

I went outside and danced to the sounds of Earth Wind & Fire.

18

Reece

I sat in the hallway, awaiting the verdict in the case of the *State of Georgia v. Cecil Jackson.* I had entered into a plea bargain with the prosecuting attorney in Wanda's case a week before. They'd dropped the charges against her in exchange for a testimony against the boyfriend and in agreement to three months of community service. Needless to say, Wanda anxiously agreed and the charges were dropped. We both showed up at Cecil Jackson's trial. Wanda was there to testify, I was there to make sure they put him away for a long time. I took a seat behind the prosecution. The jury had heard all the evidence that was presented. They'd heard Wanda's testimony and that of the doctor who had examined Jill. All the evidence was there for them to consider. He'd already admitted to some of the charges, and a conviction was inevitable. No way he would walk after the cross-examination the prosecution had just rendered, and the closing remarks were earth-shattering. Jill's testimony would have only sealed the case more, but she still refused to speak. We walked back into the courtroom. Sat down. The jury entered in single file. Couldn't read their faces, but in my heart I knew the case was airtight.

"Have you reached a verdict?" Judge White asked.

"Yes." The paper was passed along to the judge. He read it. "Proceed then."

An Asian man stood and represented the jury. "We the jury find the defendant guilty. . . ."

The courtroom was in an uproar as Cecil Jackson was found guilty on three charges and sentenced to twenty years. People were gasping for breath as they heard the verdict. Cheers. Wanda jumped up and hugged my neck so hard, I thought she would knock me over.

"How can I ever thank you?" she asked. "For everything."

"I'm sure we'll find a way," I told her.

We walked out of the courtroom together. I felt relieved that it was over.

"Can you keep an eye on Jill for a minute, Miss Jameson?" she asked as we stepped into the hallway. "I got to go pee. Been holding it all morning."

She ran off to the restroom as I nodded a yes.

Jill was wearing what looked like her Easter dress, patent leather shoes, and socks up to her knees. She and I found a seat on a bench nearby.

"Hi, Jill," I said, and smiled once we were alone.

"Hi," she responded, and that was the first time I'd ever heard her voice.

"Do you know why we were here today?"

"Yes," she said.

"You were here because something terrible happened to you, and we wanted to make sure it didn't happen again. You understand?"

"Yes," she began, "but he didn't do it alone."

My face was filled with confusion. I dropped my briefcase. Picked it up and leaned it against my hip.

"What?" I looked into those sad eyes.

"He didn't do those nasty things to me alone," she repeated softly. "Mama made him do it."

"What do you mean your mama made him do it?" I asked.

She tried that quiet game again. Silence. I realized I had to choose my words very carefully.

"Look, Jill. I know you're scared, but you have to tell me the truth. About what happened. Okay?"

"I can't," she whispered, folding her arms.

"Why not?"

"She'll beat me." She clinched her teeth when she said it, almost as if her speaking the words were the same as the beating itself.

"I promise she won't beat you. You want this to stop, don't you?"

"Yes," she said softly.

"Whatever you tell me, I promise I won't let anyone hurt you. Not even your mother."

She looked in my eyes. She was so frightened.

"You can't tell anyone," she said. "Not even her."

"I want to help you. But you have to tell me what happened."

"You can't tell anyone," she repeated. "Now that Mr. Cecil is going to jail, it won't happen again. So promise me you won't tell."

"I won't tell," I said reluctantly, knowing that I could never betray this little girl's trust, but trying desperately to think of a way to bring justice into her little life.

"Mama drinks a lot. And when she gets drunk, she makes me sleep in the bed with her and Mr. Cecil. She lets him do it. Tells him to," she said, her eyes staring at the wooden floor as if she were ashamed to hold her head up.

"And what is she doing when he does it?"

"Watching. Sometimes."

"And other times?"

"He did it once when she wasn't there. That's when she got mad. Because he did it while she was gone."

"And you told her when she came home?"

"Yes. And she was very angry with him," she said, continuing to stare at the floor. "I told her I would tell my teacher if they didn't stop."

"What did she say then?"

"She beat me." She whispered it and I barely heard her. "But later she said that she'd make him stop. That she would get him for doing it when she wasn't there."

"She confronted Mr. Cecil?"

"Yes. Mr. Cecil said he didn't do it while she was gone, but he did."

"Then what happened?"

"Then they started fighting and he told us to leave."

She went on to tell me in detail what took place with her mother and Cecil Jackson. I couldn't believe what I was hearing and remembered the day Wanda Manning came strutting into my office playing the victim. She'd sounded so sincere. But now that I knew the truth, I was mortified that she'd attempted to use me in her scheme. She played me.

"Thank you, Miss Jameson." Wanda returned from the restroom. "For everything."

"You're welcome," I said, and when I looked into her face, I wanted to slap her. I knew I had to do something. I wanted to put Wanda Manning away for so long, she wouldn't remember what freedom felt like. I just didn't know how to go about it without betraying Jill.

"Come on, Jill," she said. "Tell the nice lady good-bye."

Her little hand waved to me as her mother dragged her down the hallway. Her eyes staring into mine, pleading for help. I waved back and tried my best to smile.

"Hello, Counselor." A familiar voice whispered in my ear.

"Darren?" I turned to find his beautiful face. He was dressed · in a navy blue suit and wearing the tie I'd given him for Valentine's Day two years back. "You were in the courtroom?"

"Thought I would come by," he said. "Knew I'd find you here, awaiting Cecil Jackson's fate."

"Thank you for coming." I smiled, flattered that he was there. "You were right, Darren. There was more to that story than I knew. You know, with the little girl. She finally told me what really happened."

"What happened?"

"The mother was in on it the whole time. Allowed the guy to molest her daughter."

"You're kidding me."

"Nope."

"A lot of sick people in this world."

"I've got to do something."

"There you go, trying to save the world again," he said. "What you need to do is notify social services and walk away."

"Yeah, you're probably right," I said, but knew in my heart that it wouldn't be the end of it. Knew I would take matters into my own hands and work it out. I just didn't know how. I would fix Wanda for what she did to that little girl. I knew it and Darren knew it, which is why he changed the subject.

"Can I buy you lunch?" he asked. "No pressure. Just lunch."

"Sure. Why not? I'm hungry."

We walked over to the CNN Center. I told him about what Jill had said.

"So what are you gonna do?" he asked.

We grabbed a couple of burgers. Found a table.

"I don't know."

"I think you should just let it go. The guy is locked up," he said. "But knowing you, I know you got a backup plan."

"You're right about that," I said. "Wanda should be locked up. What if she does it again? With someone else? Another boyfriend? Not to mention the fact that she played me."

"Oh, now we get down to the real deal." He laughed. "She played you. That's what you're really pissed about."

"Got that right." I laughed too. "So, how have you been?"

"Reece, I miss you." His smile was still there, but his eyes were sad.

I missed him too. But in a different sort of way: He missed the romance, I missed his friendship.

"Miss you too," I said, in-between bites. "You look good."

"You look good too," he said.

"What you been up to?"

"My life is empty without you," he began. "What did I do wrong, Reece? Or what could I have done differently?"

"You didn't do anything wrong. I just wasn't ready for marriage. Or children. And all that stuff that we were rushing into," I said. "Darren, you are a wonderful man. You deserve someone who's going to love you with all of her heart. Look at you, with your fine self. You can have any woman you want."

"That's the problem. I don't want any woman. I want you." He was hurt. I could hear it in his voice. "Reece, I love you."

"I know you do, Darren. And I love you too. But I don't think it's the same kind of love."

"That doesn't make sense," he said. "Love is love."

"I love you as my friend. You were there for me when I needed you most. Look at you, showing up in court today for my big case. You're my friend, and I love you for that," I said, and grabbed his hand. "I don't want you to disappear from my life. I value your friendship. I just don't think we're ready for marriage."

"Is it another man?"

"I've been feeling this way for a long time. Whether there was another man or not, I would still feel the same way."

Felt that tingle in my stomach when I thought about Kevin.

"I won't stop trying, you know."

"I know you won't."

"Want to get some Chinese and rent a couple of movies this Saturday?"

"I don't know, Darren." I knew better than to give him false hope. "Call me on Saturday, and we'll see."

"I'll call you Friday night," he said, finishing his burger, throwing our trash away, and walking me to my car.

19

Charlotte

Surgery.

I was glad Reece was there. Made all the difference in the world.

"You okay, girl?"

"I'm good," I said, feeling the draft creeping up my backside through the flimsy gown I was wearing. "Just a little scared. Never been through anything like this before."

"I'll be here when you go in and when you come out," she said. "Just say a little prayer and everything will be all right."

"I wish it were that simple."

"It is. You know God got your back."

"Yeah. You're probably right," I said.

"Probably? What you mean 'probably'? You know I'm right."

Silence for a moment. The room was a cold, gloomy place.

"I talked to Maxie this morning. She sends her love. Wished she could be here for you."

"I understand. She's got other priorities right now."

"She promised to come and see you as soon as she gets back to Atlanta."

"Hopefully I'll be at home by then."

"Hopefully so."

"When I get home, I want some collard greens, macaroni and cheese, and ham. Maybe some oxtails."

"You're not hungry, are you?"

"Haven't eaten since yesterday," I said. "Can you hook me up with some of that jalapeño cornbread you make at Christmastime? Or some of your mama's sweet potato pie."

"You are trippin'. What happened to your diet?"

"Screw that diet! Girl, I'm hungry," I told her. "Besides, you only live once."

"You a trip." Reece laughed, and I did too.

"I'm scared."

"Scared of what?"

"What if they don't get it all? The cancer, I mean."

"You have to have faith that they will, Charlotte."

"What if I wind up bald and have to wear a wig?"

"Oh well. Then I guess you'll have to find a cute one that goes with your face." Reece laughed. "My mama got one you can borrow."

"That's okay. No disrespect to Mother Jameson, but I'll pass."

Silence again.

"Want me to sing?"

"Sing what? You can't hold a note to save your soul."

"I can too. What you want me to sing? Some Bootsy? Some P-Funk? What?" She started moving like there was music playing.

"You are stupid," I said. "I never really liked Bootsy Collins. But Roger Troutman. Now he was the man."

"Yeah. Zapp and Roger was the stuff. I have to agree."

"Remember when we saw them in concert?"

"Yep," she said. "Back when we were working the third shift at IHOP."

"You were in law school. I was just starting out in real estate."

"Yeah, you flunked the exam the first time." She laughed.

"Please. We won't even discuss how many times you took the bar."

"Yeah. Let's not," she said. "Those were the days, though. When things weren't so complicated."

"Tell me about it," I agreed.

Silence again.

"I broke off the engagement with Darren," she finally said.

"How did he take it?"

"Hard. But he'll be all right."

"Well, when I get out of here, I'll have to go comfort him. With his fine self."

"You really need to quit," Reece said, laughing.

"I'm serious. Can't let a chocolate brother like that go to waste." I laughed. "Heard from Kevin?"

"Not a word," she said. "But I'm okay with that. He would only complicate my life more."

"Still in love?"

"Nope."

"Liar."

Silence, yet again.

"You feel better? More relaxed now?" Reece asked.

"A little. Glad you're here."

"I wouldn't be anywhere else but here," she said. "When I was a little girl, my grandmother would always sing to me when I was scared. Would help me relax."

"What did she sing?" The anesthesia was starting to work its way through my veins. I felt myself drifting.

"She sang a song about angels watching over me." Reece started humming and singing a tune. "All night. All day. Angels watching over me."

It sounded so good in my ears. Soothed me like the Vick's balm Mama used to rub on my chest when I was a little girl. Reece was my best friend, and she was there for me. Just like she always was. And I loved her for that. I shut my eyes and fell asleep.

20

Maxie

His place.

African art everywhere. Black leather furniture, glass coffee table and end tables, black-and-gold rug in the center of the room. Incense filled the air. Plants all over the place.

"You got a green thumb, huh?"

"Guess you could say that," he said. "I love plants. They breathe life into a room."

"Not at my place. They die."

"Not if you take care of them," he said. "Just water them every now and then, give them a little sunlight. Talk to them."

"I'm not down with all of that."

"What are you down with, Maxie Pants?"

Had he given me a nickname?

"I'm down with you, man," I said.

"For real?" he said. "Because I'm definitely feeling you."

His stare and those light brown eyes made me a little nervous.

"Can I get you something to drink?"

"What you got?"

"Water. Juice. Iced tea," he said. "Beer. Jack Daniels. Wine."

"I'll just have water right now," I said, scooting my behind onto his leather sofa. Looking around the room, checking out his art, and some pictures on the mantle.

"Who's the woman in the picture?" I asked, when he returned with my glass of water. "On the mantle."

"My mother."

"She's pretty," I said.

"Ain't she, though? Love her to death," he said, and then picked up another photo. "These are my sisters Rachel and Elise. And this is my brother Duane. And of course, yours truly here." He pointed each one out to me. I recognized him, although he wasn't wearing dreads in the picture.

"Four of y'all?"

"Five," he said. "My brother Kenny is not pictured here. He's in the army. Stationed in Japan."

"Yeah?"

"Yeah. His children were born over there. They're bilingual. Speak Japanese and English." He picked up another photo of several family members. "This is Dana, Bri's mother. We were married for ten years."

He pointed her out in the picture. She was a chocolate brown like Brianna. Pretty, in a Halle Berry sort of way.

"Where is she now?"

"Split. Said she was tired of being a wife and mother and just split. Moved to Seattle and started living with some dude," he said, placing the silver frame back onto the mantle. "Been gone for two years now. Bri was six when she left."

"That must've been pretty rough on Brianna."

"It was hell on both of us, but especially on her. Cried every night for a while there." He was still angry. I could see it in his eyes. "But we're doing okay now, Bri and me. Finally got our lives back on track, with the help of my mother. Now the heifer wants to come back into her life. She's back in LA and wants to see her."

"Are you gonna let her?"

"No," he said. "I told her no. She can't complicate her life like that. Can't keep running back and forth. I'm the one who's been here for her. Homework, parent-teacher conferences, finding babysitters just so I could work. She hasn't done anything."

"I don't blame you."

"I'm about to take her butt to court to get me some child support," he said. "Then I might allow visitation."

"And then it should be supervised visits!" I was angry too. "Sorry. I just got caught up."

Rico laughed.

"Daddy. I finished brushing my teeth and put on my pajamas." Brianna appeared in the doorway, and I wondered how much she'd heard.

"Okay, baby," Rico said. "Say good night to Miss Maxie."

"Good night, Miss Maxie."

"Please, just call me Maxie," I said. "Miss Maxie makes me sound old."

"Good night, Maxie." She came over and hugged my neck. Tight. Not quite a chokehold, but firm. I hugged back.

"Good night, Brianna."

"Can you read me a story?" she asked, with those big brown eyes.

"Me?" I asked.

"Yes, you," she said, standing there in her Power Puff Girls pajamas.

"Okay," I said.

"You don't have to, Maxie, if you don't want to," Rico said.

"I don't mind," I said, and then whispered, "I'm not good at this, though."

"You'll be okay," he whispered back.

I followed Brianna to her small room with pictures of the Little Mermaid painted on the wall in pink and white tones. Her white bed frame and dresser brightened the room. The colorful comforter on her bed made you feel as if you were walking through an animated movie. She pulled out her Dr. Seuss book and handed it over to me.

"Here you go," she said, and then bounced onto her bed. I sat next to her on the edge, trying to figure out why she had chosen me to read her a story instead of her father, who was obviously more experienced than I. Didn't she know I was no good at this?

I read the title of the book, and then flipped it open to the first page.

"I have an idea, Brianna. Why don't you read to me?"

"Okay." She was happy about that. "I love to read."

She read *The Cat in the Hat* to me three times before I finally had enough to last me a while.

"Okay, I've had enough *Cat in the Hat,* girlfriend," I told her.

"Guess it's time for bed then, huh?"

"Guess it is," I said, tucking her under the covers.

"Can I read to you again sometime, Maxie?"

"Sure. If I'm around you can," I said, knowing I was going home the next day.

I looked up and saw Rico peeking in the door. A smile was on his face. I don't know what made me kiss her forehead, but I did.

"Good night," I said.

"Good night, Maxie," she said, and I turned her lamp off and shut the door on my way out.

"You're no good at this stuff, huh?"

"How long were you standing in the doorway?" I asked.

"Midway through the first round of *Cat in the Hat,*" he said. "I forgot to tell you, it's her favorite."

"I used to love me some Dr. Seuss when I was little. He was the man," I said, finding my place on the sofa again. Rico sat down next to me. He silently looked into my eyes, then leaned over and kissed me. It seemed so natural for his lips to touch mine, and even when he began to unbutton my blouse and caress my breasts, it felt like second nature. The feeling took me

145

to another place, another era, another time. I closed my eyes and swore I was in heaven, his breath on my neck, his hands warm and soft.

"Stop me at any time, Maxie Pants," he whispered.

"If that were possible," I whispered back, "I would."

I was at a point of no return. Didn't know how to get back. Didn't want to. Just wanted to be wrapped in his arms, swapping love juices with him. I was definitely feeling this brother. I grabbed for his belt buckle and he stopped me before I could undo his pants.

"What's wrong?" I whispered, my voice husky with passion. I cleared my throat.

"Nothing's wrong," he said, fixing my clothes back the way they were. "You okay?"

"Fine," I answered, a little embarrassed about wanting him so much. Feeling insecure about why he was suddenly turned off.

"Come here. I want to show you something," he said, standing, then pulling me up from the sofa. He held my hand as I followed him out onto the back patio. He leaned his back against the railing and pulled me into him from behind. His arms were wrapped around my waist as he held me close. "Look how beautiful the moon is tonight."

"Not to mention the stars," I added, trying not to notice his manhood stiffly resting against my back. Confused as to why he'd stopped right in the middle of the vibe we had going. He must've detected my inexperience. Either that or he simply wasn't interested in my body.

"What you thinking about?"

"Wondering why you stopped. I thought we were feeling each other in there. Just now."

"I was definitely feeling you, Maxie. What man wouldn't? Look at you. You are beautiful, and sexy, and all that."

"But?"

"But we were moving too fast." He spun me around to face him. "I wanted you more than anything, baby. But I don't want to rush into this. Sex brings on a lot more than either of us might be ready to deal with. Emotional stuff that people take for granted for the sake of the moment."

"Sounds like a line."

"Sorry, but casual sex is not my thing. I want us to know each other. Want to make love to your mind before I ever make love to your body."

His words made me shiver.

"That's cool," I said. "We were moving too fast. Should just take it slow. Get to know each other."

"I'm glad you agree." He rubbed my arms with his hands after noticing the chill bumps all over them. "It's a little chilly out here. Let's go inside."

I followed him back inside the house.

"It's getting kind of late. I probably should get back to the hotel."

"Probably so," he said. "I'm sorry I didn't drive you home before we put Brianna to sleep. And I really don't want to wake her, nor can I leave her here alone. You can just take my truck if you want. Or you can crash here for the night. You can sleep in my room and I'll take the couch."

"I might as well just crash here."

I followed him to the huge master bedroom, with a king-sized wrought-iron bed. I recognized my jazz print on the wall above his bed.

"I have that same jazz print in my apartment," I said. "Where did you get yours?"

"New Orleans. At the jazz festival."

"Last year?"

"Yep. April."

"I was there," I said. "Small world, huh?"

"Definitely," he said, handing me an oversized Sean Jean T-shirt. "Here, you can sleep in this."

"Thanks."

"Get some shut-eye and I'll drive you home in the morning."

"Okay."

147

"Holler if you need something. Towels are in the cabinet in the bathroom. There's an extra toothbrush under the sink." He grabbed my waist, pulled me close, kissed my lips. "Sweet dreams."

"Good night."

He shut the door on his way out. And in the morning, he drove me home.

21

Reece

When Charlotte opened her eyes, I was right there by her side. Watched her struggle to make out my face, knew her vision was a little blurred. Doctors said it would be a few hours before she came to, but I waited anyway. Wanted to be there for her no matter how long it took.

"Hey," she said, clearing her throat.

"Hey," I answered.

"I'm still alive, huh?" She struggled to give me a smile. "How did it go?"

"Um. I'll go get Gwen," I said, and got up and headed toward the door.

"Reece. Just give it to me straight," she said. "How did it go?"

Tears filled my eyes. Why was I the one having to tell her?

"That bad, huh?" She was much stronger than me.

"They didn't get it all." I lowered my eyes to the floor. "It's spread much farther than they had expected."

"Spread where?"

"They think to your lungs."

She let out a squeal, and I couldn't tell if she was crying or laughing. She turned over to face the wall. She was crying.

"Figures," she said.

Silence. I began to rub her back and wished I could change the news I'd just handed my dearest friend.

"I'll stay here if you want me to, okay?"

"I want you to go, Reece. Please just go. Nothing you can do if you stay."

"You sure, Charlotte? I've got all day."

"I'm sure. I want you to go."

"But I want to be here for you."

"Stop trying to save me, Reece!" she snapped. "You can't save everybody." She was crying harder now, and I felt so helpless.

I was hurt, but I knew she was just lashing out from the pain, angry because of her illness, and not with me.

"I'm headed to the office. If you need me, that's where I'll be," I said, and grabbed the door handle. "I'll come back later on, after you get some rest. Okay?"

She never responded. Just stared at the wall. I knew her face was wet with tears. I left quietly, shutting the door behind me.

Saw Gwen talking to some other doctors as I was leaving.

"Reece." She stopped me. "She's awake?"

Tears filled my eyes and I could barely see.

"Yes," I said.

"She knows?"

"She wanted to know and I told her," I said in-between tears.

"I'm so sorry, honey. I should've been the one."

"It's okay," I said.

"You're leaving?"

"She told me to leave. Said she wanted to be alone."

"Her anger is not toward you, honey. Just know that," she said. "Give her some time. She'll come around."

"Okay." I mumbled it. Then walked away.

Caught the elevator to the parking garage. Was glad to reach my car, so I could let it out. Cried loud enough to hear myself cry. Hadn't cried like that in years. I cried with everything in me, with all my heart and soul. Wanted to scream, and I did. Lifted my eyes toward heaven. Needed an answer. I began to question my faith but knew in my heart that God knew what he was doing.

"Why, Lord?" I asked him in-between tears. "Why is this happening to her? To me?"

I sat in the parking lot for the longest time. Had to get myself together, and when I finally did, I maneuvered my Range Rover down Peachtree.

Stopped at Starbucks and grabbed a latte. Took the elevator eleven flights to my office.

"Hey, Reece." Brenda's smile cheered me a little. "How's Charlotte?"

"Not good," I said.

"I'm sorry," she said, and then got right down to the business at hand. "I rescheduled all of your appointments from this morning. I postponed your meeting with Doug Anderson to three o'clock. And you had twelve phone messages." She smiled and handed them to me.

"Thank you, Brenda," I said, and headed toward my office.

"Hey, Reece." She stopped me. "Some guy named Kevin has been wearing the phone out."

A little sunshine after the rain.

"Thank you, Brenda."

Her smile told me she wanted details, but I left her hanging.

I plopped down in my leather chair and flipped through my messages. Two were from Maxie. One from Mama. Three were from Kevin. I called Maxie first.

"Hey, girl," I said, and was so glad to hear her voice. "When you coming home?"

"Never!" She laughed. "Tonight."

"I miss your fat head."

"Yeah? I miss you too," she said. "How did Charlotte's surgery go?"

"The cancer has spread."

"Oh man. How's she doing?"

"Hurt. Angry. I don't know. She put me out of her room."

"Typical of her." She chuckled.

"What's been going on with you? You're bubbly."

"I met my other sister on Sunday. Button, the youngest one."

"Didn't hear back from Alex?"

"Not a word."

"I wouldn't sweat it. You tried, right?"

"All I could do."

"Is that all? I have a feeling there's more," I told her. I could hear something in her voice.

"Like what?"

"I don't know. Something. Your voice is smiling."

She started laughing for no apparent reason.

"All right, Maxie. Out with it," I said, sure there was something she wasn't telling. "You met a man, didn't you?"

"What?"

"What's his name?"

"Who?"

"Don't play, girl." I knew. Knew Maxie. "What's his name?"

"You think you're so smart, don't you?" she asked. "Rico."

"Rico Suave," I teased. "Is he black?"

"Yes, he's black. What kind of question is that?"

"I was just wondering, with a name like Rico," I laughed. "What's he like?"

"I'll tell you about him when I get home," she said. "Got to go."

"I want every detail when you get back here," I told her. "You need a ride from the airport?"

"I'll ride the train."

"Okay, girl. Call me and let me know you made it safely."

"I will, Reece. Ciao."

She was gone. I called Mama. Phone didn't ring long before she picked it up. She had caller ID.

"Well, it's about time you returned my call!"

"Mama, I've been at the hospital with Charlotte all morning. She had her surgery this morning."

"How's she doing, honey?" I was already tired of people asking.

"She's okay," I lied. Didn't want to go through the whole thing with Mama.

"What is this I hear about you breaking off your engagement with Darren? Have you lost your mind, Reece Yvonne Jameson? I couldn't believe my ears when Reverend Peterson told me. And Darren was so hurt."

"Mama, I can't discuss this with you over the phone. I'll come by after work."

"Good. I'm making your favorite. Meatloaf and potatoes smothered in gravy.

"Sounds good, Ma. Bye."

I hung up before she started up again.

Contemplated calling Kevin back. Decided against it. Went to my three o'clock meeting instead.

The aroma of meatloaf and mashed potatoes greeted me at the door. Mama had already cooked and set my plate aside. I sat at the kitchen table, eating while Mama washed dishes.

"What is this about you calling off the wedding with Darren?" She started up immediately.

"Mama, I just decided that I'm not ready for marriage. Not right now. Things were moving too fast."

"Reece, what is wrong with you? You and Darren have been together for so long. And he's a good man, and he can provide a nice life for you."

"I don't argue that. He is a good man." I stuffed a forkful of potatoes in my mouth. "But I can provide a nice life for myself."

"You always have been on this independent kick. Wanting to do everything on your own. Why don't you let somebody take care of you for a change?"

153

"Mama, you're missing the point."

"What's the point, Reece?"

"Why does it always have to be about a man taking care of you?"

"Your father took care of me."

"And I don't knock that. That was fine for you." I put my fork down for a moment. "Don't you want me to be happy?"

"Of course I do," she said, wiping her hands on her apron. "But I don't want you to be a fool. And right now, you're acting a fool."

"I disagree, Mama," I said. "In all my life, besides knowing that I wanted to practice law, this is the first time I've ever been sure about anything. I don't love Darren."

"How can you say that?"

"I love him, but I'm not in love with him."

"You're making a mistake."

"Trust me on this one, Mama," I said. "I know what I'm doing."

She finished the dishes in silence. I finished my dinner, placed my plate in the sink, and then quietly grabbed my keys. Felt a little guilty for eating and running, but the air was thick, and I needed some air.

"I'll call you tomorrow, Ma," I said, and kissed her on the cheek.

"Here, take some of this meatloaf home," she said. "Will only go to waste here, and I know how much you love it."

My mother and I were two very different women, from two different eras. In her day, you married for different reasons. You married for security. And if you didn't love the man, you just gave it a little time and eventually you would. I wanted security, but I also wanted so much more.

She wrapped meatloaf in aluminum foil and placed it into a plastic Kroger bag for me. She didn't understand, and I didn't know if she ever would.

22

Maxie

Checked out of the hotel before noon. Didn't want to get stuck with an extra day on my bill. Waited at the counter for my receipt. I took a mint off the counter and popped it in my mouth.

"Here you go, Miss Parker. You're all checked out." The woman behind the counter handed my receipt over. "Thank you for staying with us."

"Thanks." I grabbed it. Folded it and stuffed it into my backpack. Threw my backpack across my shoulder and headed out the door.

Rico was waiting outside to take me to the airport.

"Maxie?" A soft voice called my name.

I looked over into the waiting area. There stood a beautiful young woman, tall, about five foot eleven, long, beautiful shoulder-length hair. Looked like a model standing there with her bronze skin.

"Yeah?"

"It's me." She smiled a nervous little smile. "Alex."

"Oh." Is all I could say at first, as I took in the sight of her. "You're a little late, aren't you?"

"I'm sorry . . . Maxie . . . I," she began. "Can we go some-where and talk?"

"Can't. I've got a flight to catch," I told her. "You can walk me outside, though."

She did.

"Button told me you came down to San Diego to see her."

"Yeah, I sure did," I said.

"Maxie, I have a really great life right now. Just didn't want to complicate things."

"It's cool. No hard feelings, Alex. Like I told you on the phone, I didn't come here to complicate your life, just trying to put some closure in mine," I said. "And seems to me that I have. I've found a great sister who's promised to come visit me in Atlanta sometime soon, and one that wasn't even woman enough to face me at all."

"I . . . uh—"

"Look, when I came here, I really didn't know what to ex-pect. It was stupid of me to think you would welcome me with open arms. Our lives were so different. A lot has happened over the years. So cut yourself some slack," I said. "I really hope Button comes to visit me. I really like her. She's all that. But if she doesn't, it's okay. I'm okay with all of this. I've put a lot of time and energy into searching for the two of you, hoping that once I found you, my life would be whole. But I've come to re-alize that I'm already a whole person with or without you. Maxie Parker is a whole person all by herself."

She nodded as if to agree. And at that moment I realized that she was the one who was incomplete. Felt sorry for her.

I continued. "Over the years I've gained two really great friends. They've been like sisters to me. Always been there when I needed them most. Get on my nerves most of the time, but hey, that's what sisters do, right?" I laughed at the thought of Charlotte especially. "All this time I've been looking for my sisters, and come to find out, they were there all along."

"I'm glad you're happy, Maxie. I really am."

"I am, girl. Especially now. I can close this chapter in my life and move on," I said. "Now if you'll excuse me, I have a plane to catch. One of my sisters really needs me right now. She's sick, and I need to be there for her."

"Take care of yourself, Maxie."

"I will, Alex." I stopped, smiled at my sister. Gave her hug. "You take care too."

I nearly skipped to the Ford Explorer and to the beautiful vanilla man who was waiting to put my bags in the back. It had been a good trip.

I tapped on Charlotte's door before opening it. She was lying there, television tuned to the channel two news, her hair in disarray.

"Hey, girl," I said quietly.

"About time you brought your behind back. Thought you had taken up residence in California."

"Thought about it. Decided against it. Besides, I had to come back and check on your black butt." I laughed. "You can't find anything better to do with your time than lay up in here?"

"Can't think of a thing. I'm getting three squares a day, room and board. What could be better than that?"

"You do have a point." I leaned over and gave my girl a hug. "Here, I brought you some flowers."

I'd stopped at the florist on the first floor. Picked up what they had left over.

"Go put 'em in some water," she said. "If you wanted to bring me something, you should've brought me a Big Mac."

I found a cup and filled it with water. Stuffed the flowers in it. Set them on the windowsill.

"With some fries?"

"Yep," she said. "And a strawberry shake too."

"I'll remember next time."

"Maxie, those have got to be the ugliest flowers I've ever seen in my life."

"You know, I thought so too. But couldn't come up in here empty-handed."

"Whatever." She sat up in bed. "How was your trip?"

"It was cool."

"Meet your sisters?"

"Yeah. But it wasn't what I expected."

"Get closure?"

"I did."

"She met a man." That was Reece sticking her head in the door. "Is it safe?"

"Girl, get your behind in here," Charlotte said to Reece.

"She put me out earlier," Reece said.

"I was having a moment," Charlotte said, and chuckled.

"I know, sweetie." Reece leaned over and kissed Charlotte's forehead. "You feeling better?"

"No. But I realize there's nothing I can do about it," Charlotte said. "What's this about a man, Maxie? Please tell me you didn't take up with some Rasta dude with a nappy beard."

"I'll have you know that Rico is fine. He's not some Rasta dude, although he does wear dreads."

"Rico? What kind of name is that?" Charlotte asked. "What is he, Hispanic or something?"

"I said he wears dreads. How many Hispanic men do you know with dreads? And what's up with the nationality issue, anyway?" I asked. "He's black."

"You just never know, with a name like Rico. And in LA, you might find a little bit of anything. Sorry."

"You're awfully testy about this brother. What's up?" That was Reece.

"We just had a really nice time, that's all," I said, and then changed the subject. "What's up with you, Charlotte? When you going home?"

"Don't know," she said. "Start radiation tomorrow."

Silence. It felt kind of awkward seeing Charlotte so vulnerable.

"All right, y'all. Don't get quiet on me now. This is real," she said. "I might as well get used to talking about it. Y'all want to talk about it? Let's talk about it. The pathologist missed the cancer that had already made its way to my precious little lungs. Maybe it's even in my liver or my brain by now. Who knows, while we sit here, it's probably working its way all over my body."

"Charlotte, try not to be so cynical," Reece said.

"Cynical, Reece?" she said. "Am I being cynical? I'm sorry. I thought I was being realistic."

Reece put her face in her hands. I started flipping through the channels on the television that was mounted from the ceiling. Stopped when I got to *Judge Mathis*. He was calling some woman ghetto as she attempted to plead her case. I cracked up at the circus they had going on in the courtroom.

"You think this is funny, Maxie?"

"I'm laughing at *Judge Mathis,* Charlotte," I tried to explain. "See, the chick with the red hair is suing her mother, because . . . she . . . it was funny. I'm sorry."

"I don't mean to be rude, but I really just need to be alone right now," Charlotte said, and turned to face the wall.

Reece had been put out twice in one day. We both grabbed our purses. Reece left without another word and began down the long corridor.

I placed my hand on the door handle.

"Could you call me and let me know if the mother or the daughter wins the case?"

"Good-bye, Maxie."

"Love you, Charlotte," I said on my way out. Wished I could've seen what verdict the judge would render, but respected Charlotte's wish to be alone.

23

Charlotte

Stage Four.

Metastatic breast cancer is what they call it when your breast cancer spreads to other parts of your body. It had invaded my breasts and lungs.

"Why didn't I have any symptoms?" I asked Gwen.

"Some women with metastatic breast cancer in the lungs experience few or no symptoms," she said. "However, you may begin to experience shortness of breath and fatigue now."

Gwen was not on my team of physicians. I had new doctors, an oncologist and a team of nurses who looked after me. She just came by to see me and explain things that I might not understand. However, she did encourage me to form a relationship with my new doctors, because we would be spending a lot of time together.

The chemo began as soon as my release from the hospital.

"We'll have you come in once a week to see how it affects the cancer. We may have to increase to every day." That was Dr. Mildred James, a black woman with shoulder-length brown hair. She seemed to know what she was doing, but she wasn't Gwen, and that depressed me all the more. "You may experience some side effects, Charlotte. Nausea and vomiting, fatigue, hair loss."

All I heard was hair loss. It rang in my ears, and the visual I got of myself was a dark, bald woman wearing a wig that looked like the one my grandmother used to wear to church. Or that same chick sporting a scarf that yelled to the world, "She has the Big C!" If I didn't lose all my hair, it would be too thin to do anything with it. I would really look like I'm sick. The world would know.

Tears formed in my eyes as I thought about it all. Not only was I going to lose my hair, something that should have been the least of my worries, but I was definitely knocking at death's door. Had a reservation and was just waiting for my name to be called. Had to be something I did wrong, I concluded. Probably because I was so shallow. Shallow Charlotte. I focused too much on making my million. Spent too much time selling real estate and not enough on my knees, thanking God for what I already had. It's true. He was punishing me all right. He was fixing me, for sure this time. Nothing could save me now.

I was depressed from the moment I'd heard the news, wanted nothing more than to be alone. Still trying to sort through all the feelings, and having people around just complicated things.

I found myself crying for hours, staring out the window as if I were waiting for that big chariot in the sky to pull up out front and honk its horn for me to come on out.

"Yeah you, girl," its driver would say. "You need to come on. It's your time."

And I would go, but not without kicking and screaming.

Then other times, when I wasn't staring out the window, I'd be smiling and saying, "At least I'm alive."

But it wouldn't be long before the tears showed back up, and the depression would set back in. Charlotte, the one who used to be so strong, wasn't strong at all. I was weak. Weak little Charlotte. Shallow and weak is what I was.

After a day of doctors and depressing news, I wanted to run home and never come out again. So I did . . . run home. I stood at the kitchen sink, washing the few dishes that had sat there since the night before. Made myself a salad of fresh spinach. Seemed gloomy all through the house. Sun wasn't shining anywhere. I glanced over at the card Mildred had given me, as it rested on the kitchen counter. A breast cancer support group. Last thing I needed was to surround myself with a bunch of women sitting around talking about their cancer like they were recovering drug addicts. What did they talk about at these things anyway? Did they just sit around feeling sorry for each other?

"Hi, I'm so and so, and I have the Big C, just like you," they'd probably begin. "I was diagnosed five years ago, and I'm going to die soon. How about you?"

The phone startled me, and I glanced at the caller ID. Reece. She was at the office. Probably wanted to stop by on her way home and was just checking to see if I was home. Wanted to come by and feel sorry for me, undoubtedly. No thanks! I was already doing a good enough job of it myself. Besides, I was meeting a client within the hour. Didn't have time.

Let it ring.

Pulled my Lexus out of my Marietta subdivision. Drove down Windy Hill Road and hopped onto 75 to 400. Was meeting my clients in Alpharetta. A married couple with two children. They were looking at a three-hundred-thousand-dollar estate. Knew that if I sold the oversized kitchen to the woman and the awesome backyard and deck to the husband, the rest was butter. Knew what they were looking for in a home and in a school for their two little rug rats. Had the sale under my belt.

The 400 was backed up as usual, at a complete standstill. Chills. Then the nausea began to set in. Shortness of breath. Had to pull over on the side of the road just to catch my breath. Felt like I had to puke, but false alarm. A horrible feeling came over me, and I couldn't shake it.

"Charlotte, get it together, girl," I told myself. "Clients are waiting. Don't blow it."

Boney James blew his horn on the jazz station, 107.5; serenaded me. I finally got my breathing under control, but the nausea was overwhelming.

"Easy now. Get it together. Clients waiting," I repeated to myself.

The chills left. But the nausea was stubborn. Wouldn't leave. Lump in my throat, stomach boiling. Couldn't get the door opened in time. Puked all over the interior and the leather door.

Everything I'd eaten that day was now displayed all over my beige leather seats. What a pitiful sight I was, head pressed against the steering wheel. Stiff. Couldn't move. Closed my eyes.

"I'm sorry, God," I whispered. "Whatever I did to deserve this, I'm awfully sorry. You must be pretty mad at me this time."

I vaguely heard my cell phone buzzing, and couldn't reach it. My hands were paralyzed. By the time I'd become stable enough to drive, an hour had passed. Not one car had slowed to help me. I could've been dying out on the road, and no one even cared enough to stop.

Had missed my clients; they were long gone by the time I reached the two-story brick mini-mansion. Tried reaching them by phone. No answer.

This can never happen again! Missed money won't pay the bills.

24

Reece

Sunday morning. It was raining; pattered against my window all night. I'd stayed up working until I fell asleep. It was a wonderful peaceful sleep, although I hate the rain. Set my alarm for church, but didn't hear it going off. Jumped up.

While in the shower, I mentally picked out my red suit, white silk blouse, and silver jewelry. Tried to decide on the shoes; contemplated whether I should wear hose. Mama had fits when I showed up without any.

"It's the style, Ma," I'd tried to explain a million times. "Plus it's hot outside. No need for hose. Give you yeast infections."

"Ain't appropriate for church, Reece." She stood by her beliefs, and most of the time I'd oblige her.

My braids were looking tired. Couldn't get in to see my beautician, Bernadette, on Saturday. Waited too late and she was all booked up. Gave me an appointment for the following week. Prayed I could last that long.

I found a pair of pantyhose and pulled them on. Decided on some shoes, and bounced out the door. Didn't want Mama to send out the dogs.

*   *   *

Reverend Peterson was in the middle of prayer, so the ushers stopped me at the door. I stood in the hallway and waited patiently. Looked through the small window in the door and saw Mama, with Sheila slouched down beside her. On the other side, a few pews back, I recognized Darren's bald head. He was dressed in my favorite green suit. Knew he'd probably missed me. Hadn't heard from him in a couple of weeks. I would sit by him today. Figured it was the least I could do.

Started my strut down the aisle toward Darren. As I approached, he leaned over and whispered something into the ear of the woman who was seated next to him. Her weave falling onto her shoulders like it was real. Her legs crossed, revealing more leg than the law allowed in a Holy Ghost church on a Sunday morning. Blouse cut low, showing way too much cleavage. Whatever he whispered caused her to giggle and she whispered a response. The way he touched her leg told me I would be intruding if I sat there. I passed on by; found my place next to Mama, refusing to even look their way.

"Glad you made it," Mama whispered.

"Me too," I said, trying to calm my nerves. Wasn't prepared for this, seeing my ex-man with someone else, at our church, when my braids were looking so tired. Could've given me some advanced warning. The nerve of him showing up with her so soon after our break up. Even if the break up was my idea, it was downright tacky. He didn't see me tramping up in there with another man on my arm. It just wasn't right. This was my church, and he was out of line.

My blood started to boil.

"Darren's here," Mama whispered.

"For real? Where?" I pretended I hadn't seen him.

"Back there on the other side," she said. "He brought a guest."

"Oh yeah, I saw them. She's cute."

"You see what you've done?" She raised her eyebrows. "Should be you over there next to him."

I began to sweat. Fanned myself. Wondered if Mama could see the envy in my eyes. I was actually jealous of this black Barbie who was whispering sweet nothings in the ear of my man. Excuse me, ex-man. We had history. Cut my eyes his way. He waved. I gave him a sweet smile, which was the best I could do. Who did he think he was? Casanova or somebody? And Barbie might as well have sat in his lap as close as she was sitting.

"I like that outfit she has on." Sheila could be so tacky sometimes. "Reece, you like that skirt?"

"It's all right." I rolled my eyes at Sheila.

"She's a nice girl," Mama added sweetly. "I met her before church."

He had introduced black Barbie to my mother! I was livid.

After the benediction, I made a dash for the rear of the church. Carefully trying to avoid uncomfortable introductions. Weaving in-between sisters gossiping about who was wearing what and why they shouldn't have. Flew past Reverend Peterson without so much as a hello. Past Mother Jacobs, whom I always chitchatted with after church, and she'd tell me about all the different medications her doctors had her on. And I'd promise to come by on Saturday afternoon and drive her to the grocery store. Breezed past Sister Little who handed me a sign-up sheet for the church picnic.

"I need to know what committee you plan to work on for the picnic, Reece."

I nodded in agreement, but kept moving. No time to talk. I was on a mission to make it to the parking lot in record time.

Slammed right into Brother Donaldson. My body collapsed onto the floor, and my pride followed. Legs gaped open. Embarrassment invaded my face. Wanted to crawl under a pew and cry. This was way too much for me to handle on a Sunday morning. Whispers filled the air.

"Is she all right?" people were asking.

"Sorry, sister. Didn't see you coming." Brother Donaldson

extended his hand and helped me to my feet. "You were moving so fast. Where you off to in such a hurry?"

Too embarrassed to respond. I knew if I opened my mouth a lie would slip out, and I was in church. Straightened my skirt. Regained my composure.

"Reece, are you okay?" Knew that voice anywhere.

Wanted to take off running, but was caught like a deer in headlights. Turned slowly and there stood Darren and black Barbie.

"So this is Reece?" she asked, looking me from head to toe. Assessing me to see what the competition looked like. "I've heard so much about you."

"Reece, I'd like you to meet Tangee." That was Darren.

Tangee? What kind of name was that? She extended her hand, nails in a French manicure. I took it.

"Pleased to meet you, Tangee," I said in my professional voice. "I'm Reece."

"Tangee's the new dental assistant in my office. Just moved here from Dallas. Been looking for a church home," Darren explained.

"And I think I've found it." She smiled. "This is the cutest little church. And the spirit is definitely here."

Her voice was a little whiny, and it annoyed me.

"We were headed to Mother Jameson's for dinner," Darren said. "You are coming, right?"

Surely my mother hadn't invited them for dinner without warning me.

"Can't." I smiled a fake little smile, and I could see the relief flash across Barbie's face. Wanted him all to herself, it seemed. "I have dinner plans of my own."

"Sorry you can't join us," Tangee apologized, relieved that I'd declined.

"Who are your dinner plans with?" Darren was prying.

"With, uh, I . . ." I stumbled over my lying lips.

"What's this about dinner plans?" Mama and Sheila had walked up and I hadn't even heard them coming.

"I was just telling Reece that we were headed to your house for some of that good old Mother Jameson home cooking," Darren said, and then kissed my mother's cheek. "Trying to convince her to come."

"Of course she's coming," Mama said. "Reece, what is this about your not coming? Sunday dinner has been a tradition in this family for as far back as I can remember. Besides, I need you to stop at the store and pick up a head of lettuce for the garden salad, and I need you to make the cornbread."

"Mama?"

"Yep, it's your turn, Reece," Sheila chimed in. "I made the cornbread last Sunday."

"And fix your skirt, girl. Why is it all twisted around?" Mama said, straightening my clothes as if I were still a little girl. This only added to my embarrassment.

"Mama, please."

"You're coming right?" she said, pulling one of my braids from my face and straightening my collar.

"Yes, Ma," I said. "I'll be there."

Darren and Tangee bounced out the door, Darren cheesing as he walked past. Tangee's lip poked out in disappointment.

I sat in the driver's seat, motor running, head leaned against the seat. Wanted to drive off into the sunset and never look back. But I knew I'd better stop by Kroger's first and pick up a head of lettuce or Mama would have my behind.

Reverend Peterson and Darren were glued to the television set, screaming each time the Lakers made a basket.

"That Kobe something else, ain't he?" Reverend Peterson was all smiles, proud as if Kobe Bryant were his own son.

"He all right. Cocky if you ask me," Darren said. "Ain't got nothing on Mike when he was at the top of his game. The Bulls used to be the stuff!"

"Oh, Mike need to go sit his behind down somewhere. Too

old to be playing anyhow." The Reverend leaned back against Mama's plush sofa. "Just ain't his season no more."

"Mike still got game though, Rev."

"He ain't got nothing. Missing shots and carrying on. Might as well sit back and enjoy them millions," Rev said. "I admit, he had it going on back in the day. When the Bulls used to play, couldn't get a seat in the nosebleed section. Folks packed the stadiums just to see Mike work his magic. But he just ain't got it no more. Need to go on home to that wife and them chil'ren is what he need to do."

They laughed like old buddies.

Tangee sat at the kitchen table. Mama had put her to work peeling potatoes, and she did so quietly, sweat popping from her forehead. Sheila was washing glasses and silverware in the sink, earphone in her ear, as she chatted to someone on the other end of her cell phone.

"Reverend, can I get you some iced tea?" Mama called, swinging her hips toward the living room. I could've sworn she had freshened her make-up since church. And why was her voice so syrupy sweet when she addressed our widowed pastor?

"That would be right nice, sister." He smiled at her, every pearly white glistening, and his voice just as syrupy.

I set the plastic Kroger bag on the countertop and proceeded to mix cornmeal and flour in a bowl for cornbread. After I placed it in the oven to bake, I escaped to the den in search of a quiet place. Grabbed the remote and flipped to Lifetime television. Leaned back in my favorite chair, the one that was so comfortable you could sleep like a baby in it.

"What'ya watching?" The voice was so soft, I barely heard it.

"Oh, I don't know. Some movie on Lifetime about a woman who killed her husband," I said, taking in the softness of Tangee's face. She was a pretty girl.

"Mind if I join you?"

"Not at all," I said. "Have a seat." *Just don't talk, though,* I thought.

She scooted her size three behind onto the leather sofa, crossed her legs.

"Your mother has a beautiful home. I bet you loved growing up here."

"It was okay."

"I love Mother Jameson. I think she's so sweet."

"She can be, if you don't get on her bad side."

"I can't even imagine her having a bad side," she said. "How long has it been since your father passed?"

"Died last year," I said, glancing over at Daddy's picture on the wall. Missed him so much. A heart attack had stolen him away from us, without so much as a warning.

"I don't know what I'm doing here today, Reece," she said.

"Excuse me?"

"I feel out of place," she said. "Aren't you the least bit curious about my relationship with Darren?"

"Not the least."

"I could never have a chance with him."

"I don't understand. You are with him."

"I'm with him today, but it's you who has his heart," she said.

Silence. I felt a relief, a sort of gladness. I smiled inside. It's funny how, even though I didn't want Darren, it was hard seeing him with someone else.

"He's still in love with you, Reece. Thought he could move on, but he hasn't. Just used me to make you jealous. I know the game."

"Then why are you here?"

Shrugged her shoulders. "Don't know. A fool I guess."

"You deserve better than that, don't you?"

"In this world, you get a man any way you can. Ratio's twelve to one here in Atlanta. Sometimes you share until you get him to yourself."

"Not me, sister. I don't share a man. He's either mine or he ain't," I said. "And you should have more self-respect."

She was silent. Took in my advice.

"Look, you're a beautiful young lady, Tangee. Why are you settling for less? No man's worth sharing. Why not be alone until the right one comes along?"

"I've never been alone. Always had a man, a lover, a friend. Something. It's lonely when you're by yourself."

"Not if you love yourself."

"It's hard," she said. "Loving yourself, I mean."

"You have to do things to build your self-esteem. Promote your own self-growth and self-worth. No man can do that for you, girl. Have to do it on your own."

I felt sorry for Tangee.

"But I'm just a dental assistant. Not a successful lawyer like you."

"Are you a good dental assistant?"

"The best in the whole office."

"Then you're not just a dental assistant," I said. "You know what my daddy used to tell me? He'd say, 'Reece, I don't care if you mop floors and empty trash cans for a living, you be the best floor-mopper and the best trash-can emptier in the world. It's not the job that you do that makes you who you are, but the manner in which you do it.'"

"Yeah?" She smiled as if she were trying to picture my daddy. I pictured him too, his tall dark frame, those dimples that I'm sure broke many hearts before Mama came along, and his receding hairline. His stomach hung over his belt a little, and I used to pat him on it and tell him how he needed to join me at the gym to workout.

"Oh girl, these are ya mama's love handles." His deep voice would roar with laughter, and he'd say, "You'd better leave 'em alone."

"Whatever, Daddy," I'd say, and then kiss his cheek.

"I'll never wash my cheek again," he'd say. He always said that whenever I kissed him.

Tangee's words made me wonder what her parents were like, and why they hadn't instilled the same values in her.

"And he taught me to be strong, and to love myself before I

try loving someone else." I continued to brag on my daddy. "And he said to always give of myself to people. Because when you give, that's when your blessings come."

"Sounds like your father was a wonderful man."

"He was."

"Darren's a wonderful man, too, Reece," she said. "And he loves you."

Silence.

"Tangee. Reece. Y'all come on in here and give me a hand." That was Mama calling from the kitchen.

Tangee stood first.

"Only a few good men left in this world. Trust me, I know. And he's one of them. I know your daddy instilled some great values in you. He taught you to be strong, and to love yourself, and all that's good. But I know he didn't teach you to be no fool."

She went into the kitchen to help Mama. Left me without words. Gave me something to think about.

25

Charlotte

The stench of urine is what hit my nose first. Strong, as if someone had just relieved themselves right there in the lobby. And I realized that is exactly what happened when I saw a male nurse escorting a short, round, white-haired gentleman to his room, wetness from the center of his pants all the way down his pant leg. I watched as they passed by in front of me and on down the corridor.

"I'm here to see Mabeline Daniels."

An older white woman with snow-white hair looked up from the pad she was writing notes on. She was new. I'd never seen her in all my visits. Didn't recognize her and obviously she hadn't recognized me either.

"Who?"

"Mabeline Daniels."

She flipped through a list of patients. Must've found what she was looking for. "Are you a relative?"

"I'm her daughter."

"Then you're here to retrieve her things?"

"Retrieve her things? What do you mean retrieve her things?"

"Didn't someone contact you? Mabeline passed on two days

ago." Her cough was that of someone who had smoked ciga-
rettes for years, raspy and deep.

"No! Nobody contacted me." I straightened the wig on my
head. I'd found it at one of the beauty supply shops in the West
End. I needed something to cover up my thinning hair. My
heart fell to the floor as I took in her words. "Are you sure it
was Mabeline in two eleven?"

"Hi, Charlotte." Finally, a face I remembered. It was
Mama's nurse, Reba. Her face was refreshing, gave me a ray of
hope. Surely this new woman had no clue what she was talking
about. She had the wrong woman. Perhaps it was Mama's
roommate, Miss Hattie, who'd passed on instead, and she just
had the names mixed up.

Reba grabbed my arm and pulled me aside.

"Reba, what is she talking about retrieving my mother's
things?"

"We've been trying to contact you, Charlotte. Didn't you receive my messages?"

"No."

"Mabeline passed on in her sleep two nights ago. It was natural causes. She'd gone to bed the night before and just didn't
wake up the next morning," she said. "Have you moved or
changed phone numbers?"

"No. I've been ill. In and out of the hospital myself. Haven't
checked my messages in a few days." I became numb. Everything
seemed to be happening in slow motion. The old man who was
traveling down the hallway, and the rhythm of his walker hitting the floor, had me mesmerized. I stared, and he stared back
at me, as if he knew me. His mouth moved up and down, as if
his toothless gums itched.

"Mama's gone?" I asked, my voice trembling, my eyes
steady on the old man.

"Yes." She said it softly.

"Oh my God." I closed my eyes in hopes of opening them to
find I'd been dreaming. But when I did, Reba was there, search-

ing my face, looking for words of comfort. The old man had passed, but turned to stare at me again.

"Honey, I'm sorry," she said. "She didn't suffer any, if that makes it any less painful."

I didn't answer. Didn't agree nor disagree that I felt any less pain. I'd just discovered that my mama, the woman who had given birth to me, raised me, loved me, then had forgotten my name, was gone. I felt a strain on my heart, a pain that was so unbearable it left me without words.

"Follow me to her room," Reba said, as she guided me with her hand. She must've noticed how frail I'd become from the cancer, and held on to me. I needed her to steady me, because I was losing strength by the minute. But I managed to stay on my feet.

I followed her down the cold hallway. A light fixture was out, making it dim and somewhat gloomy. I'd traveled these hallways so many times before. At first I'd visited Mama every weekend, trying to convince her that this was the best place for her, that with my hectic schedule, I couldn't give her the best care that she needed. Every Saturday morning, and then again on Sunday after church. I'd stop at her favorite soul food restaurant on the way over and pick her up a hearty plate of collard greens, fried chicken, and mashed potatoes. I'd sneak it in past the nurses' station and into her room.

"Now Mama, you know this stuff ain't no good for you," I'd say. "If the nurses catch us, we'll be in a world of trouble."

"To hell with them nurses! They ain't my mamas." She'd frown and stuff a forkful of collards in her mouth. "Besides, we all gon' die from something."

My weekend visits soon became less frequent. Weeks became months, and here it was an entire year since I'd visited Mama last, though I'd often called to check on her. Had spoken with Reba many times and promised to visit Mama soon, but I couldn't bear the sight of my mother being so ill.

"You need to get by here and visit your mother, Charlotte.

Her health is failing by the day, sweetie," Reba would say. "She's not doing well."

"I will," I'd promise, but couldn't bring myself to do it.

Besides that, she barely even knew who I was, and it tore me up inside having a conversation with a stranger. So I stayed away.

Guilt had brought me here, but what I found was heartache instead, as Reba escorted me to Mama's room.

"Here you are, honey." She unlocked the door, lifted the blinds, and handed me a roll of tape. "Take all the time you need. Here's some tape to seal the boxes with."

Boxes were filled with Mama's things. Clothes, the Isotoner slippers I'd given her the Christmas before, crossword puzzles, books, photo albums, and her medications. I sifted through the boxes and found a stack of greeting cards held together with a thick rubber band. Removed the rubber band and began to read the cards. There was every card I'd given her for Mother's Day, birthdays, or times when I was just thinking about her and wanted to brighten her day. She'd saved every one of them, had them in date order. Some of them had turned brown with age but were there, stuck together, my signature scribbled inside.

I wept. Wished I could've had one more day with her. Realized I had forgotten to tell her how much I loved her. Her disease had kept me away, stopped me from visiting, and here I was with a disease of my own. I'd never felt more alone.

I continued to weep as I sealed the boxes with the tape.

In the parking lot, I sat in my car, ignition on. Didn't have enough strength to put the car in gear. I called Reece.

"I'm so sorry, Charlotte," she said, after I told her about Mama. "Where are you now?"

"I'm in the parking lot. I can't seem to put the car in drive."

"I'm on my way." It was all she said before I heard the dial tone.

* * *

She was there in record time and startled me when she tapped on the driver's window. My mind was lost in a time when I wore ponytails and canvas sneakers. Thinking about Mama and how she'd taken such good care of me over the years, but when the tables were turned, I hadn't done my job of taking care of her.

Reece opened the driver's door, and I stepped out. She hugged me tightly, and I nearly collapsed in her arms. After prying my keys from my fist, she locked my car doors and escorted me to her Range Rover. I'd fainted in her car, and by the time I came to, I was at home, in my bed.

I sat up, searched the room for something familiar. I was awakened by the smell of bleach, Lysol, scented candles, and the sound of Boney James's saxophone on my stereo. I went downstairs and found Reece's head stuck in my oven, giving it a cleaning it hadn't seen in months. Bacon was frying on the electric skillet, pancakes stacked on a platter next to the scrambled eggs, and fresh honeydew melon sliced in a bowl. A glass pitcher of orange juice was resting on the kitchen table.

"What are you doing?" I asked Reece.

"What does it look like I'm doing? I'm cooking breakfast and cleaning this house that looked like a hurricane had been through it." She stood just long enough to look at me, and then popped her head back into the oven.

"You don't have to do this."

"Oh yeah? Then how was it going to get done?" She stood again. "Let me ask you something, Charlotte Daniels. I'm your friend, right?"

"Yeah."

"Haven't I been just like a sister to you?"

"Just like."

"Then why on earth did I walk into this house last night to find dishes stacked in the sink, food in the refrigerator that had already started growing things, kitchen floor needing to be mopped, and oven needing a cleaning?" she asked.

177

"I was gonna clean it." I felt like a child being scolded.

"How, Charlotte? How were you gonna clean it?" she asked. "You're sick! And you can't do everything for yourself any more. That's just the reality of the situation. That's why I'm here for you. But you won't even give me the love and respect to allow me to help you!"

"I, uh—"

"How long have we been friends?"

"Ten years." It was almost a whisper.

"Ten years," she repeated. "Ten years, and you shut me out like I'm a stranger. I haven't been around all these years just for the hell of it. I love your black behind."

"I love you too, Reece." I felt tears coming.

"Then stop treating me like you don't. It's not always about you, Charlotte."

"You said that before."

"Well, I'm saying it again," she said. "You're not the only woman in the world who's been diagnosed with cancer."

"Feels like it," I said. "It's just so embarrassing. Having to ask for help when I've always been so independent."

"You shouldn't be embarrassed. Not with me," she said, shaking the can of oven cleaner in my face. "I know worse things you should be embarrassed about."

I laughed through my tears, remembering all we'd been through, and all the dirt she had on me. Reece wasn't laughing.

"How can I help you, Charlotte?"

I stood there silently for a moment. Remembering all the things I could no longer do for myself, tears began to burn the side of my face. It hurt to feel so dependent, so helpless, when I'd been just the opposite all my life.

"I'm getting to where I can hardly drive anymore."

"Okay, fine. I'll drive you wherever you need to go from now on. Give me your schedule and all of your doctor's appointments, and a grocery list, and I'll do your shopping. If it gets to be too much, I'll hire some help," she said. "What else?"

"The dishes and stuff. I can't clean like I used to."

"Fine. I'll come over two or three times a week and help you clean," she said. "What else?"

"Sometimes, in the middle of the night, I start shaking and I get really sick. Start to sweat. It's so scary. I'm afraid that one of these times, I'm going to just—"

"Just what?"

"Die or something in the middle of the night. And no one will be here."

"Okay. That's it. You're either moving in with me, or I'm moving in with you," she said. "What's it going to be?"

I'd already been thinking about selling my house and finding a smaller apartment. Something on the ground floor, so I wouldn't have to climb the stairs anymore.

"I've always loved your condo in Buckhead." I smiled. "And you do have an elevator in your building."

"Then what are you waiting for?" she said. "Get this place on the market. Don't you sell real estate?"

"Yep."

"Then let's see how fast it sells."

"Okay."

"Then let's get some boxes and get you packed. You're coming home with me."

"Okay," was all I could say, before I silently thanked God for Reece.

26

Maxie

FSBO. Three bedrooms, one bath, Master on main, finished basement. 125K or Make Offer.

What was I doing here? Stepping onto these people's porch, classifieds folded under my arm. Had called earlier and gotten directions and ended up in a quaint little subdivision in Fayetteville. Pulled into the drive in my white Nissan Maxima I'd just purchased the day before. I took Charlotte's advice and invested in a vehicle, a temporary tag plastered across the rear of it.

"I called earlier about the house," I told the brother who answered the door.

"Oh yeah. You must be Maxie."

"That's me."

"Come on in. I'll show you around," he said. "I'm Brent."

I followed him to every room. The bedrooms were a nice size, one bath and a half in the master. Cream-colored Berber carpet. The basement was finished with a wet bar off in the corner. I liked it.

"My wife and I are moving to Houston. Being transferred. Need to sell quick."

"Price negotiable?"

"What did you have in mind?"

"One ten."

"We're asking one twenty-five."

"But I don't see anyone beating your door down to give it to you," I said, looking at the fireplace and peeking at the kitchen one last time. "Your ad said to make an offer. So I'm making an offer. One ten."

Charlotte had briefed me on the art of negotiation on the way over. Had told me to find something for sale by owner. Said I would probably get a good deal, being a first-time home-buyer and all.

"One twelve and it's yours."

"I'll take it," I said, "if you pay the closing costs."

"I can do that."

"And throw in that dinette set."

"You have a deal, Maxie," he said, shaking my hand. "You drive a hard bargain, girl. What you do for a living?"

"I'm a journalist."

"You're in the wrong line of work," he said. "If you'll have a seat, I'll draw up a contract."

I sat on the plush sofa.

"Can I get you something to drink?"

"Water's fine."

He disappeared into the kitchen and my cell phone buzzed.

"He go for the price?" That was Charlotte.

"Yep," I said. "Getting ready to sign a contract."

"I need to read over the contract before you sign it. Ask him to fax it to me. And make sure you have an inspection done. I know a guy who's good. You need to call him before you agree to anything," she said. "Get a pen and write this number down."

I did as Mother Hen instructed me.

"What price did you get?"

"One twelve."

"He throw in some extras?"

"Closing costs and a dinette set."

"Girl, you are good!" She laughed. "Try and go FHA. That way you'll have to put only three percent down, and he'll have to make reasonable repairs if necessary, and you'll get a good interest rate. I know someone in the mortgage business. Just leave it to me."

I took down the number of the inspector, stuffed it in my purse.

"I have to go, Charlotte. I'll call you back."

"Bye, girl. And congratulations. I'm proud of you."

Moving day.

Boxes stacked up against the wall. Reece was in my kitchen packing dishes, Charlotte sitting by the window on lookout for the movers, bandana tied around her head. She'd already started losing her hair, and losing weight like crazy. Greg was in the bedroom taking my bed apart. I was mopping floors and cleaning toilets to ensure the return of my deposit. Every now and then we'd move our hips to the sounds of Rasta man Bob Marley's "Get Up Stand Up."

"Can we listen to something else?" Charlotte complained. "I'm not really into reggae."

"Charlotte, you're not into anything ethnic!" I yelled from the bathroom, threw the sponge in the sink, came in the living room, and began moving my hips to the music.

"Come on, Charlotte. Get up, stand up!" I pulled her up from the sofa.

"Maxie, please."

"Come on, girl. Stop being a stick in the mud."

She started moving to the music. Reece came from the kitchen moving her hips. Greg dropped what he was doing and started dancing with Charlotte from behind. His pelvis pressed against her rear. She was enjoying herself, waving her hands in the air.

"Go Charlotte, go Charlotte!" Reece and I chanted and stood around like it was a soul train line going on.

This went on for a few more minutes before Charlotte stopped dancing.

"Okay, I'm tired." She was out of breath, holding on to her chest.

"You okay?" Reece asked.

"Yeah." She was still smiling. "I just need to sit down for a minute."

She relaxed on the sofa. I grabbed a glass of water from the kitchen. Handed it to her.

"That was fun." She was still out of breath, panting.

"Girl, I didn't know you could move like that," I teased.

"Lot of things you don't know about me."

"I believe that," I said.

"While we're all here, I need to discuss some stuff with y'all," she said. "Need to start getting my affairs in order."

"What are you talking about, Charlotte?" Reece asked.

"I have an insurance policy. Took it out before I got sick. Reece, you and Maxie are my beneficiaries." She drank down the glass of water like she was dehydrated.

"Can I have some more water?"

I took her glass and refilled it.

"I don't wanna talk about this right now, Charlotte," Reece said.

"We need to talk about it, sweetie. My health is failing every day. It won't be long, Reece. We have to accept that," she said. "I need for you to help me with this."

"With what?"

"You know, help me plan things."

Silence filled the room for a moment. Sort of a morbid silence.

"Please do not bury me in the ground. I want to be cremated. Spread my ashes across the ocean." Her face became solemn. We were all quietly listening. "Just a short little ceremony. Nothing fancy, Reece. I know you," she warned. "And just my closest friends. Instead of flowers, tell people to donate the money to a worthy cause, like some breast cancer foundation or something."

"Dag, you've thought this through."

"Plenty of time on my hands," she said. "Can't work anymore."

Silence. We all digested what she said. Greg excused himself and went back to work at taking my bed apart.

"I don't want to die in a hospital room, either. Tell them to send me home."

"Okay, Charlotte, you're freaking me out!" Reece yelled and went back to the kitchen.

"Me too," I said. "Can we talk about something else?"

"We have to talk about this at one point or another."

"Well, how about another day. This is my moving day. My first house and all. I want it to be upbeat."

"Have I told you how proud I am of you, Maxie?" She smiled at me. "Girl, you finally purchased a vehicle! And invested in a very nice piece of real estate."

"Yeah, I'm proud too!" Reece yelled from the kitchen.

"Must be that man you met," Charlotte continued. "Got you changing the way you dress and everything."

"I agree with that one," Reece said.

"What's up with that? Are y'all getting married or something? He moving to Atlanta? You moving to LA?"

"Of course not," I said, blushing.

"Well what then?" Charlotte pried. "What are his intentions, girl?"

"We're just friends."

"Okay, friends."

"That's why you been running up your phone bill since you got back from LA?"

"How you know how much my phone bill is?"

"It was just lying there, all open one day. Couldn't help but look."

"Charlotte, you a trip."

"I know that," she said. "So what's up with Rico Suave?"

A knock on the door saved the day. The movers had arrived.

27

Reece

The minute we stepped into Rich's, I immediately headed toward the fragrance counter. I picked up a bottle of cologne and sprayed a little on my wrist.

"Ooh, Mama. Smell this." I held my arm up to her nose.

"Smells good," she said, picking up the bottle and searching for the price.

I sprayed a fragrance from another bottle onto the other arm.

"And this one?" I asked, holding my other arm up to her nose.

"That's nice too."

I put a dab of different cologne on my neck, and another behind my ear.

"Reece, if you put one more fragrance on, you're gonna smell like a cheap floozy." Mama held my arm and stopped me from spraying another. "Now come on. I need to find me a dress."

I followed my mother past the fragrance counter, past jewelry, and over to the women's section of the store.

"Tell me again why we're looking for a dress, Mama."

"I need something to wear tonight."

"And you're going where?"

"Reece, I'm going—" She lowered her voice as if she were giving me the ingredients to one of her secret recipes, or telling me where to find some money that she'd buried underground somewhere. "I'm going on a date."

"A date?" I stopped dead in my tracks. "A date, Mama?"

"Yes. Now keep your voice down." She pulled me over into lingerie.

"With whom do you have a date?"

"You don't know, do you?" She searched my eyes for any indication that I knew whom she was talking about.

"No, I don't know."

I followed Mama over to the women's section, and she started sorting through evening dresses.

"What about this one?" She held up a fire-red evening dress.

"It's nice," I said, half looking at the dress. "Tell me."

"Tell you what?"

"Mama, don't play."

"Okay. Okay." She laughed like a little schoolgirl. "The Reverend."

"The reverend who?"

"Reverend Peterson," she said. "Keep your voice down."

"You and Reverend Peterson?" I held my hand over my mouth. "Ooooh."

"Shhhhh."

"How long?"

"Well," she contemplated, "he's been coming around now for about six months or so."

"Coming around?" I said. "You mean more than just on Sundays for dinner."

"Sometimes during the week." She laughed that schoolgirl laugh again. "Sometimes we sit on the porch and chitchat. Sometimes we just talk on the phone for hours. He's such a nice man."

I tried to picture Mama on the phone whispering sweet nothings to Reverend Peterson.

"You think I'm terrible, don't you?"

"No, Mama. I don't."

"Well, what do you think, Reece? What would your father think?" she said. "He and Reverend Peterson were such good friends. Your father was a deacon at the church for many years, not to mention we were best friends with the Reverend and Paulette."

I silently listened to Mama.

"Started out, we were just keeping each other company. I started inviting him over on Sundays for dinner, because I knew he didn't have a wife at home to cook for him. Then one Wednesday night after Bible study, he drove me home."

"Where was your car?"

"In the shop."

"In the shop?" I started thinking back to when Mama's car was having a transmission overhaul. Started to count the months. "That was eight months ago. You been seeing Reverend Peterson that long, and you never said a word."

"I guess it's been about that long."

"And this is your first date?"

"Yes," she said. "We've been taking it slow. Keeping it on the good low."

"You mean the down low, Mama," I said, still in awe. "Wow, eight months."

"What have I been thinking? Running around here acting like some little schoolgirl. This is all wrong," she said, suddenly feeling ashamed of her secret love affair. "Let's go, baby. I'm sorry I dragged you out here to this mall. You must think I'm a fool."

"No, I don't Mama. There's nothing wrong with you dating Reverend Peterson. Daddy's gone and so is Mrs. Paulette," I said. "I'm happy that you have somebody to keep you company."

"Really? You mean that?"

"Yes, Mama. I mean that. Maybe if you get you some business of your own, you can stay out of mine."

"Reece Yvonne." She cut her eyes at me. "Then you're not mad at me?"

"Mad at you?" I laughed. "Because you trying to get your groove on with the Rev?"

"Reece, behave."

"No, Mama. I'm not mad at you. I'm glad you've found someone who makes you smile. Look at you, all giddy about going on a date and stuff."

"What would your father think?"

"Mama, Reverend Peterson could never take Daddy's place. But Daddy is gone. And it's not like you're getting married or anything. It's just a date. So you should have some fun."

"You're probably right."

"I know I'm right. Now come on," I said. "Let's find you a dress."

I started sorting through the clearance rack.

"What about the red one I just showed you?" she asked, searching for it on the rack. When she found it, she held it up again.

"That's too conservative. Look at this one."

I held up a black dress with spaghetti straps, low-cut front, short, with a split up the side.

"Reece. The Reverend is a God-fearing man."

"Yes, Mama, but the operative word here is *man*," I said. "You got to give him something to think about when he drops you off at home."

"You're a mess," she laughed. "Now find me something with a little more on the shoulders, a shorter split, and showing a little less cleavage."

"Okay, Mama," I laughed.

"Reece." She started the whispering again. "What do you think the people at church will say?"

"Who cares?" I said. "But if you really want to know, I think the deacons and the congregation will be okay with it. You're a well-respected sister at our church." I hesitated, smiled. "But those women. The ones who sit on the front row every Sunday trying to get his attention—they gon' kick your butt."

We both laughed.

"Tell them to bring it on," she said, and then sashayed on into the dressing room to try on the dress I'd suggested.

I treated Mama to lunch at the Macaroni Grill. We searched the menu for something to satisfy our hunger pains after a Saturday morning full of shopping and girl talk.

"Now remember to eat light. You know you're going out to eat tonight," I warned. "And when you get to the restaurant, don't be ordering just a salad, trying to be cute and all. You order something good. Get your grub on, you hear?"

"I ain't afraid to eat," she said.

"That's good, because I've seen him eat. And he can put some food away. Ain't no shame in his game."

We both laughed. The tables had definitely turned. Here I was giving my mother dating advice.

"Reece, what's going on with you and Darren?"

"Nothing since we called off the wedding. We're just friends."

"That boy loves you."

"He's got Tangee now," I said, taking a drink from my water.

"Are you serious?" she asked. "He don't care nothing about that girl. He just brought her to church that day to make you jealous."

"Well, it didn't work."

"Is that why you ran out of church like you were running down a football field? Trying to score a touchdown? Fell flat on your behind."

She was laughing at an incident that I didn't find the least bit humorous. It had to have been the most embarrassing moment of my life.

"I, uh—"

189

"You were jealous, Reece," she said, laughing so hard she had to wipe the tears from her eyes with her cloth napkin. "Plain and simple."

"I was jealous, Mama," I confessed. "When I saw him with another woman, I went crazy. Mama, I'm so confused."

"Look, baby. I'm not trying to tell you how to run your life. Not trying to tell you who to love and who not to. But good men are hard to come by. And when you got one, you don't just throw him away like he's nothing."

"But if I don't love him like he loves me, isn't that selfish?"

"That is selfish," she said. "But I think you love him more than you're letting on. I think you have these preconceived notions about what love should feel like. Like you should see butterflies floating around, and feel a tingly feeling in your stomach. That's what Hollywood tells you, when you see these movies about people falling in love, and they can't eat or sleep. That ain't real life. Love don't always come that way."

"Well, how do you know? When you're in love, I mean?"

"You just know." She placed her hand over her chest. "In your heart, you know."

"So you were head over heels in love with Daddy?"

"Not right off. Took years for me to get to know who he really was. But I knew right off that he was a good man. He was hardworking, and I knew he'd take good care of me. I was right about that. And I loved him more the day he died than I had in all my life. The love grew. You understand?"

"Yes."

"The person that you see in the beginning is not the same person you end up with years later."

"Mama, I met a man when I was in the Bahamas," I confessed. "And when I was with him, I felt that tingly feeling in my stomach. So it really does exist."

"Where's this man now, Reece?"

"He's in the Bahamas," I said. "That's where he lives."

"And how many times have you talked to him since you've been back?"

"I haven't."

"Still get that tingly feeling when you think about him?"

"Sometimes," I said. "But I don't think about him as often."

"What are his intentions? He moving here?"

"No. We never even talked about it."

"And you fell in love?"

"I thought I did," I said.

"You had a fling. That's all it was," she said. "I had a fling once, before I married your father."

"You, Mama?" I asked. "With who?"

"Chester Williams. He was a Navy man. Served in World War II. He was home on a pass with one of his buddies when I met him at a dance at the Union Hall. He was handsome, I tell you. Knew all the right things to say."

"What happened?"

"Your father caught wind of it. Threatened to kill him if he called on me one more time. Nearly ran the man out of town."

"Did you see him again?"

"Never," she said. "I married your father two months later."

"You loved this man, Chester?"

"Thought I did," she said.

"Mama, I'm so confused."

"I can't tell you what to do with your life, baby," she said. "You should search your heart. You'll know what to do."

The waitress placed a basket of bread on our table, and I went for it like a hungry beast. Hadn't eaten all day.

"I will, Mama," I said in-between chews, "search my heart."

28

Charlotte

By the second week, I was already sick of Reece's place. Her phone rang constantly; phone calls from her mama, her sister Sheila, clients, Darren. Most of the time, I just unplugged it and let it roll over into voice mail. And Reece was always fussing over me, forcing me to eat healthy things like yogurt, cottage cheese, calling me ten times a day, checking on me all through the night as if I were a child.

I couldn't work anymore and spent my days at home, usually in front of the television. Had gotten into the soaps and could tell you everything that went on with Victor Newman and the rest of the cast from *The Young and the Restless*. Had my afternoon all lined-up: *Ricki Lake, Oprah,* and *Judge Mathis.*

Maxie would come by once in a while to hang out with me. One afternoon she brought me some fried fish from Bankhead Seafood, a place that I had only heard about. Bankhead was an area of town that I never frequented, and had no desire to. We ate fish and watched *Oprah*. Coretta Scott King was a special guest on this episode and was receiving a makeover.

"Girlfriend got it going on," Maxie said after the makeover was complete. "Almost look like she had a face-lift."

"For real," I said, squirting mustard and hot sauce all over my fish, a combination I'd never tried, and only did so after Maxie kept saying how good it was. "You want something to drink?"

"What you got?"

"I have some beer hidden in the vegetable bin," I said, in a whisper, almost certain that Reece had the place bugged. "Want one?"

"Yeah, I'll take one." She looked up from the television set. "What you doing drinking beer, Charlotte? That can't be good for you."

"Don't you start," I said. "You sound like Reece."

"Well, I'm sure she's just looking out for your health."

"Maxie, it's one beer," I said, and went to the kitchen. "What harm could that be?"

"Okay, one beer." She licked her fingers and shut the Styrofoam carton that held the other half of her fish, fries, and hush puppies. It was way too much food to finish in one setting. "You won't tell Reece will you?"

"Not me. My lips are sealed," she mumbled, mouth full.

I opened the refrigerator, searched the vegetable bin for my six-pack of Heineken. Looked behind the milk, underneath the eggs. Searched the entire refrigerator. It was gone.

"Never mind. She's already found me out," I laughed. "The heifer."

"Water's cool, Charlotte." Maxie laughed too.

"Then water it is," I said, and grabbed two bottles of water.

"You wanna go somewhere, Charlotte? You need to get out of this house. It might do you some good." She stood, stretched, and then wiped her mouth with a napkin.

"Yeah, I could go somewhere," I said. "Where?"

"I don't know. Let's just ride."

We ended up at a concert in Centennial Park, listening to a calypso band that closely resembled the one we'd heard during our visit to Nassau. We dragged fold-up chairs from the trunk of Maxie's car, strolled the three blocks from the car to the park. Maxie carried both chairs, while I struggled just to make it. We set up right at center stage, taking in the crowd that was rapidly forming around us. A homeless man stretched his body across the lawn as he took in the sun and the sounds of the band. I tiptoed around him, careful not to get too close. Another man searched the trash for leftovers, his hair and beard matted, and when he smiled at us, his teeth were coffee brown.

"Sisters, can you spare some change?"

Maxie immediately reached into her pocket and pulled out a bill. Handed it to the stranger and he thanked her.

"What are you doing?" I couldn't believe her. She didn't know this man from Adam.

"He asked for some change. What?"

"So you give it to him, just because he asked? We work hard for our money. He should go get his, like we got ours."

"Charlotte, you can't possibly be that selfish," Maxie said. "The man doesn't have a job, nor food, probably lives in this park. He's scrounging around in trash cans for God's sake!"

"He should get a job then."

"And how do you propose he do that?" she asked. "You gon' give him one?"

"All I'm saying is he's an able-bodied person. He could work."

"I'm sure he *could* work, if someone offered him a chance to. Probably would be grateful to. But what are the odds of that happening?" she asked, her stare making me uncomfortable and ashamed of my earlier comments. "He's probably a decent person, just down on his luck right now."

"And you think that by giving him a dollar, that's going to bring him up on his luck?"

"Charlotte, just shut up."

"No, I'm serious Maxie," I said, really needing an answer.

I'd never considered this before, never probed into the life of a homeless person before. Never even looked their way when they begged on the street. Considered them a nuisance. I usually just kept walking, looking straight ahead, careful not to make eye contact. If I made eye contact, they'd ask me for money, I'd say I don't have it, and that usually resulted in being cursed out. So I never bothered. But the look in this stranger's eyes startled me. I'd never seen such desperation. And he was grateful and even gave Maxie a warm thanks.

"Giving him a dollar won't make him rich, Charlotte. But it'll buy him a cup of coffee at McDonald's. Or if he collects enough dollars, maybe he can buy himself a real meal. You just never know."

"The people who usually beg from me appear to be alcoholics just looking for a drink," I told her. "How do you know who's for real?"

"It's not your place to know who's for real. If they ask, then apparently there's a need. You just do your part, and the rest will take care of itself. Now can we move on to something else?" Maxie stood and began to sway her hips to the music. She was so sure of herself. I envied that about her. Wished I were as sure.

But the reality was, my illness caused me to doubt myself more and more each day. Questions were always haunting me, like "Will I see next year, or even next month? Will I make it through the week without getting sick in the middle of the night?" I used to have such a vibrant life, made good money. Now I just strolled through hospital corridors, finding intimacy with nurses and oncologists. I constantly questioned my Christianity, and my fear of dying was almost overwhelming. Many nights I'd wake up before dawn, panting, sweating, and thanking God that I was still alive.

Went to a breast cancer support group meeting once, and was still trying to decide if I wanted to return. Though everyone was cordial, I felt uncomfortable hearing stories more devastating than my own. Met some very nice people who'd lived with the disease for five, ten, and some as many as fifteen years.

It was encouraging, gave me a new perspective, but frightening. When reality sets in, there's not much you can do about it but face it.

People started moving toward their cars when the band began to pack up their instruments.

"You ready, girl?" Maxie asked, patting her neck dry with a napkin.

"Yep."

"I'll go get the car. You wait here."

"No." I folded my chair. "I can walk. Don't be treating me like some invalid."

"Okay," she said, folding her chair, stuffing it in its carrying case, and throwing it over her shoulder. "Dag. Don't start tripping, Charlotte."

"I'm not tripping. I'm just saying I can walk." I attempted to stuff my chair into its carrying case, but couldn't get it in. Maxie watched. "Are you gonna help me or what?"

"I thought you didn't need any help," she said sarcastically. "You're not an invalid, remember?"

"Maxie, just put the chair in the bag!" I said, handing her the contraption. "And let's go."

Maxie swung the chair over her other shoulder and we headed toward the parking lot. Halfway down Marietta Street, I was tired, but continued. Knew I should just sit down until I could catch my breath, but I refused. Needed to feel strong and independent again.

"Is she all right?" a brother in khaki shorts and a white silk shirt asked us as he passed on the street. He slowed.

"What's up with you, Charlotte?" Maxie asked nervously. "Are you okay?"

I stood in the middle of the sidewalk; couldn't take another step. Before I knew it, Khaki Shorts was on his cell phone, explaining to someone on the other end that an ambulance was needed. People stopped and stared. Their conversations were muffled, their faces a blur as my eyes began to close.

The sirens were loud. Knew they were coming for me, but I still couldn't open my eyes.

"Is she going to be okay?" I heard Maxie asking the paramedics. "What's wrong with her? Is she going to be okay?"

"Ma'am, could you step aside, please?"

"What's wrong with her?" Maxie asked again, and I wanted to tell her I was just fine. She was frantic, and my heart went out to her.

"Ma'am we really need for you to step aside."

"Look!" I heard Maxie's voice again, and I imagined that she probably had someone by the collar. "I asked you a simple question. Will she be okay? She is my friend, almost like a sister to me. And I am very concerned about her right now. I'm scared. And when I get scared, I get violent! Now, I need to know that she'll be okay."

"Look, ma'am, I understand your concern. We are doing all we can for your friend here. Now if you want to ride with her in the back of the ambulance, you're certainly welcome to. But until then, I have to ask you to step aside so we can do our job."

It was a bumpy ride to the hospital in the back of the ambulance. My eyes opened a bit, and I watched as Maxie stared out the window. She was scared. This whole incident had taken her by surprise, and she was still shaken. I listened as she called Reece and explained the details of the incident, told her which hospital they were taking me to, the cell phone shaking in her hand. After she hung up, she caught me watching her.

"You all right, girl?"

I nodded my head a little.

"You scared the holy crap out of me," she whispered, a half smile in the corner of her mouth. She was relieved that my eyes were opened. "Had me about to jump on somebody."

I laughed inside.

"Reece will meet us at the hospital. Matter of fact, she's probably already there, as slow as these dudes are driving. I could've driven you there faster myself. You just relax. We'll be there soon, okay?"

I nodded again.

She grabbed my hand and held on to it until we reached Emory. The doctors ran some tests, and after a few hours, I was released.

My heart smiled when I replayed Maxie's words in my mind. It felt good that she cared, and when we left the emergency room, I almost told her so. But I decided against it. Didn't want her to know that I'd heard.

29

Maxie

I was excited and nervous all at the same time. I had checked my hair and lipstick a thousand times. Had changed clothes at least a dozen, before finally deciding on a cream pantsuit with strappy, sexy heels. I'd stocked the refrigerator with tons of fresh seafood, chicken breasts, steaks, fresh fruits, and vegetables. Had even scoped out a couple of sushi bars in the metro area and made a note of their addresses.

My heart began to beat rapidly as I spotted him. His smile was the sunshine when he saw me, and his eyes followed mine as he rode the escalator up to where I was standing. I waved. He waved back.

When he reached me, it felt as if time stood still, his arms wrapped around my waist, his lips against mine.

"Hi." I'd heard his voice a million times on the phone, but it sounded as if I were hearing it for the first time.

"Hi." I'd never been more nervous before in my life.

He handed me a bouquet of flowers. Not like the ones I'd given Charlotte in the hospital. These were a pretty array of exotic flowers. I'd never been much of a flower person, but these were so beautiful, I couldn't stop looking at them.

"You look good, girl." Rico grabbed my hands and spread my arms apart in order to get a better look at me. "Very good."

"You don't look too shabby yourself," I said, and that was an understatement.

His dreads brushed his shoulders. His hand warm and sort of rugged as it held on to mine all the way to baggage claim. I loved the ruggedness of his hands. Hated a man with soft hands; wasn't sexy at all to me. His face was beautiful, but not pretty; told a story of a hard life that comes along with being a black man, but his eyes were gentle and revealed the wisdom that is gained through experiences.

"I have missed you!" His lips swept across my cheek. "Talking on the phone wasn't enough. Had to see you."

He held me in his arms, kissed my lips again and again. I wasn't used to all the attention, and definitely not in a public place. Public display of affection was never my thing, but here I was with a man who made everything else around me seem to evanesce. I kissed back, and before long, everyone had picked up their luggage, met their parties, and vanished to go do whatever it was they came to Atlanta to do. Rico's brown leather bag was nearly the last one, spinning around endlessly on the carousel.

"How did Brianna take your leaving?"

"She was pissed. Wanted to know why she couldn't come. Cried all the way to the airport." He threw his bag over his shoulder. "She sent you something."

He unzipped the front pocket of his bag, handed me a Dr. Seuss book.

"What do you know, *Green Eggs and Ham*," I laughed.

"I think she wrote something inside," he said.

She had. I read it and my heart danced when I saw her handwriting. Reminded me of my own third-grade penmanship.

To Maxie, I miss you and love you.

"This is sweet."

"Where are we going?" he asked.

"You hungry?"

"Starving," he said.

"Well, let's grab something to eat."

We ventured down to Son's Place, a little soul food spot near the Little Five Points area, for lunch. Our plates were loaded with collard greens, mac and cheese, candied turnips, buttery lima beans and whipped potatoes, and, of course, their famous fried chicken. The noisy atmosphere made you feel as if you were at a relative's place. And you just made yourself at home.

After lunch, I drove down Moreland Avenue and gave Rico a tour of Little Five Points, Atlanta's version of New York's East Village. It was quiet during the day, but I explained that at night you'd see street musicians and folks with mohawks and tattoos. Lining the streets were tattoo parlors, head shops, and vintage boutiques with their psychedelic storefronts.

"Turn that up," he said, trying to sing the words to Earth Wind & Fire's "Boogie Wonderland."

We both danced in our seats and were tempted to get out of the car and start a soul train line on the sidewalk. But we refrained and kept on rolling. My cell phone buzzed.

"Well?" Charlotte asked when I picked up.

"Well what?"

"Don't play, Maxie. You know we're waiting," she said. "When are you bringing him over here?"

"We're busy," I said. "Can't make it."

"Don't make me hurt you, girl. We have been waiting all day to meet your little Rico Suave. Where are you anyway?"

"In Little Five Points."

"Why on earth would you take that man to Little Five Points? There is so much to see in Atlanta, and you take him straight to the ghetto."

"I would explain it to you, Charlotte. But you wouldn't understand."

I could hear Reece in the background yelling, "What did she say? Where are they? When are they coming over?"

Finally she just grabbed the phone from Charlotte.

"Hi, sweetie," she began. "Are you coming over or what? We can't wait to meet Rico."

"I'll be there in about an hour." I hung up before either of them could say another word.

"My friends are dying to meet you," I told Rico, who was still wrapped up in the oldies station.

"And I'm dying to meet them," he said, and started singing again.

In no time, they were old friends. Reece and Rico were discussing their favorite stocks, how to successfully cheat at blackjack, debating over whether or not Tupac was really dead.

"I think the brother is hiding out overseas somewhere, myself," Rico said. "Just got a feeling he's still alive."

"Nah. He's dead," Reece insisted. "People saw him die."

"You think so?" Rico was skeptical. "Then why did he change his name to Machiavelli? You know who Machiavelli was, don't you?"

"Yeah," Reece said. "But he was always talking about dying. He was sort of morbid, if you ask me."

"But a poetic genius, no doubt."

"Now, I agree with you there," Reece said, and she and Rico shook hands like two brothers on a street corner. "You want something to drink, Rico?"

"Whatever you're drinking," he said.

I knew Reece would like him. If she hadn't, she would've faked it for my sake. But she wasn't faking; she was enjoying his company. Charlotte, on the other hand, was busy observing, and I was waiting for her to tell me what his flaws were.

"Rico, I understand you have an eight-year-old daughter." Charlotte started with her third degree.

"Brianna," he said proudly. "That's my baby."

"It must be tough raising a child all alone," she said.

"We have our days, but overall it's rewarding," Rico said, and didn't hesitate to pull out Brianna's picture. "Here she is."

"She's cute," Charlotte said, and then passed the picture to Reece. "Where's her mother?"

"Charlotte, you're prying," I stepped in.

"It's all right, Maxie. I don't mind," Rico said, and then continued with Charlotte. "Brianna's mother walked out on us, ran off with some other dude. So I've had to raise my daughter on my own."

Reece handed him a glass of lemonade.

"I'll take one of those," I told her, my mouth watering at the sight of it.

"You know where the kitchen is, girl. You're not a guest." Reece collapsed into the oversized chair in the corner.

I pouted, and then headed to the kitchen.

"So, Charlotte," Rico took a long swig from his glass, "tell me about your illness. What type of cancer do you have?"

I stopped dead in my tracks and shot him a look that said, "What are you doing?" But his look said, "She's all up in my business, so I'm about to get up in hers."

"Breast cancer." She answered as if they were discussing something as simple as the weather. "But it's spread into my lungs."

"So you're taking chemo?"

"Yes."

"Are you happy with your oncologist? Because you know, if you're not happy, you can always find another." He sounded like an authority on the subject.

"I'm happy with my oncologist."

"That's good." He took a second swig from his glass, and his eyes landed on her hair. "Is that a wig?"

"Sure is," Charlotte said proudly, patting it as if she'd just left the beauty shop. "You like it?"

"It's working for you."

Rico was more charming than I suspected. The four of us spent the evening chatting like old friends and caught a couple of movies on DVD. Rico fit in as snugly as O. J.'s leather glove.

Although I was enjoying the rapport, I couldn't wait to get him all to myself. I thought of an excuse.

"You must be tired, huh?" I smiled at him.

"Exhausted." He must've felt my vibe. "You ready?"

"Yep," I said, slipping my shoes on. "Good little ride from here to the south side. We better get going."

"Whatever, Maxie." That was Charlotte. She couldn't just let it go. "We know what's up."

"What's up, Charlotte?" I asked.

"We know you just trying to go get your groove on," she continued. "I ain't mad at you, girl. Go handle your business. Lord knows you need it. There's probably cobwebs up in there."

"That's it!" I snatched my earrings off. "I'm kicking your butt."

"Don't pay Charlotte any mind, Maxie." Reece stepped in between us. "You'll have to excuse her, Rico. She can be just downright tacky sometimes."

"You got that right," I said.

"I just tell it like it is, that's all," Charlotte said.

"No need to apologize, Reece." Rico took my arm and pulled me toward the door. "Good night, ladies. It's been real."

"Yes, it has." Reece gave Rico a hug. Then me.

"Good night, Charlotte," Rico said.

"Good night," Charlotte said, never looking up from the television. Guess she was in one of her moods all of a sudden.

The ride to Forest Park seemed endless, radio tuned to the Quiet Storm on V-103. Before we made it out of Buckhead, Rico's head bounced against the leather passenger seat, mouth open, light snoring sounds escaping from his beautiful lips. Guess I'd have to tackle those cobwebs another night.

30

Reece

Old. Abandoned. Rotten boards covered every window. I slowed at the curb, looked through the passenger window, contemplated going inside.

"I'll wait in the car." Charlotte locked her door.

"I'll be right back," I told her, flashlight in one hand, key in the other.

I approached the building, looking around at the dirt that was once a lawn, crickets chirping. I nearly took off running at the sight of a Siamese cat crossing my path. He stopped, his green eyes met mine, and we stared at each other for a moment. My heart pounding so hard, I thought I felt it throbbing in my temples. I grabbed my chest, and he took off around the side of the house.

I exhaled, stuck the key in the door, and pushed it open, dust floating through the air as if it had been waiting years for someone to release it. The smell was that of an old basement, and I held my breath. The wooden floorboards made a squawking sound each time I took a step. Walls were mildewed from the same water damage that had caused damage to the ceiling.

"They actually want money for this?" I whispered to myself,

shining the flashlight into the corner where a cobweb had found its home.

I looked around. It was a good-sized house, four or five bedrooms. It had possibilities. The room where I stood would be the common area, a place for dominoes and television. My eyes searched the small area in the corner, where I would put a desk and a phone for a receptionist. The large room in the middle would be the kitchen area and could easily hold tables and chairs for dining. There was a room for the children to play, and a room to store donated clothing and shoes. I ventured upstairs, where there were three huge bedrooms and two bathrooms.

The place was old, funky and boarded up, but nothing a little Lysol and elbow grease couldn't change. I saw through the mess, and envisioned a fully equipped shelter for homeless men, women, and children. My adrenaline began to flow, heart pounding. I began to imagine the hardwoods brought back to their natural wood-grain finish, the dull floral wallpaper removed and replaced with something that promised hope and provided a ray of sunshine. The boards would be removed and replaced with windows, and paintings would cover every wall. It would take more than bleach to replace the stale basement stench with the smell of honeydew melon in the afternoons and pancakes and sausage on Sunday morning.

I wanted it.

Saturday morning. The sounds of reggae being pumped from Maxie's boom box were refreshing. She and Rico had escaped to one of the upstairs rooms where they claimed to be removing wallpaper but were doing more dancing and talking than working. Charlotte sat in a patio chair facing the opened back door, catching a morning breeze and reading Malcolm X's biography, a book Rico recommended she read. She actually took his advice, and was so engaged in the story line, she'd stopped complaining about the stench and how loud the music was.

I'd hired Jerome, one of the brothers from the neighborhood, to replace the windows and to help paint. When he said he had been out of work for two months, I didn't hesitate to offer the job. In the next breath, he'd managed to convince me that his buddy Rob could make the hardwoods shine so bright, I'd see my reflection in them. I hired him too. And Rob magically brought the floors to life. I'd never seen anything more beautiful.

By the early afternoon, boarded windows had been replaced, floors redone, dull wallpaper removed, and walls had been sanded and prepped for painting. Boxes of pizzas were stacked atop the second-hand desk I'd purchased from goodwill.

Mama and Reverend Peterson stopped by on their way to the flea market to bring a pound cake and a gallon of iced tea.

"This is coming along quite nicely, honey," Mama said, looking around at our hard work. "A lot better than what I saw the other day."

"You should be very proud, Reece." That was Reverend Peterson.

They looked like two high school kids, wearing identical T-shirts and baseball caps. They were cute together, and I smiled at the sight. It had been a long time since I'd seen my mother so happy.

"Thank you, Reverend."

"You know, we're gonna have to come up with another name for you to call me. Reverend's fine, but—"

Mama jumped in. "But it's not personal enough. Not something you would call your stepfather."

My eyes found Mama's. Hers danced. I checked the Reverend's eyes, and they did the same.

"I wanted to be the one to tell her, Pearl!" He pouted. "You promised."

"Tell me what?" I knew, but I wanted to hear the words.

"I asked your mother to marry me last night," he boasted, his chest stuck out like a rooster who'd just rustled his hen's feathers.

"And I said yes!" Mama just couldn't wait to get that out. Her face wore a beautiful glow, and her finger wore a stunning rock that she dangled in the air.

"Oooh, Mother Jameson!" Charlotte closed her book and came over to observe the ring, for its value no doubt. "Girl, that's a nice ring. Must've cost a fortune. Congratulations."

"Thank you, honey." Mama's face glowed even more.

"What's going on down here?" Maxie and Rico came out of hiding.

"Mother Jameson and the Reverend are engaged," Charlotte said.

"Get out of here!" Maxie's eyes found mine immediately. Searched for what my reaction had been. Knew how I'd felt about my father. She hugged Mama, but her eyes remained on me. "Congratulations, Mother Jameson."

I was thrown off guard by the news. Was happy for Mama when I thought she was just having a fling, but marriage was something different. Marriage meant that the Reverend would be replacing my daddy; trying to fill his shoes. My daddy's memory was sure to fade away. I didn't like it; not one bit. I loved the Reverend and had a great deal of respect for him, but he wasn't Daddy. And it unnerved me to stand by and watch him steal my daddy's place.

"When's the wedding?" Rico, who never seemed to meet a stranger, jumped in.

"We haven't set a date," the Reverend said. "Edward Peterson here."

Rico took the Reverend's hand in a strong handshake.

"I don't believe we've met, young man," Mama said. "I'm Reece's mother. Everyone calls me Mother Jameson."

"I'm Rico." He hugged Mama, as if it were the most natural thing to do. "I'm a friend of Maxie's."

"Well, Maxie, you didn't tell us you had a friend. You'll have to bring him by for dinner tomorrow," Mama said.

"What about church?" Reverend Peterson asked. "You should

both come to church in the morning. Get fed with the Lord's food first."

"Church is good," Rico said, before Maxie could protest. "What time does it start?"

"Eleven thirty."

"We'll be there." Rico sealed the deal.

Maxie was unsure about the commitment that had just been made without her consent. Especially since she hadn't set foot in church since one year ago Easter Sunday. And even then she'd tiptoed out long before the benediction. I'd invited her a few times since then, but respected her position that she didn't need to go to church to worship the Lord.

"Most of the folks up in there are the biggest sinners in the world anyway," she'd claimed. "I got a better chance at heaven than they do."

"You're probably right," is all I would say to her, and then I'd just leave it alone.

Mama also invited Charlotte to dinner, and then commenced to introduce herself to Jerome and Rob, my hired help. Before long, she'd invited them over too, claiming it was a celebration dinner. They accepted once she told them how happy I'd be to bring them if they didn't have a ride.

"Is everything all right, Reece? You look a little flushed." She finally turned to me. "You haven't said a word about my news."

"I'm happy for you, Mama," I lied, knowing I was more than uneasy about the whole idea.

"Thank you, baby." She kissed my cheek. "Try and be on time for church in the morning."

"And Reece, try and think of something else to call me, other than Reverend. It's just so formal. I'm family now." Reverend Peterson kissed my forehead, just like Daddy used to do. "Call me Dad if you want to."

"Dad's good," Mama chimed in. "Now come on Edward,

209

we've got some shopping to do. Before everything is picked over."

Mama pulled Reverend out the door, but their words lingered. *"Call me Dad."* How could I ever form my lips to call another man Dad?

Suddenly my big day didn't seem so big at all.

31

Maxie

The choir was jamming. They wore royal blue robes with big yellow letters down the front: CC for the Christian Center. I clapped and swayed from side to side right along with them. Their voices were strong and they sang with such intensity, I couldn't help but feel it. I was into it, until the song was over and the congregation was asked to be seated.

Every time we'd get comfortable in our seats, it was time to stand again. Stand up. Sit down. Wished they'd settle on one or the other, because all this work was wearing me out. And I swore the collection plate came by at least three times. Already I'd given fifteen dollars; five each time it came past. Once more and I'd have gone home broke.

Rico sat next to me, dressed in his gray pinstripe Sunday suit with the full-length jacket, his dreads falling onto his shoulders, his goatee trimmed to perfection. Each time he clapped his hands, his cologne crept past my nostrils and filled me with de-sire for him. And when he held my hand, something deep down inside of me began to dance. Charlotte sat to my right, her short wig twisted a little, but I didn't bother to tell her. On the other side of her was Reece, who seemed to still be pouting over her mother's announcement. Next to her was Sheila, then Mother Jameson, who couldn't help smiling at her man who was now smiling back from the pulpit. When he stood to speak, he reminded me of a little boy who'd found a quarter on the sidewalk and thought he had hit a gold mine; wanted to share the fact of it with the world.

"I have an announcement to make," he began, looking around at his congregation. His smile piqued everyones's curiosity; people looking at each other surprised. "Sister Jameson, can you join me up here in the pulpit for a moment?"

Eyes searched the room for Mother Jameson, and once found, followed her all the way to the pulpit. She almost danced until she reached her prince, who was waiting, hand held out to her. He helped her up the three steps, her beautiful white dress swaying with every step. I always thought of her as a pretty woman, not fat, but pleasantly plump, her mocha skin matched Reece's, and her hair was always together; never a hair out of place. Must've gone to the beauty shop every week. She had a beautiful smile that I guessed had broken a few hearts in her day.

"As you all know, I've been a widower for almost two years now. And I've been praying that the Lord would send me a wife," he said. "Well, the Lord has answered my prayers."

The whispers were coming mostly from the women in the front row, who were staring at each other in amazement. Other whispers came from the couple seated behind me, and when I turned to look at them, they handed me innocent smiles.

"I've asked Sister Jameson to marry me, and she's said yes," Reverend Peterson continued, holding on to Mother Jameson's hand as if he were afraid of losing her. "We haven't set a date yet, but I'm sure it will be soon."

The congregation applauded the announcement. Deacons stood in respect for their leader's announcement, cheesing from ear to ear, and clapping their hands. The organist played a tune that caused the heavy sister in front of us to get the Holy Ghost. Before long, the entire church was standing, clapping and dancing to the tune. Mother Jameson blushed like a schoolgirl. The women in the front row fanned and continued to whisper. Reece excused herself and headed for the ladies' room. I followed, and Charlotte wasn't far behind.

"What's up with you, girl? I thought you were happy that your mother had somebody," I said, locking the door behind us. I checked the stalls to make sure we were alone.

"I am happy."

"Then why are you tripping?" Charlotte asked.

"I'm not. I just needed some fresh air."

"Whatever, Reece," I said. "You been tripping since your mama said she was getting married. I saw the look on your face the other day when they made the announcement. What's up? You don't like the Reverend?"

"I love Reverend Peterson."

"Then please help me out. What's the problem?"

"I just think they're rushing into this. Why is she in such a hurry to replace my daddy?" Reece sat on the edge of the plaid sofa in the ladies' room, her chin resting in her hands.

"Reece, I don't think they're trying to replace your daddy. Have you looked at your mother lately? She is in love with that man," Charlotte said.

"They only been dating eight months."

"Eight months is a long time when you're that age."

"Not to mention, they're probably tired of waiting around to have sex." Charlotte freshened her lipstick. "You know it's been a long time for the both of them."

Reece and I both looked at Charlotte, but neither of us responded.

"Reece, I think eight months is long enough to know that you love somebody," I said. "I've only known Rico a couple of months, and, uh . . ."

"And what?" Charlotte asked.

"And I'm really feeling him."

"Do you love him, Maxie?" Reece's eyes brightened a little. I hadn't really given it much thought.

"You know, I think I might."

213

"For real?" they both asked almost in unison.

"Yeah." I smiled, got lost in my own thoughts for a moment.

"What do you have to compare it to? I mean, when was the last time you had a man?"

"Charlotte, shut up."

"No, I'm serious, Maxie. Have you ever had a man? Because as long as I've known you, I've never seen you hang out with anyone except that Greg person who used to live across the hall."

"I've had plenty of men, for your information, Charlotte," I lied. But the truth was, the only man I'd ever known sexually was my foster father who raped me at fourteen. Still remembered it like it was yesterday, how he'd pinned me down to my twin-sized bed. Waited until Mrs. Robinson, his wife, left for the grocery store one afternoon, and took advantage of me. He'd threatened to do it many times, but that day he actually carried it out. Forcefully, he pressed his overweight, funky body against mine. I fought it with everything I had in me, screamed at the top of my lungs, but to no avail. He took my virginity and left me to bleed, alone, tears streaming down my face. A week later, I was sent away as if I'd done something wrong.

Every man that I dated after that suffered because of it. Whenever I suspected sex as being a part of the agenda, I'd end the relationship. Afraid. Didn't want to relive the past. But with Rico, it was different. Wanted to be with him. Even fantasized about what it would be like. Couldn't wait to find out what it was like to be with a man that you wanted to be with.

"Have you and Rico . . . you know?" Charlotte asked, straightening her wig in the mirror.

"Why are you so concerned with my sex life? When's the last time you had any?"

"It's been a while," she laughed. "My days of having sex are long gone."

Reece and I were silent, and then Reece went back to pouting.

"Reece, you're being selfish." I finally broke the silence. "Mother Jameson deserves happiness. And you should give her your blessing."

"I agree," Charlotte said.

"You don't understand," she said.

"Well help me understand, then."

"Just forget it," she said, and stepped into one of the stalls.

I straightened my locks, freshened my lipstick, and headed back to the sanctuary.

After church we all gathered at Mother Jameson's for Sunday dinner. She put me to work peeling potatoes, while Reece finished the dishes, Sheila cut slices of tomatoes and onions for the collard greens, Charlotte made the cornbread, and the men gathered around the television set in the living room, shouting at it as if the Lakers could hear their screams.

At dinnertime, Rico blessed the food, and I was amazed at how well the words rolled off his tongue. He hadn't stumbled once, but instead gave wonderful words of thanks. I could never do that. Rarely even said grace myself, just an occasional "God is great, God is good, let us thank him for our food," and then a quick "Amen" before my food had time to get cold. But his prayer was so powerful. Made me love him more. While everyone else's eyes were closed in prayer, I checked him out. Took in his facial features, the way his lips curved when he spoke, his muscular arms bulging through his silk shirt.

When he opened his eyes, he caught my glance. I blushed and turned away. Everything in me wanted to take this man home and show him what I was made of. I did; take him home that is.

"I drew you some bath water," he said, drying his hands on a towel. He grabbed my hand, pulling me up from the leather sofa—where I'd collapsed the minute we walked in.

"You drew *me* some bath water?" I asked, just to be sure.

215

"You're the only other person here." He smiled, his strong hands around my waist leading me to my bathroom. "What? You surprised?"

"Very."

"Why?" he asked, unbuttoning my blouse. "Hasn't anyone ever pampered you before?"

No one had.

"No. I can't say that they have."

"Well, let me show you what you've been missing." His lips brushed against mine as he removed my bra and began to undo the zipper on my skirt.

I shivered as I stood butt-naked in front of the man I was falling head over heels for. He took my hand as any gentleman would, and helped me into the tub, bubbles everywhere, candles burning on the side of the tub and sink. The water was perfect, just the way I liked it; hot, but not scalding.

He began by washing my back, then front, and then kissed my lips so gently it nearly brought tears to my eyes. No one had ever treated me with such delicacy.

"Don't you want to join me?"

"No." His lips brushed the back of my neck. "I just want to bathe you."

India Arie was singing "Brown Skin" on the CD player in the living room, and I closed my eyes to take in the words.

Just about the time my toes were beginning to wrinkle, he grabbed a towel, wrapped it around my wet body, and escorted me to the bedroom.

We stood in each other's arms, kissing, touching, loving. I could've stayed that way forever, and when he lifted me onto the bed, my eyes stared into the flame of the candle that flickered on the nightstand. I'd had sex once before, but this was my first time making love, and it was an experience that I would remember for eternity.

"Was that your first time?" he asked.

"What? No," I lied. "Why do you ask?"

"Just felt like it was."

"It's just been a while."

I wasn't ready to reveal my horrible truth yet. Just wanted to lie there, nestled in the curve of his body, his chin resting against my shoulder, his fingertips caressing my arm softly, and fall fast asleep. So that's exactly what I did.

32

Charlotte

"The problem with people of color is that we don't educate ourselves."

The words rang in my head all the way home. She was right. I hadn't taken the time to find out anything about my disease. Just hoped I would wake up one morning and realize that it had all been just a bad dream. In my dreams I'd find my weight at its norm, my hair would be full again, and my cancer, the monster that was running rampant through my breasts and lungs, would be just a figment of my imagination.

I'd decided to go back to the support group a second time. It was actually comforting to be around women who, like myself, were fighting the same demon: breast cancer. Everyone had a story to tell; some more devastating than others, but all resulting in the same conclusion. We all had cancer.

Leslie hosted the meeting at her home in Suwannee, which by the way, she'd gotten a great deal on: five bedrooms, three baths, master on the main, a beautiful abode for a mere three hundred thousand. It was a steal.

She was a short, dark sister, who wore her hair nearly bald, she was forty-five and had been diagnosed with breast cancer ten years prior. Her cancer was in remission. She was so full of fire that I was drawn to her right away. Reminded me of Maxie with her I-don't-care-what-you-think-about-me attitude.

"The reason we don't educate ourselves is because it's easier if we don't know the truth. The truth hurts." Leslie and I stood in her kitchen sipping iced tea before the meeting. "But if we don't know what we're dealing with, then how can we ever have a chance of fighting it?"

It was a rhetorical question, but I had an answer. "We don't."

Gladys was a thirty-nine-year-old white woman who'd been diagnosed five years prior. Tammy was forty-seven and hers had spread to her liver, but she'd been maintaining for two years. Ophelia was fifty-two and had been diagnosed fifteen years prior.

We all shared the same fears, and it was encouraging to see women who were fighting the same disease that I was and were actually winning. I left the meeting feeling empowered, a feeling I hadn't owned in quite a long time. But once I got home, I was weak again.

"That's when you pray," Ophelia told me when I shared my feelings with the group. "The group is here to support you, but you need something greater for the times when you're alone."

"Get used to spending time with God," Gladys had chimed in. "He's pretty much the best thing you've got going."

I knew how to pray, and I was pretty good friends with God—up until he allowed this terrible thing to happen. I hadn't spoken with him in quite some time. I was still pissed. He owed me an explanation, and thus far I hadn't received one. So I shut down all lines of communication between God and me. But according to my support group, I'd made a terrible mistake by doing that. Not only that, but I was also lacking in knowledge. I hadn't bothered to educate myself about my disease. There was so much I didn't know, and realized I had some catching up to do.

I had Ophelia drop me off at Barnes and Noble on the way home, told her I would call Reece and have her pick me up. I

219

checked out the health section, bought some books on breast cancer. Sat in a plush chair in the corner of the bookstore, a café latte in one hand and a book in the other. I got lost in the information as if I were reading a romance novel.

"Ma'am, we're closing in five minutes." The red-headed Opie Taylor look-a-like with buck teeth was putting me out of the bookstore.

"What time is it?" I asked, looking up from my book.

"Almost ten," he said, straightening books on a display table.

I'd lost track of time and had completely forgotten to call Reece.

"Where have you been?" she nearly screamed into the phone. "I've been worried out of my mind, Charlotte!"

"Sorry. I meant to call."

"You meant to call."

"Is there an echo?" I asked, looking around.

"Don't be smart, Charlotte. This is not funny. I thought you were getting a ride home with one of the ladies from your group. And when you didn't show up, I got worried."

"I did get a ride. I had her drop me off at the bookstore." I felt like a child explaining to my mother why I'd missed curfew. "Can you pick me up or not?"

"I should make your behind walk since you have no regard for other people's feelings."

"I can walk," I threatened, and started out across the parking lot.

"Whatever, Charlotte."

When she pulled up beside me, I was so grateful for the ride, I'd forgotten why I started off walking in the first place.

33

Reece

The floors had been restored, walls painted, windows replaced, pictures hung. I stood in the middle of the floor, looked
around, smiled. The tap on the door startled me for a moment.

"Just came by to see if you needed some help." Darren stuck
his head in.

"Hey."

"Hey," he said. "I got something for you outside."

"What is it?"

"I'll be right back."

He stepped outside again. In a few minutes he came back in,
he and Jerome carrying a beautiful mahogany desk. Rob carried the chair. I stared in amazement, as they placed the furniture in its rightful place in the corner.

"I see you've met Rob and Jerome."

"Yep." He smiled, and there were those beautiful dimples
that I hadn't realized I'd missed so much.

"Thank you for the desk."

"You're welcome," he said. "There's more."

The three of them headed back outside and came in with

rollaway beds, a couple of foldaway tables, chairs, and a thirty-six-inch color television.

"Thanks, guys." Darren handed them each a twenty dollar bill.

"You want us to carry these beds upstairs?" Jerome asked.

"Naw. I think we can handle it from here," Darren said, his eyes on me.

He gave them each the official handshake, shared only amongst black men.

"I'll come by tomorrow and give you a hand, Reece." That was Jerome. He'd been coming by every day, helping me to put the finishing touches on the place.

"Okay," I said, and before I could finish my sentence, they both were gone.

Darren pulled me close, and gave me a strong hug. I hugged back; had missed him.

"I'm proud of you."

"Really?"

"Yes," he said, looking around at all my hard work. "I guess I just didn't understand how important this was for you, Reece."

"And now?"

"And now I do," he said. "The place looks good."

"Thanks," I boasted. "It's hard to believe it myself."

"When are you gonna start soliciting clients."

"Clients?"

"You know, homeless people." He laughed. Embarrassed.

"I won't have to look far. Just drive down the block and you'll see what I'm talking about," I said. "It won't take long for the word to get out."

"What about work? Who's gonna mind the shop while you work?"

"Well, Jerome and Rob have agreed to run the place during the day. I'll come by in the evenings and take care of things. When things pick up, I guess that's when I'll decide whether or not to quit the firm."

"I guess you have it all worked out, huh?"

"I've thought things through," I said, almost flirting. "What's going on with you?"

"Not much."

"Haven't seen you at church lately."

"Been going to one in Stone Mountain. A little Baptist church near the house."

We stood there, had an awkward moment. I looked at my watch.

"It's early. You wanna catch a movie or something?"

"Can't."

"Come on. We could probably catch a matinee."

"Reece, I can't," he said. "Tangee's outside waiting for me. I used her truck to bring your furniture over. She would've come inside, but didn't want to make it awkward for you."

"Oh," I said, unsure of how I felt about what he'd said.

"Reece, we're living together now. Tangee and I," he said, turning his back to me, taking a peep out the window. "I moved her into my place a couple of weeks ago."

"Oh." I couldn't think of anything else to say.

I prayed my voice hadn't revealed the jealousy that I felt inside. Tried to stay strong, but the news was a slap in the face.

"I guess you're pretty serious about her then, huh?"

"We share a lot of the same dreams," he said. "We're going in the same direction. Got a lot in common."

"I'm happy for you, Darren," I said, and my voice cracked a little. "I wish you both the best."

"You okay?" He grabbed both my hands.

"Of course."

"Sure?"

"I'm fine, Darren. Tangee is a nice woman. I've had a conversation with her, and I must say that she's quality."

"No matter what happens in either of our lives, we'll still be friends, right?"

"Always."

"Because I care a lot about you, Reece."

"Feeling's mutual."

"Good," he said, relieved that I hadn't acted a fool about his news. He hugged me again, and before I could say another word he was heading for the door.

"Take care of yourself, Reece." He smiled. "If you ever need anything, please call."

"I will."

He was gone, and now belonged to someone else. I was happy for him. Happy that he'd found someone who could love him completely, the way I never could. As for myself, I felt pity. I sat in my new leather chair, tears falling from my eyes. Felt more alone than I had in all my life. Everyone had someone, except me.

I spotted Mama and Sheila at the food court, and they waved. I stood in line and ordered a burger and fries before joining them.

"What took you so long?" Mama asked. "I've been calling your house all morning. Where were you?"

"Went for a run this morning. When I came home, I crashed." I placed my tray on the table and took a seat in the wrought-iron chair.

"Are you okay, baby? You don't look so good." Mama placed her hand over my forehead, checking for a fever.

"Ma, I'm fine."

"I'm glad you showed up." Sheila took a huge bite from her sandwich. "If I have to look at another wedding dress today, I'm going to puke."

"We've only been to five stores, Sheila."

I ate in silence.

"You gon' eat those fries?" Sheila asked, and grabbed a handful before I could answer.

"Set a date yet, Mama?" I asked.

"Well, honey. That's what I wanted to talk to you about. We were thinking about June twenty-eighth. Since you and Darren aren't getting married now, and the church is already reserved for the day," she said. "Is that all right with you?"

"Yeah," I lied, and felt like I'd been punched in the stomach.

"You sure? Because we can change it if it's awkward for you."

"The date is fine, Mama," I said. "But why so soon?"

"Well, we just want to get it over with. The formalities and all," she said, still glowing. "Just ready to get on with our lives."

"You gon' finish that burger, Reece?" Sheila grabbed the remainder of my cheeseburger, stuffed it in her mouth with one swift movement.

"What have I told you about stuffing your mouth, child?" Mama scolded her, and then turned to me. "I want the both of you to stand up with me. You will, won't you?"

"Of course, Mama. Why wouldn't I?"

"I don't know, Reece. You've been acting mighty strange lately. Like you don't want me to get married or something. I saw the look on your face the other day when we announced the engagement. And then the way you behaved in church the other day. I saw all of it."

"She's just being a brat, Ma."

"Shut up, Sheila."

"You are, Reece," she said. "You're just being your usual selfish self."

"Excuse me?"

"You're selfish. You have a heart of gold, but if things don't go your way, you pout like a little kid."

"I just don't want someone trying to replace my daddy, is all."

"No one's trying to replace your father, Reece. Edward has a great deal of respect for your daddy, and he would never try to be your father, nor try to erase his memory."

"What do you mean I'm selfish, Sheila?"

"You are," she said. "Look what you did to Darren. He didn't fit into your perfect little world, so you pushed him away. Right into the arms of someone else. Now you're moping around here wanting someone to feel sorry for you."

"I'm not moping!"

"Then what's wrong with you? Surely you knew that he and Tangee were a hot item."

"Of course I knew, and I'm very happy for him."

"And now that Mama has a chance to be happy with someone, you're trying to mess that up too."

"Screw you, Sheila!"

"Girls," Mama said.

"You always got your way, even when we were little. It was always your way, or no way. When I wanted to play Barbies, you wanted to do something else. And we always ended up doing whatever you wanted to do."

"And I guess you been holding on to this for all these years."

"I guess I have."

"Well, I'm sorry you feel that way."

"You got issues, Reece." Sheila pushed the knife further into my heart.

I got up and walked away.

"Reece!" Mama called, but I kept walking. "Reece, you come back here."

I walked briskly until I reached my Range Rover in the parking garage of the mall. Never turned back. Once inside, I cried so hard I thought my heart was going to explode. She was so right. I did have issues. I was all messed up, and selfish, and didn't know a good thing if it slapped me in the face. And here I was trying to save the world when I couldn't even save myself.

I drove home, barely making it because the tears blurred my vision. Prayed that Charlotte was still with her support group and hadn't made it home yet. Once inside my condo, I locked the door behind me, headed for my bedroom, got under the covers, and wept.

34

Maxie

Breakfast in bed. Waffles with strawberries and whipped cream on the side.

"Want some OJ?"

"Nope. Warm milk."

"Warm milk?"

"The acid in the orange juice doesn't agree with my stomach."

"Warm milk it is, then."

I'd missed him already, and he'd just gone to the kitchen.

"Miss me?" he asked, handing me my glass of warm milk.

"How did you guess?"

"You play hard, but I know you got a soft spot for me."

"What makes you think that?" I teased. "I don't like you."

"That's why you were screaming my name so loud last night?" he asked, changing his voice to a high-pitched screeching sound. "Oh, oh, big daddy, don't stop!"

"Whatever." I punched him in the arm.

"I know that was your first time too."

I was silent. Hoped we could change the subject.

"Good milk." I burped, and wasn't even embarrassed. "Excuse me."

He smiled, grabbed my empty glass and set it on the night-stand.

"Got something you want to tell me?"

"No."

"Ask you something?"

"Yeah."

"I'm leaving tomorrow, you know. Where do we go from here?"

I shrugged. Didn't want to think about tomorrow. Just wanted to enjoy what we had left of today.

"We should probably talk about it, Maxie. I mean, I'm dig-gin' you, baby. And uh, I don't think I can just go home with-out knowing where I stand."

"Well, I think you're forgetting one small detail."

"What's that?"

"I live in Atlanta. You live in LA," I said. "Worlds apart."

"Yeah, you're right."

"However," I started, and his eyes lit up with anticipation, "you could always move to Atlanta, you and Brianna."

"Can't," he said it so quickly, I was sure he'd already con-sidered it. "Can't uproot Bri like that. Plus my family's in LA. Need to be near my family."

"Yeah. I guess you're right."

"Why don't you move to LA?"

"Can't. Just invested in a piece of real estate here. Would have to put it on the market and all," I said. "Plus, my girls are here. You know, Charlotte's sick and all. And Reece is gonna need all the help she can get with the shelter. Now's not a good time to be relocating."

"Yeah. That's cool," he said. "Then I guess we just continue like this, huh?"

"Guess we do."

He took my empty plate and headed to the kitchen. Came

back into the bedroom and changed into a pair of sweats and a T-shirt.

"I saw a gym around the corner. Going to workout."

"Okay, baby."

"I'll holler at you later."

I heard the front door shut, and knew we'd reached a cross-road.

I showered and threw on a pair of jeans and my Malcolm X T-shirt. Put the dishes in the dishwasher and took some shrimp out of the freezer for dinner. Lit some candles and put in a Miles Davis CD. Waited for my prince to come back. Missed him like crazy.

I dozed on the sofa, and when I heard the door shut, I thought I was dreaming.

"Daddy's home," Rico whispered; he kissed my forehead and took a bag to the kitchen. I was on his heels.

"Where you been all day?"

"Went to workout. Then started walking, just to clear my head. Ended up at this little bar around the corner. Watched the game. Stopped and got us some grub on the way back." He took two plates from the shelf. "You like Chinese?"

"It's all right."

He dumped fried rice onto our plates, topped it with Szechwan shrimp.

"It's spicy," he warned, placing a forkful up to my lips. "Taste."

"Rico. I can't just up and relocate to LA. I just bought this house. My friends are here. Besides, I don't really know what your intentions are. And we haven't known each other that long." I took the forkful of food into my mouth.

"I agree."

"But at the same time, I don't want you to leave tomorrow and not know where we stand."

"We just take it one step at a time. If it's meant to be, it will be."

229

"Will you see other people?"

"Will you?"

"I don't want to."

"Me either," he said. "But it's ridiculous to put unrealistic expectations on each other. You might meet someone, and so might I."

"You looking for someone?"

"No. But you never know." He sat at the table. "Sit down and eat your food before it gets cold."

"Not hungry." I walked out onto the deck. Checked out the stars.

I had just closed my eyes when I felt Rico's arms wrapped around my waist.

"I'm falling in love with you." I said it first and immediately regretted it. Felt like a fool. Wished I could take it back.

"I don't plan on seeing anyone else, Maxie. But I'm just being real. Long-distance relationships never work. I can stand here all day and tell you that it will, but we both know the reality of it." He'd completely ignored what I'd said.

"You're right."

"I can't make any promises, baby. Not right now."

"That's cool. I can't make any either." I pulled away from his embrace. Opened the sliding glass door and went inside.

Hartsfield Jackson Airport was as busy as Wall Street in the middle of the day. Since September eleventh, unless you were a ticketed passenger, you weren't allowed past check-in. We stopped in a little shop at the airport, where Rico picked up a T-shirt for Brianna. Added it to the collection of other items he'd purchased for her: a sterling silver necklace with a Mickey Mouse pendant, a pair of Nike sneakers, a Barbie doll, and a pair of silver earrings that I'd bought.

"You spoil her."

"She's my baby. I have to," he said.

"You better go on and get to your gate."

"You in a hurry to get rid of me?"

"Got some laundry to do."

"That's cool," he said. "Tell Charlotte and Reece good-bye for me."

"I will."

He kissed me deeply, his tongue probing the roof of my mouth. I wanted to cry but had to be strong. Glad I was letting go before I was too far gone. I was in love, but I was still in control. Enjoyed the time we'd spent, but knew it was just that, a good time. He'd go home to life as he knew it in LA, and I'd continue with mine. Fun while it lasted, is all I could say.

"I had a good time."

"Me too."

"Guess this is it, huh?"

"Guess it is."

"Call you when I get home."

"That's cool," I said, but I wouldn't hold my breath.

One last hug and he took his driver's license out and headed toward the check-in line. I turned to walk away, wanted to get to my car before I broke down. He was watching me; I knew it. Could feel his eyes watching me.

"Hey, Maxie Pants," he called.

I turned around, teary eyed. His eyes found mine.

"I love you too."

I'd waited all night for those words and was relieved to finally hear them. Wanted to dance through the airport. But I played it cool. Instead, I watched him place his bag on the luggage belt and walk past security. Once he disappeared, I skipped to my car. I loved him, and he loved me, but neither of us knew what to do about it.

35

Reece

Saturday. A beautiful, sunny June afternoon.

Couldn't have been more perfect if it were my day. The church was decorated in lavender and white. Ribbons and flowers were everywhere.

"Hi, Mama." I peeked into the restroom. Wanted to make sure it was safe.

Sheila was straightening her pantyhose. Charlotte was doing Mama's make-up, while Sister Phyllis was putting little Shirley Temple curls in her hair. Maxie sat on the plaid sofa and smiled at me, probably relieved that I'd shown up.

I'd taken a leave of absence from the office and locked myself in my bedroom at home for so long, everyone had begun to worry. Mama had called every day just to make sure I was at least eating. She'd left my bridesmaid dress with Charlotte and hoped that I would show up. Sheila had called twice to apologize for some of the things she'd said; not all, but some. Charlotte had pretty much given up on trying to talk to me. It was Maxie's voice on the other side of the door that ultimately convinced me to come out of hibernation.

"Reece, this is Maxie." She tapped lightly. "I know there's probably nothing that I can say that hasn't already been said. And I respect your choice to continue to be locked up in that funky room of yours. I hope you got a window opened in there, and a flyswatter to kill the flies. And girl, you probably need to burn some incense. And you should probably consider taking a shower!"

She made me smile, at least.

"I know you think that the whole world is against you. But you really need to get over yourself. You call yourself a support system for displaced men, women, and children. Got your shelter looking all beautiful and everything. When you gon' start helping somebody? Huh? How you gon' help somebody when you can't even help yourself? That's foul, girl! I thought you were stronger than that. I remember your daddy, Daddy Jameson. And he would not be happy with you right now. I know that for a fact."

The truth always hurt.

"And as for your mama, I think Daddy Jameson would be proud to have the Reverend take his place for a while. At least he'd know she was well taken care of. Now I love you, girl, and you can be mad at me for the next ten years, but I'm always gon' tell you the truth. Now tomorrow's your mama's wedding day. And you can choose to stay up in that funky room all day, or you can put this beautiful dress on and stand up with her like you're supposed to. She don't need your permission to get married, Reece, but I know she sure does want your blessing. And if you don't give it to her, then you're not half the woman I thought you were." She stood there for a moment, waiting for a response. "That's all I got to say. Take it for what it's worth."

By then I was in tears. She was right and I knew it. I stayed locked in my room for the rest of the night, but by noon the next day, I was showered and dressed in lavender and lace.

* * *

233

"Hey, baby. Come on in, let me see you." Mama wasn't even mad that I hadn't returned any of her calls. She looked relieved and happy that I was there. She took me in her arms, and then stepped back to get a better look. "Oh, you look so pretty."

My eyes found Sheila, who was wearing an identical bridesmaid dress. Unspoken apologies were exchanged.

"Come here, let me do something with those braids, girl," she said. "Why didn't you get your behind up and go to the beauty shop this week? Those edges need some work."

"Got that right," Charlotte chimed in, and went back to painting Mama's lips.

Maxie's words had stuck with me through the night: *How you gon' help somebody when you can't even help yourself?* She was right. I had work to do.

"Thank you," I mouthed to her when she looked my way.

She never said a word, just winked, smiled, and ran her fingers through her locks.

Mama was just about ready by the time Darren knocked on the door.

"Mother Jameson, you ready?" he asked. "It's time."

"Give me just a minute, honey."

He waited patiently while Sister Phyllis finished Mama's hair. Then we all held hands and stood in a circle for prayer.

Mama opened the door and Darren stood there, hand held out to her, that black tuxedo only making him all the more beautiful. His eyes searched the room for me, and once found, he gave me a warm smile. Mama took his arm and headed toward the sanctuary. The music began to play, and Sheila and I took our places.

Sheila danced down the aisle, arms locked with Deacon Adams, who was the Reverend's groomsman. Deacon Jones, who was the best man, stood next to Reverend Peterson at the front of the church. They were both sweating bullets. I was Mama's maid of honor, and danced down the aisle alone, a bouquet of white roses in my hand. Reverend Peterson searched my face for acceptance. I gave it to him with a wide smile and even blew him a kiss. Wanted him to know that I was honored to have him take my mother's hand in marriage.

I watched Mama stride down the aisle, escorted by a handsome Darren; her cheeks were rosy, her face glowing like that of an angel's. She was happy, but nervous. Darren was like a proud father giving his daughter away.

A white Rolls Royce awaited the handsome couple in front of the church, and as it pulled away from the curb, the crowd waved and wished them blessings. I cried, not because I was unhappy, but because Mama was such a beautiful bride. And because she'd managed to find happiness twice in a lifetime. She was so lucky, and if I found it only once, I'd have thanked God for it.

"How you doing?" Darren's hug caught me off guard.

"Good." I smiled. "You look so good."

"So do you," he said. "Glad to see you. Mama Jameson was getting a little worried that you wouldn't show. I think it meant the world to her that you did. She didn't care if the good Reverend showed up, as long as her baby girl did."

I smiled because I knew he was right. "Where's Tangee?"

"She's around here somewhere." He searched for her, and we both found her across the lawn, talking to some of the sisters from church. Her mouth was moving, but her eyes remained on us. Wanted to make sure we didn't leave her sight. I waved to her, and she waved back. Her smile was genuine.

"I'm happy for you," I told Darren. "But you know, y'all can't be shacking up like that. When you gon' ask that girl to marry you?"

"Not ready for that just yet. Think we'll just take it slow." His eyes never left mine. "For now."

"That's cool. Slow is good."

"Well," he straightened his bow tie, "a few of us are heading over to the Westin for cocktails. Want to come?"

"Nah. I've got some work to finish up at home."

Charlotte and Maxie headed my way.

"I know she's not over here talking about work."

"For real. It took us a week to get you out of the house. There's no way we're letting you back in now."

"I'm having a little get-together at my place," Maxie said. "A few of my neighbors, Greg, and a few other folks from my old apartment complex. You should come, Reece."

"I, uh—," my eyes shot across the courtyard; familiar eyes were observing me, a smile like the sunshine. I blinked. Wanted to make sure my eyes weren't playing tricks. They weren't. It was really him, dressed in a white tuxedo, looking like a prince who'd undoubtedly rode in on a white horse to match.

Kevin smiled and waved. I waved back, made my way over to him, leaving Charlotte, Maxie, and Darren—and their whispers—behind.

"What are you doing here?" I asked, standing face to face with the man of my dreams.

"I came for your wedding like I promised," he said. "What happened to my invitation?"

"I didn't get married."

"I realize that now. But then, I knew that you wouldn't."

"You were so sure, huh?"

"I hoped."

"How did you find the church?"

"Your secretary is very resourceful," he laughed. "Very nosey, too, but very resourceful. She thought you might be happy to see me."

"She was right." My heart was fluttering. "You look good."

"Not nearly as good as you." He grabbed my hand. "Can I kiss you, or would that be inappropriate in front of the church?"

"Who cares?" I looked around at all the eyes that had settled on us. Whispers filled the air, but I didn't care. "Let's give them something to talk about."

Kevin took me in his arms, his lips covering mine. I felt that tingle in the pit of my stomach and knew that it was true what they say about love, that you'll know when it comes along. I knew that I had found it; I didn't care what anybody else said.

36

Maxie

My place was jumping. Music playing loudly, folks at the dining room table playing spades, empty paper plates all over the kitchen counter. Charlotte was dancing with one of my neighbors in the middle of the living room floor. Reece and Kevin were nestled in the corner whispering sweet nothings in each other's ear. And I was missing Rico.

I was late; had missed my period by at least two weeks, and knew what I was facing. After two home pregnancy tests and one from the doctor, it was official. I was three months along. Part of me wanted to run to my man, tell him the news, and live happily ever after. But the level-headed part of me knew that happily-ever-after only happened in fairy tales. I had to come up with a solution, and fast. I was running out of time. If abortion was an option, it had to be done before the risk factors were elevated to a higher level.

"What's on your mind?" Reece finally pried herself away from her prince and joined me in the kitchen.

"Nothing," I lied, and started dumping paper plates into the trash, loading dishes into the dishwasher, and covering the food with aluminum foil.

"Something's on your mind. You haven't been yourself all day." Reece wrapped up what was left of the ribs, and stuck them in the refrigerator. "You miss Rico, huh?"

"Yeah. Something like that."

"Maxie, it wouldn't be the end of the world if you moved to LA, you know."

"My home's here, in Atlanta. That's where all my friends are."

"Friends are friends wherever you are," she said. "Whether you're here, or in California, we'll still be your friends. Its just geography, sweetie."

I was silent. Contemplated what she said.

"Besides, don't count on me being here forever. I've got some decisions to make myself, about where I want to end up. Never know what could happen a year down the road. You just never know, Maxie."

"You're right about that."

"Now," she looked me square in the eyes, "you want to tell me what's really going on?"

"Nothing's going on."

"Now, Maxie. We've been friends for how long?"

"Too long."

"Spit it out. I know you all too well. What's really on your mind?"

"You're beginning to act like Charlotte. All up in my business and all."

"It's my job to be up in your business. That's what friend-ship is about."

"Whatever," I told her, and poured myself a glass of iced tea. "I'm pregnant."

"For real?"

"Yes, for real. Can you keep your voice down?"

"Sorry," She whispered. "Does Rico know?"

"No. And I want to keep it that way. I've got an appoint-ment at the abortion clinic this week."

"Maxie, you're not serious."

239

"I am," I warned. "And don't try and talk me out of it, Reece. I've made up my mind about this."

"Abortion is murder, Maxie. And murder is a sin."

"God doesn't see me the same way he sees you. He knows that I'm not equipped to be bringing no illegitimate children into this world."

"He doesn't expect you to be perfect. No parent is perfect, Maxie."

"Got that right. Look at my mother and what she did to us. She screwed up every one of our lives, and left us here to pay the price. No way would I ever do that to a child. Nobody deserves that."

"You're right, Maxie. Nobody deserves anything that you went through," she said. "Have you considered adoption?"

"Are you kidding me? Do you really think I would put my child into the system to go through the same crap I went through as a child?"

"I don't mean a foster home. I'm talking about a real family."

"No way. It's all the same. Once a child is in the system, that's it. Their whole life is messed up."

"Maxie, you have to tell Rico. He should have some say in this."

"Can't."

"What do you mean you can't?"

"He has his own issues, his own family. Can't lay this on him."

"Maxie, you didn't get pregnant by yourself. This is just as much his issue as it is yours."

"Reece, let it go. I ain't telling him."

"How far along are you?"

"Three months."

"When's your appointment?"

"Wednesday."

"I'm going with you."

"Be better if I go alone."

"I don't care what would be better," Reece insisted. "I'm going."

"Going where?" Charlotte caught the tail end of the conversation as she walked into the kitchen carrying empty glasses she'd collected from around the room.

"Going to Kevin's hotel when I leave here." Reece was quick. "So don't wait up."

"You fast heifer." Charlotte smiled. "I'll get Maxie here to run me home."

"Good," Reece said, leaving the kitchen. "I'll call you in the morning, Maxie."

"Okay."

I put everybody out, cleaned the house, and drove Charlotte home. Came back and poured myself a glass of warm milk. Put on a jazz CD to soothe my nerves. Sat on the deck and mentally prepared myself for what was ahead. I didn't sleep at all that night.

My knees locked as I sat in the waiting room. Reece looked up every now and then from her magazine, searched my face for any sign that I'd changed my mind. I silently wished she'd been more proactive in talking me out of it, because I was so afraid of what was ahead. Wanted her to tell me that I was making the biggest mistake of my life. The truth was, I didn't have a clue how to handle the situation and needed a little persuasion. But she sat there, pretending to support my decision.

"How can you just sit there and read that magazine?" I asked her. "I'm going crazy over here."

"Your decision, sweetie. I'm just here for moral support."

I looked around at all the worried faces in the room; panic-stricken women with limited options. And I was one of them, except I had a few options. I started going over them in my head: I could go through with the pregnancy and have the baby, find a nice, loving family for him or her. One that I could be sure would love the child, and provide a nice home. Or I could raise the child myself. Mama had three of us. Maybe if I just

241

had the one, it wouldn't be so bad. Rico was doing it with Brianna; raising her all by himself. Surely I could handle it, if he could. How bad could it be anyway?

"Okay. Let's go," I told Reece.

"For real?"

"Yeah, for real."

She followed me out the door, and once outside, I was grateful for the air. Felt like I had been suffocating.

"I'm proud of you, Maxie," she said, giving me a tight squeeze. "You made the right decision."

"Yeah, well I hope so," I said, my heart pounding. "I don't know what I'm doing, Reece. I don't know jack about raising kids."

"No mother does the first time, Maxie. You just do your best. That's all you can do."

"What if my best is not good enough?"

"It will be, sweetie. I promise." She grabbed my hand and drove me home.

Once home, the only thing left to do was call Rico. Needed to hear his voice.

I'd picked up the phone three times, dialed the number, and hung up before it rang. Picked it up once more, to check for a dial tone.

"Hello?" A sweet vanilla voice was on the other end.

"Hello."

"Maxie?"

"Who is this?"

"It's me. Rico," he said. "What are you doing?"

"Nothing." I'd been crying and tried to hide it. "What about you?"

"Just sitting here. Thinking about you."

"Nothing better to do than that?"

"Guess not," he said. "Have you been crying?"

"No."

"Sounds like it."

"I think I'm coming down with a cold or something. Sinuses all messed up too." I tried to make my voice smile. "Where's Brianna?"

"At Mama's. She spent the night over there." His voice sounded like music in my ears. "She loved the earrings you sent her."

"Yeah?"

"Yeah." We were both silent for a moment. "Miss you."

"I miss you too."

"Really? Maxie, why don't you come out here for a visit?"

"Can't."

"Why not?"

"Because, um . . ." I had to think quickly. "I just took a job with one of the local magazines. A nine to five. And, uh, they need me to be here."

"Maxie, you're lying. You would never take a nine to five. What's going on? Why haven't I heard from you? Are you seeing somebody else?"

"No," I said.

"You sure? Because I'm feeling this vibe."

"Well, maybe I am. Nothing serious, but I'm going out." I bit my bottom lip, and wondered what I was doing.

"Oh." He was hurt. "Didn't take you long to jump right out there, huh?"

I was silent. He was taking the bait, and I'd convinced myself that it was better that he did.

"Gotta go. I'll call you some other time," I said.

"Cool," he said, and then hung up on me.

I buried my head in the toilet bowl, puking. Seemed it was all I did was puke. Many women got morning sickness, but mine came in the morning, noon, and night, every single day. I was sick all the time. Not to mention, I cried all the time, even when there was nothing to cry about. My emotions were all out of whack, and I couldn't seem to get a grip on them. Wanted to sleep every day away. Never been so tired in all my life. Surely this didn't last for nine months. If so, I'd never survive.

Thought about picking up the phone a thousand times to call him back, straighten things out. But I couldn't bring myself to do it. Instead, I told myself that I was doing the best thing for everyone involved by leaving him out of it. It was best for me, for him, best for Brianna, and best for the baby. What kind of life could a child have sharing parents between two cities that were worlds apart?

The phone rang three times before I decided to pick it up.

"Yeah, Maxie, it's me." Rico's voice was calm and cool. I hadn't heard from him since he'd hung up on me three days prior. Thought I'd never hear his voice again, but was so grateful to God for allowing me another chance. "Been checking out schools for Brianna in the Atlanta area. Been thinking about it, and maybe the east coast ain't so bad."

"What?"

"Yeah," he said. "Shouldn't be too hard to find a job. They have construction sites there. I got skills, and I'm a hard worker. I've been tightening up my resume."

"Rico, wait," I said, before he got too carried away. "I can't let you uproot your daughter like that. She has a stable environment there with your family and all. The last thing she needs is to be dragged across the country."

"Maxie, I thought you loved me." His voice was soft and gentle. "Were you just caught up in the moment when you told me that?"

"I do love you."

"Then what's up?"

"Rico, I'm pregnant." There. It was out in the open.

He was silent at first, and I thought he'd hung up.

"Whose is it?" His words were as sharp as a knife.

"What do you mean, 'whose is it?' "

"Whose is it?" His voice sounded angry.

"It's yours! What the hell do you mean, 'whose is it?' "

"Are you sure it's mine, because just three days ago you were bragging about seeing somebody else."

"I knew it was a mistake to tell you." It was me who hung up this time.

In less than thirty seconds, the phone rang again.

"How far along are you?" His voice was gentle again.

"Four months."

"And you're just now telling me?"

"I didn't want you to feel trapped. You have your own life."

"Did it ever occur to you that I deserved to know, Maxie?"

I didn't have an answer.

"You had no right to keep this from me!"

"I'm sorry," I said, and I really was.

"I'll call you later. I need to think this through."

He was gone.

When he called back, he was much calmer.

"Move here with me, Maxie," he said. "If you don't want me to move to Atlanta, then move here."

"Don't feel like you have to do the noble thing, Rico. I'll be fine."

"I want you here whether you're pregnant or not."

"Under what conditions?"

"No conditions," he said. "I mean, I'm not sharing you with no other man, if that's what you mean."

"Fine," I said. "And I'm not sharing you."

"Fine."

"And I'm not ready for marriage, either."

"Cool. Neither am I."

"And I'll need my own place. We ain't shacking up," I said. "Somewhere with culture. Not in the hood, but not far from it."

"I got some areas in mind." His voice smiled. "Anything else?"

"Yeah. When you coming to move me?"

"I got some time off in a couple of months," he said.

"I'll put my house on the market."

"I'll talk to Brianna."

"I'll break the news to Charlotte and Reece," I said.

"Good."

"Pregnant or not, huh?"

"Pregnant or not," he said. "I'm thrilled that we have a baby growing inside of you, Maxie. But even if that weren't the case, I'd still want you. Baby or not. I love you, no conditions."

"Okay," I said, and was so happy I didn't think my heart could take it.

"No more secrets, though. Okay, baby?"

"No more secrets."

When I hung up the phone, I did the Cabbage Patch dance, rubbed my stomach, and couldn't believe there was actually life growing in there.

37

Charlotte

I found my home in the vegetable section of the grocery store. Picked up some broccoli, zucchini, squash, and cauliflower. Planned on firing up Reece's gas grill the minute I got home. I was in a hurry to get out of the veggie section, considering someone's child was screaming at the top of his lungs and getting on my nerves so bad, I wanted to beat his behind myself. No wonder I never had children.

I grasped the handles on my basket a little tighter and made a mad dash for the checkout line.

"Look Mommy, she doesn't have any hair." The little rug rat stopped screaming just long enough to make that observation.

"It's not polite to point and talk about people." The caramel-colored mother handed me a smile of apology and grabbed a tighter hold on her son's hand. "I'm very sorry."

"It's okay," I said.

It was the first time I went out without my bandana or before throwing a wig on my head. I just took my chances this time. Had become more daring and surer of myself since my support group had come into my life. Had started driving again and was feeling pretty good about myself. Had even considered wearing my hair natural, like Gwen's, if I could find a good barber to line it up real nice for me.

"He's always misbehaving," she continued. "I don't know what to do with him sometimes."

"Beat his behind!" is what I wanted to scream, but instead I said, "Children are a handful."

"Yes. They are." She chuckled. "You must have some of your own."

"No. I don't. But I've been around enough to know that they're a trip."

"Umm hmm."

It was then that I noticed the baby in a carrier in her basket. She definitely had her hands full.

"How old is the baby?"

"Four months."

"She's cute." I couldn't believe I was standing there admiring someone's baby. I'd never cared for children, but she was so beautiful I couldn't help watching her; her round little caramel face with chubby cheeks. She had a head full of hair and the fattest pair of legs I'd ever seen on someone so small. I touched her little hand, and she grabbed hold of my finger and wouldn't let go. Tried to put my finger in her mouth.

"She's teething," her mother explained. "Wants to gnaw on everything she gets her hands on."

"What's her name?" I smiled at her.

"Imani."

"Hi, Imani." I spoke to the child as if she could understand. She smiled, and my heart melted. Her brother started pulling on my purse in a fight for the attention I was giving his little sister.

"Look what I have." He pushed his robot toy toward me.

"Oh wow. What is it?"

"It's a robot, silly. What did you think?"

I wanted to slap him into next week for being so disrespectful to adults, but had to remind myself that he was merely a child. I wondered if Imani would grow up to be such a terror. I continued to play with her.

"Charlotte?" The voice was so familiar, but I couldn't place it.

I turned to find William, the old flame that'd broken my heart.

"I see you've met my family," he said, referring to the woman, the annoying little boy, and the beautiful Imani.

"Well, I guess I have."

"Charlotte, this is my wife, Tonya."

My mind immediately went back to that dreadful morning that he awoke and said that he was going back to his wife. I replayed it in my mind.

"Hello, Tonya. Very nice to meet you."

"So this is Charlotte?" She knew me already. I immediately became a threat to her, and her body language changed. Her tone told me that there had been more women, more uncomfortable encounters, lies had been told, and old wounds were still open. She observed me. She was a woman scorned, and I knew it. But what William and I had was long over, and if anyone should feel betrayed, it should be me. He left me to return to her. What did she have to be pissed about? But who knows how the story went once it left his lying lips. I gave Tonya a warm smile that said, "I'm not your enemy. He is."

Immediately she became withdrawn, not so friendly. I wondered what he'd shared with her. Had he given her every detail of our sexual escapades or just part of them?

"You cut your hair," he said.

"Something like that. Yes." I was too embarrassed to blurt out that it had fallen out because I had the Big C. Didn't feel the need to go through all the details of it.

"Looks good," he lied. "And you've lost weight."

"Yep. That too."

"You're not sick, are you?" Didn't he know anything about discretion?

"Well, since you asked, I've been diagnosed with breast cancer."

"Wow. Sorry to hear that, Charlotte."

"It's okay. I'm doing great." I searched for another subject. "So you live in this area?"

"Yes," he said. "What about you? Don't live in Marietta anymore?"

"Nope."

"So how've you been?"

Tonya was eyeballing me, a look of betrayal on her face.

"Good," I said, thinking of a way to end this line of questioning. "Look, it was very nice seeing you, William. And nice to meet you, Tonya, but I've really got to run. I've got this thing . . . this meeting to go to."

"Hey, do you have a business card on you? I'd like to call you about some real estate."

Tonya's eyebrows rose.

"No. No. I'm sorry. Don't have one on me."

"Well here, let me give you my card." He pulled his wallet out, handed me a card. "Give me a call."

I took it. Rushed to the checkout line, and then to my car.

Breathless. All of these feelings and emotions rushed through me like a freight train. I had loved him once. He had been my whole world, but I was sure he was out of my system. Wasn't he?

It was late. I turned off the television but left the light on the nightstand burning. Wasn't sleepy, and didn't feel like reading. Pulled the card out of my purse and looked at it. It was the number for his place of business.

I remembered how much I'd missed him when he left. Had been a while since I'd felt those feelings, and longed to just hear his voice. I would call and listen to his voice mail at the office, then hang up, and take myself to sleep.

I dialed. It rang.

"William speaking." He picked up. I was at a loss for words. "Hello?"

"Hello. William?"

"Charlotte?"

"Yes."

"What's up?"

"I didn't expect you to be at work."

"I'm not. I have my business phone forwarded to my cell phone," he explained. "I'm glad you called."

My heart skipped a beat. He was glad I called, and I immediately was too. Thought about inviting him to a secret place, just to feel his arms around me again. Just to feel the touch of a man, period. It had been so long. Yes, I was glad I called.

"I've been looking at this place in College Park. A piece of real estate. I can't get the guy to budge on the price. I know you're the best at what you do and thought maybe you could give him a call for me. Hold on a second while I get his number. Maybe you can negotiate that price for me."

"You want me to negotiate the price on a piece of real estate?"

"Yeah. Why did you think I was so anxious to talk to you?"

I was silent. My heart began to ache.

"You didn't think that I was still interested in you . . . did you?"

"I did."

"Come on, Charlotte. I'm a married man. Not to mention you're sick. You have . . ." he struggled just to say it, "you have cancer."

I hung up, but his words lingered. How dare he be so insensitive?

"You have cancer," he'd said in such a way that I felt as if I were HIV positive or something. I hated him.

I'd never been so humiliated in all my life. After all the self-worth I'd built up, he'd managed to diminish it in two minutes flat.

*   *   *

"He was a sleazeball anyway. What did you ever see in him?" Ophelia had to work at helping me build up what William had torn down. "Now get yourself together, girl. If anything, you should feel sorry for his wife. She's the one who has to put up with his trifling behind."

"You're right. It was just such a low blow, that's all."

"Well, you put yourself out there for it. What were you really expecting?"

"It gets lonely sometimes. I miss the touch of a man."

"Then find you one, girl. There are men out there with brains. Not like William, the jerk, who doesn't even know he's a jerk."

"Well where are they?"

"You won't find them stuck up in your bedroom, at home. You have to get out and do things, Charlotte," she said. "What did you do before your illness?"

"I have to admit, I was a workaholic. Didn't have much of a social life."

"Well all that's about to change," she said, and pulled me out of the chair. "Come on, let's find you something to wear. We're going out tonight."

We ended up at a blues and jazz spot in College Park. Music pumped so loud I couldn't hear myself think. The place was packed and we barely captured a little table in the center of the room. Before we could sit down good, a tall dark gentleman was asking me to dance.

"I'll watch your purse, girl," Ophelia said, and took it off my arm as I was swept away to the dance floor.

"I'm Herb. And you are?"

"Charlotte."

"Come here often?"

"First time," I said, moving to the music. "What about you?"

"I've been here a few times. It's one of the places I like to visit when I'm in Atlanta. I'm here on business."

"Where are you from?"

"Dallas," he said. "I'm here for a convention. Leaving first thing in the morning."

The Z.Z. Hill tune was encouraging the crowd to bump and grind, and most of them obliged. But my look told Herb that I wasn't about to bump and grind with a perfect stranger. He must've understood the look, because he didn't try any sudden moves. Instead we danced and talked the whole night through.

When the issue of my illness came up, all he said was, "I'm sorry to hear that, Charlotte." And in the next breath, said, "Can I call you next time I'm in Atlanta?"

"That would be nice."

"Maybe we could go out for a bite to eat or something."

"I'd like that."

I scribbled my phone number on a napkin for Herb. He stuck it in his pocket and we continued to swing to the sound of the blues.

Before I closed my eyes that night, I remembered Herb's words as he had walked Ophelia and me to our car.

"Life is a gift, Charlotte, and you can either take it or leave it. If you take it, then you must live it to its fullest, regardless of the hand it deals. If you leave it, then you only have yourself to blame."

"You're right."

"I know I'm right," he said, and then gave me a strong hug; his cologne pleasantly filled my nostrils. The touch of a man is what I'd been yearning for, but I received so much more.

He opened my door as I stepped into the passenger's seat. "I think you should choose life."

"You think so?"

"I know so," he said. "How else will I get to spend any time with you?"

"You have a point."

"I'll call you when I get back to Dallas, just to see how you're doing."

"I'd like that."

"I thought you might." He shut the door, and I gave him a warm smile as we drove away. Even if I never saw him again, I was grateful for his kindness.

Before I dozed off, I said a little prayer. Thanked God for life.

38

Reece

Those sad eyes.

I recognized them the minute I looked up. I turned my glance from Jill to her mother.

"Good to see you again, Miss Jameson. I heard you had started a shelter and came by just to say hello and to let you know that Jill and I are doing well."

"I'm glad." My eyes searched Jill's.

"I was able to find me a steady job, and I'm renting an apartment not too far from here," she said, looking around. "This sure is a nice place you have here."

She was right. It was a nice place. All the work had been completed, and I'd opened my doors just two weeks before. People were knocking each other over in search of a warm meal and a place to sleep. I'd hired Jerome to run the place during the day, and I would take over in the evenings. Rob was my maintenance man. Mama prepared meals and brought them over each day. Maxie helped out on the weekends, but was working for some magazine, which kept her pretty busy during the week; that and being pregnant. And since Maxie couldn't devote as much time as I'd expected, Charlotte decided to help out with the children. Darren and Tangee even helped out in the food kitchen from time to time.

"How are you, Jill?" I asked with a smile, and her look told me she knew exactly what I was referring to.

"Fine," she said, and I was glad that she responded. She even smiled a little.

"Good. I'm glad to hear it."

I was just about to confront Wanda with the information that I had, and expose her for the sleaze that she was, when I noticed the Bible she was carrying. She noticed me looking at it, and held it up.

"The Good Word," she said. "Been going to church, you know. Went to a revival a few months back and done got saved. Can you believe it? Found me a church home, and even joined the usher board. Figured I needed to be a better mother for my baby, and needed to stop all the foolishness I was carrying on."

I just stared.

"I know you know the truth, Miss Jameson. Jill told me. And I want you to know that I'm real ashamed of what I did. Real sorry too. I was living in sin and couldn't see my way out. But I done found something better. Took everything I had to come and face you, and let you know that I done changed, and ask your forgiveness. Would mean a lot to me. And I appreciate you not taking action against me."

I was at a loss for words. She was different, I could tell. She even had a glow about her.

"I done asked the Good Lord for forgiveness. Now I need yours."

"Why do you need mine?"

"I just do. Would feel mighty blessed if you allowed me to do something nice for you. Like help out around here. I get off work at four o'clock in the afternoon. I could come over here for a few hours each day and work the intake desk, or read to the children, or I could help serve the meals. Anything you need me to do."

"I sure could use some help around here."

"I'd be happy to do whatever I can."

Mama came through the door carrying a huge pan of fried chicken.

"There's more in the car, honey," she said.

"Excuse me, Wanda," I said, and then helped Mama and Dad bring in roasting pans filled with fried chicken, a huge pan of macaroni and cheese, cornbread, and at least ten gallons of fruit punch.

When I walked into the kitchen, Wanda had an apron around her waist and had already started preparing plates to be served. Jill was at a corner table reading a story to a group of younger children who were waiting to be fed.

In my heart there was forgiveness.

I put on an apron and gave her a hand with the plates. Folks formed a line in anticipation of the wonderful meal Mama had prepared. The dining room was filled with men, women, and children, and I couldn't help but smile. Dad said grace after everyone was served, and after that it was on. The only sounds in the room were forks hitting the plates.

My smile told Wanda that I appreciated her help. I think she took it as forgiveness as well. Maybe it was, I don't know, but it truly wasn't my place to judge anyone.

By the time Kevin came by to pick me up, it was late and I was exhausted.

"You're a sight for sore eyes," I said, planting a kiss on his lips.

"So are you," he said. "You ready?"

"Let me finish the dishes and I'll be ready."

He rolled up his sleeves and helped me wash and dry dishes. We talked about what took place during the course of our day. I was juggling my work at the firm and struggling to keep up with the shelter. It was becoming extremely difficult to maintain both, and I was starting to wear down. My body felt as if it were going to collapse.

"Why don't you quit the firm, and just focus your attention here?" he asked, as I handed him a plate to dry.

"I want to. I'm just a little scared."

"Scared of what?"

"Failure."

"Are you kidding me? This here," he stretched his arms out, "this is no failure."

He was right. It was a success. There were six families of displaced men, women, and children living at the Jameson Home. At least fifty more came by for a hot meal each day. Still others needed warm beds, but the space was limited, much less the food. I had turned many families away because we couldn't accommodate them. Mama did what she could as far as preparing meals, but her small kitchen couldn't handle the growing number of hungry mouths to feed.

Soon businesses began donating food. They delivered it by the truckloads. People brought clothing and linens. Besides Wanda, I had at least three other volunteers who rotated shifts to help clean, serve food, answer phones; whatever needed to be done. But even with that, I still longed to be there full time. My heart was there.

Kevin had moved his practice to Atlanta and was pounding the pavement for clientele. In his free time, he painted and sketched. He was preparing a piece to be displayed at the upcoming African American Arts Festival and was like a child in a candy store with excitement. It was all he talked about, and I was so proud of him.

"Maybe you should just be an artist full time. Sell your paintings," I suggested. "It's really what you love to do."

"I would starve."

"Not if you're good."

"I have to be able to pay the bills. Have to be able to support my wife."

"Your wife?"

"Yeah, my wife. That is, if she'll have me."

He dried his hands and placed the last plate on the shelf. He reached into the pocket of his pants, pulled out a small box, opened it, and held a beautiful diamond ring between his fingers. Got down on one knee. "Reece—"

"Yes?"

"I've loved you from the moment I laid eyes on you. You are the most beautiful woman I've ever met in my life." He kissed my fingertips. "Will you be my wife?"

"I don't know what to say."

"Well, can you think of something, because this floor is a little hard on my knee."

"Say yes, girl!" That was Wanda who had come downstairs from cleaning toilets and helping the women put their children to bed.

"Say yes, Miss Jameson," Jill chimed in.

Even Jerome stuck his head in the door to see what all the commotion was about. I had an audience and a handsome man on his knee awaiting my answer to the question that women wait their whole lives to hear.

"Yes," I whispered, but everyone heard.

Everyone applauded. Kevin slipped the ring on to my finger, took me in his arms, and kissed me.

It was the second time I'd said yes to a man, but this time was different. This time I was sure.

39

Reece

I sat in Bernadette's chair, her skinny fingers pulling on my hair, tightening my braids. My head hurt from her pulling so hard, and I popped an aspirin into my mouth to relieve the pain. Charlotte sat across the room getting a French manicure and a pedicure by Dante, the gay nail technician who had women standing in line for his services. Portia was giving Maxie a facial.

Five hours at a beauty shop was more than enough time to make us all beautiful. Afterward we headed over to the Cheesecake Factory in Buckhead to add some pounds to our hips with huge chunks of strawberry cheesecake.

We were spending as much quality time with each other as possible since Maxie and her unborn child were LA bound. Rico was coming to pack and move her within the week. Although I hated to see her go, I was happy that she'd chosen love. I knew she'd be a perfect mother for her baby. I just wished she'd known it. But in time, she'd see that just because her mother made mistakes didn't mean she had to make the same ones.

Maxie had placed her house on the market, using the expertise of Charlotte, who by the way, was working again. Her cancer was in remission, and she was stronger than ever. Had made some lasting friendships with the sisters from her support group. She was sick of me breathing down her neck, acting like her mother, and decided to move in with her friend, Ophelia. I was a little jealous at first, hurt. It felt like a slap in the face. But after I thought about it, I realized that it was good for her to be around someone who shared her illness and her fears. Someone who understood exactly what she faced every day. We were still friends. That would never change. But she needed the other women in her support group. Her life depended on them.

The shelter was doing so well I had to quit the firm in order to handle all the business. Between that and planning a wedding, I barely had much time for anything else. We'd immediately set a date. It would be on the beach in Nassau, but we'd reside in Atlanta. We would live in my condo in Buckhead, and enjoy the view. I couldn't wait to tell Mama my news, and to ask her and Dad for their blessings.

"Let me see that ring again," Charlotte said, after stabbing her cheesecake with a fork and stuffing it in her mouth.

I held my hand out to her.

"That boy got taste."

"Umm hmm," Maxie agreed, and rubbed her growing stomach. She'd already gained at least twenty pounds, and she was glowing.

"When's Rico coming to move your things?"

"Next weekend." She beamed. "He found me a place."

"I don't know why you don't just marry the man and stop playing," Charlotte said.

"Because I want it to be right when I do. I'm not ready for marriage just yet."

"And you have every right to wait," I defended her. "Rico's not going anywhere."

"What about you and this man from Dallas?" Maxie asked.

"Oh, he's just a friend." Charlotte brushed her off, and stabbed another piece of cheesecake. Her blushing told us that she was lying, but we left it alone.

I watched my girls and smiled, grateful that I had them in my life. Would miss our threesome, but knew it was time for change. It was what we'd waited our entire lives for.

After church on Sunday, Kevin and I stopped at Kroger to pick up a head of lettuce, some cucumbers, and a tomato for the salad. I grabbed a watermelon and a bouquet of flowers for the table. When we got there, I immediately lost Kevin to the basketball game that the other men were screaming at the television about. I smiled as he fit right in, then made my way to the kitchen. I'd finally found peace in my life. Finally found happiness that was worth waiting for. I thanked God for it.

I started pulling lettuce apart for the salad, cut the watermelon in half, and tasted how sweet it was. There was nothing like Sunday dinner at Mama's.

AS REAL AS IT GETS

MONICA MCKAYHAN

ABOUT THIS GUIDE

The questions and discussion topics that follow are intended
to enhance your group's reading of AS REAL AS IT GETS by
Monica McKayhan. We hope the novel provided an
enjoyable read for all your members.

Reading Group Questions

1. Reece is in no hurry to meet Darren at the altar. Do you think she ever loved him or did her love for him change over time?

2. Do you think Darren ever really loved Reece, or did she just fulfill the need in his life to be needed by someone?

3. What do you suppose Darren's insecurities are?

4. Do you think that Reece's meeting Kevin caused her feelings for Darren to change?

5. When Maxie's mother committed suicide, she and her sisters stayed with Uncle Walter until the night of his arrest. What do you think the three girls' lives would've been like had Uncle Walter not gone to jail that night?

6. Why do you think Maxie's mother committed suicide? How did this change Maxie's views about motherhood?

7. Charlotte was really down on herself when she learned she had breast cancer. She often thought that God was punishing her. Do you think this was about her guilt for not visiting her mother as often as she did?

8. Do you think that Charlotte's illness changed her relationship between her and her girlfriends? Did it draw them closer or force them to move in different directions?

9. Would you have forgiven Wanda Manning for what she did to her child?

as your reaction to Mother Jameson and Reverend
ᴎ dating each other? Were you surprised by the
of their engagement?

w did Mother Jameson's views about love and relation-
ᴘs differ from Reece's views?

These three women endured life-altering changes. In what
ways did their attitudes and views about life and each
other change as the story progressed?

13. What do you think became of Reece, Charlotte and Maxie?